JANET HOBHOUSE'S
DANCING IN THE DARK

"Few fiction writers have as keen a sense for the contemporary moment or as classical and rigorous a craft as Hobhouse."
— WOMEN'S WEAR DAILY

"Janet Hobhouse is a fine writer and *Dancing in the Dark* is a colorful book, detailed and intelligent."
— THE SAN FRANCISCO CHRONICLE

"Janet Hobhouse has a great talent for cutting through to the core of her characters and revealing truths that lie beneath their delicious, cruel or tiresome games. Her analysis is so precise it takes on a mathematical quality."
— THE BERKELEY GAZETTE

"Hobhouse writes in a beautiful and mannered style, full of glimmering and special lucidity, full of moments of instant and complete awareness."
— THE LOS ANGELES HERALD EXAMINER

"*Dancing in the Dark* reads as though it were choreographed by Hermes Pan for a 1930's Hollywood musical."
— THE HOUSTON CHRONICLE

"A tense, engaging novel."
— THE LOS ANGELES TIMES BOOK REVIEW

DANCING IN THE DARK

DANCING IN THE DARK

Janet Hobhouse

VINTAGE CONTEMPORARIES

VINTAGE BOOKS · A DIVISION OF RANDOM HOUSE · NEW YORK

First Vintage Books Edition, September 1984
Copyright © 1983 by Janet Hobhouse
All rights reserved under International and Pan-American
Copyright Conventions. Published in the United States by
Random House, Inc., New York, and simultaneously in
Canada by Random House of Canada Limited, Toronto.
Originally published by Random House, Inc. in 1983.
Grateful acknowledgment is made to Thames and Hudson
Ltd., London, for permission to reprint excerpts from
Mexico by Michael D. Coe.
Library of Congress Cataloging in Publication Data
Hobhouse, Janet, 1948-
Dancing in the dark.
I. Title.
[PS3558.03369D3 1984]   813'.54   84-40003
ISBN 0-394-72588-3 (pbk.)
Manufactured in the United States of America
Front page photo copyright © 1984 by John Timbers

For Cable, Jean-Loup, Michael,
Larry, Annie, Judy, Murdoch
and for Tory

DANCING IN THE DARK

THEY HAD COME BACK FROM dancing at four o'clock and were still up drinking brandy. A long, low fatigue held them in their places, and beyond that, according to Gabriella, the intense pleasure of the moment. More than happiness, it floated as peace.

Those three sprawls, frank in Morgan's case, naturally decorous in Gabriella's, more studiedly so in Claudio's, were all that was left of an evening that had begun with a large dinner party downtown and progressed in a brief tour of the clubs in the usual small company. The party clothes hung about them now, spent, limply brilliant. In the disarray was a kind of nakedness, wholly unerotic, a childlike absence of defense.

Only Claudio's dress might have suggested that the guard was somewhere still up; because though the black tassled loafers had been removed to free his absurdly elegant and silk-covered feet, the satin jacket remained tight in its descriptive embrace of his small torso.

Opposite Claudio, in a deep armchair, Morgan sat and spoke across his own long legs, played at discussion, discursive, only occasionally passionate, the apparent conflict an excuse merely to maintain them, all three, on the scaffold of what Gabriella took to be a miraculous harmony.

Morgan looked over to where his wife sat next to Claudio on the blue sofa and wondered whether she was happy. At four-thirty this anxiety presented itself as problematic and distinct, like a distortion of stereo when a record has come to an end. The appearance of joy was convincing, expressed itself in Gabriella's quick response to what was said, to whatever wit was still going at that late hour between Claudio and himself, and along the length of her arm, as it lay in contact now with Claudio's, as relaxed as a courtesan's, full of its own power and assurance of pleasing.

For no reason, Gabriella laughed again, just as she had laughed all evening in a way Morgan had not seen for years until these past weeks when the new—or revived—Gabriella had announced itself as a kind of challenge to their life together, an ultimatum inside the invitation, plea, that he, Morgan, join her dance.

Claudio, smoking gently, shifted his position on the sofa, taking the ashtray with him in his left hand, Gabriella's arm in his right, a man in command of his universe, in total possession, here on the Callaghers' sofa, where eventually he would spend the night, where for the past few weeks he had felt himself at home. As Claudio moved, Gabriella lifted her hand to accommodate him, let it hover above his by way of reassurance; and Claudio, resettled, in gratitude for her constancy, had bent his head, raised her knuckles to his lips, kissed them and then buried her hand between both his own, inside the warmth of his lap.

All this Morgan noted as a sign of something arrived at. No longer on the brink of it, each now had his place inside the threesome, and what anxiety Morgan perceived as the undernoise of their evening, had nothing to do with a situation in the process of forming, but rather with his own surprise at discovering himself and Gabriella so firmly inside.

But while Morgan sensed near him the metaphor of trap, it was his wife's projection of her own freedom that held him. He'd not seen her so gay for months, perhaps it was years—but he could not calculate that length of time without consciousness of his own failure.

Now again Claudio said something that provoked Gabriella's smile, disrupting her features and letting slip for a moment the face of a Gabriella years younger than the one Morgan had been able to lead in to the present that he'd provided for them. Again, he felt the reproach and wondered at it, the extent to which his wife was not simply saying, You see, Morgan, how simple it has always been, if only you could have tried, or at least thought about it a little.

But Morgan also saw in her joy a promise of peace inside the diversions of their present life, saw confrontations evaded, and maybe better than that, if he had it in him to hope for it, a second chance, not only for them but for himself. For that smile which lifted the weight of her wary dissatisfaction also took him, Morgan, back to their first days in college when Gabriella had seemed to offer him a way out of his own drab and unhappy existence by the sheer force of her capacity for pleasure.

Peculiar that he should have forgotten that thing in his wife, let her appetite and talent for joy pass with all the other vulnerabilities of youth as something best not dragged into middle age—not that at thirty-two they were middle-aged; they were simply no longer young, prematurely wizened, perhaps, by the normal processes of marital attrition. Well, if Claudio, himself forty, was able to release Gabriella from the stony consequences of being Morgan's wife, then he, Morgan, was willing to let it happen. Not just for himself, though abandoning power over his wife's happiness made him a little ashamed, but because it seemed more terrible that Gabriella should be allowed to arrive at whatever was coming next without having first been happy (by whatever means) in her early life with Morgan.

Gabriella looked over to where her husband sat and wondered if he was genuinely happy. Or rather if he was engaged enough by all of this to let her go on being happy. She was not certain what it meant that he did let it go on. Perhaps Claudio's being gay made all the difference and allowed Morgan to discount it.

Yet it was beneath her to believe that he would dismiss the changes in their life simply because Claudio fit no crude notion of where happiness for women conventionally derived: children and lovers. Claudio was neither, or perhaps a little patchwork of both.

Still, Morgan's complicity in all this surprised her. And Morgan's new hours—he who used to scowl at midnight when people stayed at dinner, used to turn down parties in order to be up early for work—Morgan now burned on no sleep and constant hangovers. And beyond this, there was the great surprise of his sudden docility. He had simply followed her lead and in the last two months let her alter the shape of his life and his own firm direction over it.

Morgan's face had two major expressions: impassive-mysterious (the most attractive to strange women) and engaged, querulous or questioning (the most attractive to Gabriella). A third expression could interrupt either of these in a sudden storm and then as quickly disappear. This was Morgan laughing, when as tonight a great flash of teeth and stretch would jump from his features, and a noise like a starting engine would rise from his throat, pick up and declare itself as the pure, unguarded joy of a three-year-old. When that happened, Morgan's eyes often registered surprise, as in "Who said that?" or "Where did that come from?" Gabriella knew it came from Morgan's New England childhood, which she pictured set among red barns and corn-shucking contests, despite Morgan's insistence that there had been nothing more idyllic than a dead-ivy–choked little house near the university where his parents taught.

Actually it was the rarity of Morgan's mirth that had seduced Gabriella, and the reliable sobriety that had held her. Morgan wore his drabness lightly. And gallantly. And until now it had seemed to Gabriella an adequate protection against the wilder possibilities of life. Thus sheltered, Gabriella had herself been daring, had chased to the edges and returned unscathed, letting her husband bear the weight of his dullness while encouraging his small escapes—as this evening when he'd gone out, sneakers under his pinstripes. Since it couldn't be Gabriella, perhaps Claudio would be the one to release the being that burned and dazzled inside him: this familiar Morgan, who, banging his heart against his duty and apologizing for his capitulations, had let his wife, in compensation, go free.

And their pied piper? He sat quietly and sipped his brandy with a certain modesty, as though aware of the thoughts his presence brought with him into the house, unwilling to take credit for the revolution at hand, calm and stately among the speculations that bounced between his hosts.

When Gabriella thought about Claudio, on the rare occasion he was absent from them, she tended to add to his features a small, rather military mustache, in keeping with the alert set of his brow and the long thin nose that descended full of purpose, dividing the pale soft cheeks and jutting out over his round and rosy mouth. Claudio's eyes, in daylight a distressed, blinded baby blue, took on in night lighting, or when momentarily illumined by the flare of his Dunhill, a pensive, ironic character, the look of a Prussian officer who sits solitary in the café of some occupied capital, sipping *fine* and speculating on the horrors of war. And this despite the constancy of his laughter and companionship, the customary insistence on his own *joie de vivre*.

This little alter image of Gabriella's shone all the more brightly Germanic once she had learned from Claudio the circumstances of his Italian first name. John Shreiber, Claudio's father—flat-footed and long-jowled, according to his son's description—had seen in the occasion of his last child's birth the opportunity to embrace tradition, and with a chauvinistic and tribal pride previously abandoned at Ellis Island, had given him the family name Claus. But after years at school, jeered first as Santa Claus (he had been quite a fat little boy) and later, more wittily, when he had grown some way toward his present small but languid self, as

7

Dangling Clause, he had taken advantage of his move to New York to abandon "Claus" with the rest of the Shreibers. On Christopher Street in the late fifties he became Claudio, by early self-mocking analogy with Daddy-o, and then not so self-mockingly, but in a spirit of aesthetic aspiration—as though to breathe out at every self-naming the very air of the Renaissance, or at least, of the Mediterranean. Shreiber he was more or less stuck with, but Shreiber appeared only under summons of taxmen, employers, landlords. To his lovers, friends and fellow waiters, whether or not they were aware of the thud of his real name, he existed properly as Claudio, which despite the blue of his eyes suited him better than Claus, being, unlike the latter name and like himself, not simply short but light-footed and dapper as well.

It was Claudio's continued capacity for self-invention, itself an American heritage of course, which appealed to Gabriella. Surrounding himself with the stage effects of other pasts (Paris in the '90s, for example, Weimar Berlin), he felt it his privilege to forgo the accident of his own. More than this, he refused to let a sense of the past hamper his cult of the moment. That was part, according to Gabriella, of Claudio's gay life. Morgan thought it more likely simply part of New York, where no one was ever born, but arrived like Claudio sprung whole and discontent from Ohio, desperate to begin again.

But Gabriella had been born in New York, and not just Gabriella, but her great-great-grandparents as well. Morgan had been shown a photograph of a squat couple in horse and carriage outside a house on Riverside Drive. Gabriella was actually fifth-generation New Yorker, a rarity to say the least. In spite of this, however, not one other member of family still lived in the city. There had been extravagant deaths, and moves to California.

Gabriella stood now and provoked, in the flash of knee and thigh, just before the fall of silk skirts, Morgan's memory of Gabriella twelve years ago, when at a Yale production of *The Bacchae*, his own retranslation, he had first seen her, a Chorus girl in chiton with Busby Berkeley legs. But the pride of initiative she had subsequently denied him when at dinner their first night she had told him, "I only joined this play because I wanted to meet you." And after that night, Gabriella's long legs had marched like a drum majorette's across Morgan's own sense of himself. Ennobled by association, hallowed by use, enshrined by tradition, for twelve years they'd carried Gabriella in and out of Morgan's past, like two dipped *madeleines.*

Gabriella walked across the room and sensed how her movements attracted the impassive gaze of her husband and the benign approval of Claudio. She heard them hover in their talk, reassure themselves she was returning, and then begin again as she moved away noiselessly in her stockinged feet. Happy in the renewed circulation of her body, tall, powerful, she knew herself to be loved by both, aware that Claudio's adoration incited the love of her husband as at the same time it confused him, unused as he was to an unmenaced recognition of another man's regard for his wife.

In the bathroom, Gabriella turned on the tap and ran cold water over the low sounds of the men's voices in the room outside. Braced against the sink, she looked down at her feet, which were blotched and swollen from the dancing, and at her eyes and the smudges of kohl that had come adrift during the night. She took a towel and held a corner under the water, then shifted the mascara under her eyes onto the terrycloth, leaving a dark streak that Morgan would find later in the morning. It was her pleasure to scatter such clues of female life where either of the men might find them. Kate used puffs of oiled cotton for such removals, and disposed of them considerately under the sink, into a small Peruvian basket. Gabriella, despite four years of marital debate on this issue, continued to mark the towels.

Just now Kate was sleeping in the small room next to the bathroom, having returned four hours previously from dinner with her former husband. It was the first time she'd seen him since their separation six weeks ago, when she had arrived, apologetic and overwhelmed, to stay with Gabriella and Morgan.

The Callaghers had met Claudio often through Kate, but not until Richard's treachery (and that was the word they all used, for Richard had gone off, cliché fashion, with Kate's best friend) had Claudio occupied any position in their lives. Before that, only Gabriella had seen him, and of course Kate, to whom he'd almost belonged. Morgan's perception of it was that he had accompanied Kate into the Callagher home, along with the ten suitcases, the violin and the bear.

Actually Claudio's arrival had been something so sudden or so gradual that it now existed simply as fact and lay between Gabriella and Morgan uncharacteristically unscrutinized. Others, as Gabriella sensed, were mystified by his continued presence in the Callagher household, by Claudio's shaving brushes in the Callagher bathroom, by Claudio's voice on the Callagher phone, sweetly intimate and expansive: "I hope your dog is better, Bernard, Morgan told me"; "Gabriella's in the shower right now"; "I'm so relieved about your mother's operation."

Complementing their refusal to explain the situation either to outsiders or themselves was Claudio's own vagueness about his whereabouts, so that though there were whole weeks when Claudio lived more with them than not, bringing his laundry to be washed in the Callaghers' building's machines, stocking their fridge with the necessities of his own nutrition—his little jars of artichoke hearts, his ginseng, his wheat germ—nevertheless he convinced himself that it was the logic and pressure of the moment that conveyed him there: the lateness of the hour, an appointment in the morning on the Callagher side of town, and just at the present, and good for the long haul, a rent-strike organized by the Hispanic tenants of Claudio's heatless building.

But Kate in her sadness accepted neither the evasions of Morgan and Gabriella nor the paraded tentativeness of Claudio. For if Claudio had arrived as one of Kate's possessions, then it had to be said that Gabriella had taken him away. And while neither

Claudio nor Gabriella would have admitted this, Kate felt it as a third loss, after Richard and Liza, though she was too proud or too demoralized ever to mention it.

In any case, Kate was just now, as she told Gabriella, rather confused over questions of friendship and trust. She had come to trust Richard after a reasonable calculation of the odds of betrayal, and then had kept a relaxed watch, bumping along, like any other wife of an attractive man, in a small range of sensation— as small as she could make it—between alarm and apathy. On that course she had expected to sail without disaster till the end of her days. On that assumption, and as though there were all the time in the world, she had let their lives build slowly around them, piece by piece bought furniture, gathered friends, created habits which she expected to abandon one day out of boredom alone, and not like this, all at once, on the simple say-so of Richard.

Gabriella turned off the tap and heard the sounds of Verdi's *Requiem* coming from the living room. That was the last time they had all seen Richard, when he'd gone with Kate and them eight weeks ago to the Musica Sacra concert. Gabriella had sat on the edge of her seat; Richard had slept through the second part. Kate, hearing the music, would remember.

It did occasionally occur to Gabriella after Kate's arrival to doubt her own security with Morgan, or at least to wonder at her complacency. Others were there to reassure them, to name them the great married couple, just as of course they had named Richard and Kate. But then, she and Morgan, as Kate had told her, were evidently close, at times to the point of excluding others, as when, as often happened, a table full of guests had to hang in anxious space while their hosts debated a point of art/literature/ politics or that mercilessly cherished biography which took them, Gabriella and Morgan, twelve years into the past. It was this liveliness about their sense of themselves and their own freedom to draw on it, touch it, talk it, that Claudio had once pronounced "impressive," something achieved rather than merely fallen into.

11

What might appear to outsiders, Gabriella could imagine, as inconsiderate squabbling, shone in Claudio's description as the great connecting fabric of Gabriella and Morgan's "wonderful marriage." Kate said it was likely that Claudio was right because Richard had once used that phrase to her, had said that he and she never "talked." Well, they certainly were not talking now.

Gabriella stepped out of the bathroom and passed the door of Kate's room, sensing for a moment that it had been shut in hostility. The slightest guilt slowed her there, as she looked down at her own glamorous dark skirts and pictured Kate in the nightgown that had so surprised her when first she saw it six weeks ago, a pale dress, flannel, infantile, as though enforcedly virginal, things being what they had now become. Gabriella thought of Kate waking now and finding the others together, still talking or slumped, but with the evidence of their private happiness around them. Yet it couldn't hold her; she returned to her place on the sofa, returned her arm to Claudio's, so that the three of them could continue to sit, stuck in that heavy atmosphere of cigarettes and brandy, aware that the city slept around them while they, blessed, apart, kept watch over their feelings.

ON ONE SIDE OF A SMALL ZINC table covered with empty glasses and overloaded ashtrays—the tables on the mezzanine overlooking the dance floor were barely served by the waiters: drinks were acquired between dances, consumed upstairs and there abandoned—Morgan sat between Kate and Claudio. Across from them was Gabriella, having a noisy good time with Preston and Mickey, friends of Claudio's that had once made a fast trio with him in a recent era of Fire Island weekends and all-night city cruising.

Across the drinks, old jokes and private references flew from these two to Claudio, and some flirtatious banter to Kate, whom they'd known from the old days with Richard. Morgan they left as usual almost superstitiously alone, as though if addressed he might turn nasty, despite Claudio's evident safe rapport. Responding with delicacy to their precaution, Morgan paid attention mostly to Kate, trying to draw her out, to adjust the balance tipped by Gabriella's revelry, though he did this as much to protect his wife's ease, as to add to Kate's.

From time to time he allowed himself to watch the floor show, or rather air show, that began on a small stage just above the mezzanine level where the acrobats stripped and pranced to music before diving into a net which stretched a perilous few feet over the heads of the dancing crowd. Only occasionally did the patrons stop to watch what was happening above them, craning their necks while knees and feet kept time. But then, quickly bored, they returned their attention to their partners, or else, eyes rolled inward, to the demands of the dance.

From the mezzanine, however, the show was irresistible, and to Gabriella, who like Morgan had not been to this club before, as spectacular as the circus it was based on. The free-for-all of the place, the combination of childishness and sexual abandon, made her high and flirtatious—with Mickey, with Preston, with faces across the room, to every sign as ponyish and self-loving as a teen-age vamp.

Claudio watched Gabriella with his best friends, pleased to sense the beginnings of an extended band. He had not often been able to see his friends really "mix." In the old days Kate had brought it off at dinner parties where straights and gays had mingled only a little nervously under the indifferent gaze of Richard. But the Kate-Richard dinners had been half-hearted, and apparently doomed. As Gabriella in her innocent cruelty had recently passed on to Claudio, it was Richard and Morgan's colleague Otto's firm knowledge that Richard had left Kate because he'd been outnumbered by what Otto (and possibly Richard, Claudio was not certain) had referred to as "Kate's fags."

Preston made a little signal to Claudio and they went downstairs to dance. Mickey, isolated and unable to carry on the hilarity alone, drew Gabriella unsteadily to him and disappeared with her below. And Kate, in panic, it seemed to Morgan, or to spare him the obligation of taking her onto the dance floor, withdrew in smiles toward the Ladies'.

Alone, Morgan emptied his glass and concentrated on the movements around and below him as people entered and exited from each other's lives, made passes, arranged meetings, lost their partners, reattached. Beneath the cool surface was an earnestness of pursuit, and clear declarations of lust inside the self-disguise:

young men and old dressed as truckers, dressed as aristocrats, dressed as thugs, dressed as chorus girls, dressed ostentatiously as ladies. Some of the women, likewise in drag, held their places in this glamour-loving crowd, in hobnailed boots, forty-inch waists, shorn heads and full jowls, dressed as their fat older brothers.

On the platform to Morgan's right, now moving his feet and hips in time to the music, was a good-looking tough in sequins and lavender hose. On the face of this street kid—the kind, as Morgan remembered from school, who'd break your arm if you called him a sissy—there was no register of what he was up to, only a kind of desperate dedication to what he was doing, and, it seemed to Morgan, not doing very well. In his effort to concentrate on the music the boy's head was down a little. When he looked up, giving the *caput mortuum* smile of the professional go-go girl, all teeth and tension, Morgan saw the disasters of street brawls and malnutrition in his mouth, guessed that he was working here to pay for his dentist. When the music paused in its drive, the boy made his joyless drop and swooped like a plucked turkey into the far corner of the net. There he lay, shiny and sullen, until the spotlight went out, when he collected his unshattered limbs and skulked toward the wings.

Kate took a long time coming back, and when she did, she was repainted and apologetic. "Sorry, Morgan," she said, "there was heavy traffic in the Ladies'. You know, they still lock the doors when they do coke so you have to wait. Half the line got bored and went to the Men's."

"Which is probably what they are, anyway," Morgan said.

"Probably."

"Do you want a drink? There was a waiter up here a minute ago."

"Thanks." Kate settled into her chair and pulled her cigarettes from a small bag.

"Vodka?" Morgan asked. He lit her cigarette.

"Yes," Kate said. The urbane ritual was pleasing.

A discreetly made-up waiter in black T-shirt and shorts took their order and disappeared downstairs.

"You should be dancing with Gabriella," Kate said. "Please don't feel you have to stay here with me. I'm fine alone, not likely to get into any trouble." She smiled.

"I prefer it up here," Morgan said, "and it's good to have you out with us. Though I wish you looked happier about it."

"Sorry," Kate said.

"I only mean I wish you *were* happier," Morgan said, "in this pleasure palace."

"Well, I shouldn't have come. I only cast a pall. Bad fairy at the feast."

For a while they said nothing, pretending to listen to the music.

"Have you seen Richard?" Kate said.

"Just at the office, and not much of that. Our lunches seem to have stopped."

"That's because Richard's feeling sheepish. I've made you into the shelterer of the wronged wife. But you should see him if you want to, Morgan; there are no sides."

"Perhaps there are sides," Morgan said quickly. "How was your dinner with him?"

"Painful," Kate said.

"Yes."

"He says he still loves me."

"Of course," Morgan said.

"He says it's six years of his life."

"Yes," Morgan said.

"Then why does he stay with Liza?"

The waiter came back with the vodkas. Morgan paid cash, not willing to trust his credit card to make the long journey down and back. All the while he was engaged with the drinks Kate had been waiting. Now she was oddly cheerful.

"I'll tell you something, Morgan. That may have been my last husband, but it's almost damn sure to be my last friend. She practically lived with us those six months, looking for the loft. Six months. If I'd known."

"You don't know," Morgan said.

"Oh, come on. You know, I really don't blame Richard. Odd, isn't it? I knew him so well, you know I always knew it was possible he'd be led off like a pet lamb."

Morgan felt caught, hearing the description, incompetent and allied by gender to Richard, yet unable to contradict Kate. He simply refrained from nodding.

Kate went on without him, shouting over the music, "But I do blame her. In a weird way you expect more of your friends than your husband. It's all simpler how they're expected to behave. And Liza is female."

Morgan agreed that Liza was female, uncertain what it was that Kate invested in that fact.

"If it was the other way around, I think I'd feel more loyalty to Liza than to Richard. She is my sex."

"Yes," Morgan said uncertainly.

"I mean, I'd never have betrayed Liza."

"No."

"Well, I trusted her friendship, and see where that's got me, husbandless and friendless."

Morgan saw the opening: "Not at all friendless, Kate, there's Gabriella, and me and Claudio . . ."

"You have each other," Kate said mysteriously. "Richard's put an end to my friendships."

"But I would have thought—"

"Because in a perverse way," Kate said, "I haven't got time to have friends anymore, make them or be one, I have to spend the whole time looking for a lover. Liza was a luxury that having Richard allowed me. Ironic, isn't it?"

Kate sat back, pleased with her syllogism. It was Morgan who found it depressing.

"And another thing," Kate went on, sitting forward again, "I

17

hadn't any idea of how cut off single women are from single men, precisely because they're single."

"Surely, Kate—" Morgan said.

"No, when I was married to Richard," Kate said, "I was free to make friends with all kinds of men. Now because there's a possibility of sex between us, everybody gets categorized—brutally. *I* do it. I can't be in conversation with a man for twenty minutes without all the time having to scatter my conversation with clues as to my sexual interest or indifference; my eyes either shine or they sink to my shoes. Before there was this awful cheapening issue I was free, I could get to know him, hear if he had anything to say, apart from the thing that always gets said first: 'Might we or might we not go to bed?' "

There was a sudden burst of laughter on the small staircase that rose to the mezzanine, followed by Preston on his way up, his arm around Gabriella. The laughter came from behind them, from Claudio collapsed against a wall, supported by Mickey: "You're falling on me, Claudio—come on, it wasn't that funny."

"Oh, it was!" Claudio collapsed again theatrically against the wall. Gabriella sat down next to Kate and addressed Morgan: "I'm dancing, right?" Morgan nodded. "I hear the following conversation behind my back: 'She's a drag queen.' "

" 'Never.' "

" 'Is.' "

" 'Too tall.' "

" 'For a queen?' "

" 'Drag queens are thinner.' "

Gabriella and Claudio laughed again. Morgan managed a smile.

"Why aren't you dancing?" Claudio asked Morgan.

"I've tried Kate, she won't, I was waiting for Gabriella."

"What about all us other girls?" Mickey had his hand on his hip, the outraged Southern belle. Still, he did not try to catch Morgan's eye but looked at Claudio.

"Okay, let's go," Gabriella said.

"Miss Energy. Whatever is she on?" Preston said.

"Just her own natural juices," Claudio answered. "Give some of it to Morgan, sweetums, he looks a little flat."

Gabriella stood up and took Morgan downstairs. But the moment she had him on the dance floor, her energy seemed to leave her. Away from her audience, she found it strangely dull to be there. A sense of obligation filled her, like someone who has brought a homely cousin to a ball.

It was true that Morgan cut an odd figure on the dance floor. Taller than most of the other dancers, and more heavily boned, he had a Huck Finn look about him, an unguarded pleasantness of expression, emanating sweet indifference to the surroundings. Gabriella was touched and exasperated by his tolerance of their whereabouts, by the goony smile he offered her, like someone at a country-club barbecue. In fact, Morgan was simply grateful to be away from Kate and the others. He was not enjoying being the only straight male in the group, longed vaguely for Richard's company, or at least for a sense of what he was meant to be saying to Richard's wife. In this particular party it was, as always, easiest for him to be alone with Gabriella. Dancing in his usual way, he sunk comfortably into habit and smiled again at his wife.

Gabriella turned her back on him and was brought face to face with two men in Mexican gear, bare torsos under leather vests, studded belts, Pancho Villa haircuts and mustaches. As she turned, the smaller man flashed his teeth and lifted a glass vial toward her. Gabriella inhaled, and signaled by the Mexicans, passed the popper to Morgan. Politely, Morgan declined, and then, when Gabriella insisted, sniffed, waited for the palpitations and resumed his dancing, unaffected by the drug. His movements were charmingly simple, crudely rhythmic and private, the hard work of someone stamping grapes. When, every now and then, Morgan looked up at the performers diving into the net overhead, not quite remembering each time to keep the rhythm with his feet, a small anxious look came over his face.

Under the effect of the popper, Gabriella watched Morgan and felt proud to possess him. It connected her with the gay males here that she was partnering such a good-looking man, and in that there was a bond of taste and power. If, on the other hand, male beauty was something you had rather than accompanied, it would be Morgan and not she who belonged. The thing confused her. What she least wanted to be was half of a married couple. She tried to think of Morgan as a trick; it was almost impossible.

The disco number went on and on. As it slowly became a different song, Morgan bent toward her and shouted, "I ought to go back and get Kate."

"Why?" Gabriella was now dancing full rhythm; having cleared a little space around her and the Mexicans, she was able to do five steps back and three to each side, no mean territorial victory on the packed dance floor. "It's a good track."

"It's late."

"Only three."

"Yeah, late. I've got to be at work tomorrow and so have you." Morgan had now stopped dancing and was standing still, shouting at Gabriella as she went on with her dance.

"You go," she said.

"I can't leave you here."

"Stay."

"Let's go, Gabriella," Morgan said. He took her arm. "Kate's not having a good time and I've got to be up early."

"You go," Gabriella said. Again, she turned her back on Morgan and joined the Latins, again she took a whiff of the popper. When she spun around to offer some to Morgan, she saw that he was gone.

Morgan made his way with difficulty to the edge of the dance floor. It was impossible to move in a straight line, impossible even to move the way he did daily in the downtown rush hours, half turning every now and then like a game of Streets and Avenues, until he carved his Z-shaped exit from the crowd. Here he had to dance his way out, following the beat of the music, mimicking the steps of people in his way until he could get past. Moving like this, and sensing himself ridiculous in his impersonations, he took some ten minutes to get through the crush and back to his table. There he saw Kate staring straight ahead in exhaustion, the bottom half of her face still hanging on to its fixed expression of courteous merriment, the eyes dark and tragic, far-seeing: the eyes of an old gypsy at a campfire. She was asleep.

Next to her, but facing the other way, was Claudio, his long thin hands drooped over the balcony rail, his blue eyes unfocused and weary: Cocteau in a rough crossing, Proust on the Titanic. Between them in a red plastic ashtray, a Gauloise burned.

"Well, this is a lively group," Morgan said, "Who's for bed?"

Kate stirred and found the smile there waiting for her on her face. "Where's Gabriella?" she said. She had picked up her small bag and was collecting her cigarettes and matches. Claudio, in no hurry, continued to stare vacantly ahead.

"She wants to stay awhile longer. You want to go don't you, Kate?"

"I wouldn't mind."

"What about Claudio?"

Claudio turned. "Where are Mickey and Preston, sweetums?"

"Mickey was with a blond in lederhosen," Morgan said. "Seemed very attached."

"Heinz," Claudio said. "Nazi trash. You go. I'll wait for Preston."

Inside the taxi Kate sat backed into the corner, looking bundled and apologetic. Her evening bag dangled from her hand onto the dirty cab floor, where it had been knocked by one of the driver's more violent swerves.

"Jesus," Morgan said as he swerved again.

"You wanted to stay," Kate said.

"No, I didn't. I've got to be at the office at nine tomorrow. Nine today."

"I could have taken a cab myself," Kate said.

"It's fine," Morgan said irritably. Then gently, "I'm pretty tired." Morgan bent down and picked up Kate's bag. Its dark sequins shone under a red traffic light as the cab went full speed through it.

"Probably can't stop," Morgan said. "Another one with no brakes."

"I was a bit overdressed for that place, wasn't I?" Kate said. "Imagine taking an evening bag. I suppose I haven't been to a disco for ages."

"I thought there were quite a few evening bags," Morgan said, "and high heels, and tiaras. I thought we looked perfect. Anyway, Kate, who cares? That's not why you didn't have a good time. We should have left sooner."

"You're so gallant, Morgan, one in a million, thanks."

Morgan sat for a while, silenced by the compliment, trying not to see out of the window.

"Actually I always did get rather depressed at discos. I'd forgotten. Richard hates to dance and there was a lot of table sitting. Which means watching people go up and down and repeat their two to seven movements, and listening to what is, after all, the world's most boring music."

"What would you like better?" Morgan asked. He turned his body rapidly toward Kate as the driver slalomed among the jaywalkers.

"Well, rock," Kate said. "Something with a human being inside it. The point about disco is that it's meant to work like a synchronome so even the tone-deaf and spastic can get up and pack the floor. It's not meant to be treated like music."

"I used to like the Stones," Morgan said wistfully. "But then

I gave up, around twenty-seven or so. It was full-time work keeping up, and I suppose I thought I was too old. And here I am, five years later, out all night."

"Born again," Kate said and smiled at him, "born to boogie. Maybe you don't really like it," Kate said to Morgan, "do you like it?"

"Well, I must."

Kate said nothing.

"Or do you think I've been brainwashed?" Morgan asked her. "By Claudio? By Gabriella, by the music?"

"No one, nothing." Kate laughed. "I'm only asking."

"I'll think about it," Morgan said defensively.

"I'll sleep on it," Morgan said as the cab came to a sudden silent stop outside the building, and the doorman, ostentatiously discreet, managed to open the door on Mr. Callagher at three-thirty A.M. in such a way as not to seem to notice the presence of his companion in the absence of his wife.

Gabriella, left unpartnered on the dance floor, expressed solemn concentration as she pushed her feet and tried to hold back a creeping self-consciousness. For a while she had felt safe thinking no one would notice her bobbing about alone, but as that security faded, found herself setting her face to indicate that solo dancing was her brave and customary intent.

Through the mask of self-involvement Gabriella's anxiety could be read as she scanned the horizon for signs of Claudio, Preston, Mickey. Morgan's easy departure without her began to seem alarming. She told herself that Morgan was simply tired. It was true they had been to bed after three twice that week. Unlike the crowd tonight they almost never took drugs of any kind. Nothing kept them up but their own curiosity.

At first Gabriella had been overwhelmed and impressed by the size and energy of the great night public, convinced that not all of them had, like Claudio, afternoon or night jobs or, as some of the costume was meant to suggest, a private income. She guessed, and later found out, that a certain amount of cheating went on to transform the nine-to-five people into one-till-dawn partygoers, namely the unconfessed naps between performances of working and playing selves. Some, of course, had no regular jobs, but not many, Gabriella thought, disco fees and leather costing what they did. Here everyone kidded everyone else, about stamina, about gender, about their daytime lives. Here at least they were free of the facts: the dance celebrated their freedom. But she and Morgan weren't going to be able to sustain their bluff much longer; the present frolic would be limited.

And most of these dancers were in far better shape than Morgan and she. Not just from the dancing, night after night, but from the habit, then at the height of fashion, of working out at a gym two or three evenings a week. It was part of the Gay Strikes Back movement, as Claudio—whose rippleless torso and narrow shoulders belonged to an earlier era—had explained to her. A "Never Again" chauvinism prevailed, fairies no more, gays would be muscle men, or as the song had it, Macho Men. That partly explained the pectorals and short hair and the prevalent S-M look that menaced Gabriella, while for Claudio, provocatively dandyish as he was, it was simply a matter of style. At times Gabriella would think of the tender Claudio, out on the prowl downtown, in and out of the bars in the meat district, like a mewing kitten among the bone-crunchers and switchblades, and she would shudder. Claudio, however, laughed at her fears and told her that the leather mob wasn't really so tough, and that after twenty-five years on the job, he could look after himself.

"Hi," someone shouted behind her. "Where's Morgan?" Gabriella turned and saw Preston bobbing on sneakers behind her.

"He's gone home," Gabriella told him, affectedly casual.

That was the end of the conversation, apparently, for Preston, willing enough to stand there and dance with her, had no further inclination to talk. In front of her he moved, eyes shut, the sweat running freely down his neck, the smile of greeting affixed and drying out across his face. Alone again, face to face with Preston, Gabriella felt her nerves arriving. Preston, for example, one of the gym regulars, was certainly in good, and for Gabriella now, exhausting shape. She was out of breath, would have liked to sit the next one out. Unfortunately, the music didn't seem to work that way, but went on and on in Wagnerian arcs and without perceptible interval. Looking around now for Claudio, she knew the mask of her good time to be fading fast; and she was ruining her clothes, not having worn the workout gear that Preston had on, the black T-shirt made all the blacker by the patches of sweat under his arms, across his back and down the central line of his chest. On Preston all the funk was sexy; on Gabriella it was simply further evidence that she should go home.

Preston, Gabriella noticed, now no longer even glanced her way as he moved, up and down, loose-spined, one arm held ramrod stiff by his side. At moments he even lost her altogether as the crowd shifted along the floor. Then Gabriella had to side-step gauchely in order to keep her claims on him current. But for her nervous vigilance, Preston was likely to come out of his disco trance as someone else's partner.

Gabriella tried again to pick out Claudio among the dancers and noticed that there were suddenly no longer any women on the dance floor, neither real nor presumptive, nor anything now remotely female. Only men, chains, tattoos, stomach muscles, and what Gabriella in her panic read as increasingly hostile faces. Desperate to wake Preston, to take herself out of the momentary nightmare, she shouted his name.

Preston's brown eyes, glazed, looked blankly at her for a while, then registered. He smiled. "How you doing?" he said.

"I think I'd better get home."

Preston took Gabriella's arm and tried a little fifties twirling, but they crashed into the couple next to them in such a way that it seemed Gabriella's fault.

"Sorry," she said. She smiled. With synchronized two-step the couple turned from her. Preston, when Gabriella looked back, had his eyes closed once more and was bopping solo.

"Preston!" Gabriella shouted.

Preston looked up.

"I'm going now; you stay."

"You want me to get you a cab?" Preston asked her.

Gabriella shook her head, but was grateful. Preston's eyes closed again when Gabriella kissed him goodbye, and as she moved off, remained closed. Preston was one of the all-nighters; he took his naps on the disco floor.

Out on the street, without Morgan or Claudio, Gabriella felt a little vulnerable in that district. But the pounding music had stopped, and the air, cold and blue with the beginnings of morning, smelled clean. On the block the hookers had gone home. A tramp or two, wrapped against the cold, muttered under the neon signs as she passed. Gabriella heard the slow noise of a cab behind her, and turning, saw that he was free. She was lucky; her adventure tonight would end well: lone girl plays safely in all-male club. She gave the driver her address, relaxed her leaden body against the unsprung seats and happily noted the potholes that marked her way home.

But with the fatigue, a sadness descended, that however much she braved this world, Gabriella was never going to be anything but a coolly tolerated part of it; never going to be in any real sense welcome, no matter how noisily she announced her presence. And she sensed, too, that things might become tricky with Morgan. It would be best to avoid that confrontation; they simply wouldn't do the clubs so much anymore. And she ought to retrieve a little credibility at work. She would start again sane on Monday.

Gabriella got out of the taxi and moved past the doorman, up in the elevator, past the sleeping form of Claudio on the sofa, past the locked door of Kate's room. Undressing quickly, she crept into bed next to Morgan and curled her form like an apology around his own.

CLAUDIO SAT AMONG THE covered pillows of the Callaghers' sofa and held carefully above the blankets a gold-rimmed demitasse of black coffee. He had moved once this morning, left his lair, made his coffee, greeted the hungover Morgan on his way to work; and then he had retreated, wrapped in the red-silk dressing gown he'd brought with him from the West Side. Now he sat motionless, engaged in the effort to return to a state of peaceful readiness for waking: a gerundial arc of movements so slow and continuous that it brought him bumpless in to the present tense. Claudio's mornings, no matter where he found himself, nor after how much or how little sleep, demanded a careful languor. No knocking out of his dreams, but a slow coming to, an unperceived sitting up, an unalarmed opening of the eyes and determining of whereabouts had to precede the silk-wrapped saunter to the bathroom, the semiconscious preparation of coffee and lighting of the first Gauloise of the day. Then, with the edges of these acts still soft, Claudio's waking would take place by itself, and he would be delivered through the agencies of coffee, cigarette and the *New York Times*, properly detached from his sleeping persona, ready for his shower and the closely attended acts of dressing. All of this, performed with control and at the pace of a dignified pavane, normally took him until noon.

Since it was crucial to Claudio's happiness that no part of the ritual be hurried or omitted, he seldom stayed out whole nights with his tricks and never brought them home. On weekends away he made sure his hosts would expect him no earlier than lunchtime. Even so, there were weekends when Claudio's matutinal needs were not to be satisfied, either because the water was no longer hot, other guests having used the bathroom first, or because some plan (antique shops, distant beach) demanded early rising. On such occasions Claudio would meet the day courteous and good-humored as always, but just a little put out, and as the day wore on, increasingly prone to sarcasm or sulks.

This morning, though the slow reintroduction of Claudio to the day was proceeding along its solemn, measured path, Claudio felt imperfections in his accustomed ease. The sight of Morgan on his way out—his face drawn, his shoes unbrushed, the color of his tie doing violence to the color of his shirt—had upset him, together with the recollection that last night Morgan had preceded Gabriella home. He himself had left the disco after a long search for Gabriella among the dancers, but when he'd got in, Morgan was still up, reading, and there had been no sign of his wife.

Claudio's worry attached itself less to Gabriella's recent whereabouts than to the possibility of Morgan's irritation. He wished neither to be blamed for Gabriella's high spirits nor to be viewed as an agent of discord between man and wife. All of this Claudio had attempted to convey this morning, standing in the kitchen over the little espresso pot and looking as pensive and sympathetic as his pre-caffeinated self was able to look, while Morgan seemed in any case hardly able to focus.

"Are you all right?" Claudio had ventured. And Morgan had said, "Just about," a reply which, it seemed to Claudio, probably referred to Morgan's hangover. And then, as unsubtly as Claudio dared to, he'd asked, "Is Gabriella all right?" To which Morgan had replied, without much affection, Claudio thought, "Dead to the world."

There they'd left it, with Claudio uncertain as to what Morgan thought about last night, or about Gabriella, or about Claudio, but with a faint suspicion that a shadow was over their friendship. And it seemed suddenly a good idea to leave husband and wife alone for a few days, for him to move back to the unheated flat on the West Side, where, if he really couldn't stand it, he would ask Preston to put him up—always supposing Preston was alone —on Preston's filthy floor.

The thought of this small martyrdom now made Claudio somewhat happier. He was able to imagine Morgan in one or two days' time not only forgiving Claudio whatever might be held against him, but, impressed by his delicacy and lonely without him, ready to demand his return. Lifted by this thought, Claudio rose from his pillows and headed for the shower in the full flush of *amour propre*. As he passed Kate's room, however, Claudio paused and then entered. Kate had left the house before Morgan, and like him had been in a rush. Her bed was unmade, her nightgown lay on the floor next to the bear and the novel she'd been reading for the past two months. Around these things, like corpses on a field of battle, and making passage almost impossible, were dozens of pairs of Kate's shoes: red satin stilettos, green crocodile slingbacks, gold-lamé mules, bunny-fur slippers and woven *après*-ski boots, cast off and discarded over the weeks Kate had been with the Callaghers; and among the shoes, shopping bags full of papers from Kate's work in advertising. In the far corner of the room was a pile of Kate's dirty laundry, and next to it an open address book on the floor. The room resounded with the frenzy with which Kate had led her life since Richard's departure, as though by fleeing from the consequences of his action, as though by her rushing from job to cocktail, from lunch to movie, from female friend to female friend, Kate was going to outrun the pain that pursued her and threatened, if she ever slowed down, to come crashing round her head.

And this bothered Claudio too, this morning: his neglect of

Kate. Moving cautiously around the shoes, and going through one of her large leather bags to find a pen and a piece of paper, Claudio wrote a note and put it as visibly as possible in that disorder on her pillow. Then, intending more seriously to catch her eye, Claudio picked up the bear, set it on the pillow and attached the message under its arms:

"Please have dinner with me tonight (Friday) or tomorrow, or whenever. I miss you. Claudio. P.S. I am at home. Call me when you get in."

Then Claudio proceeded at his normal rate toward his shower, where once again he noted with disapproval the skin-drying soap the Callaghers used and the hideous can of shaving cream that sat shamelessly red on the shelf of the pale Callagher bathroom.

Under the covers of the far bedroom Gabriella came slowly awake and understood from the temperature of Morgan's side of the bed that she was going to be late for work. Delicately she got out of bed, trying not to wake her hangover, feeling as guilty as when she'd been a student cutting classes. At thirty-two, she still retained a childish dread of bosses, unimposing though the present ones were, casual, not to say comatose. And though neither Max nor Stephen, the heads of the lecture agency where she worked, was liable to register her presence much before two in the afternoon, when the office came to life as though on signal—the phones beginning to ring in response to the sound of the Dixie cup (Max's fifth black coffee) thrown with final accuracy into the chipped green bin—the understanding was that Gabriella was meant to be there beforehand, shepherding whatever calls and emergencies fell outside the prime hours of Max and Stephen's competence. Over the reality of this bohemianism, Gabriella imposed her conventional notion of authority, something to be alternately obeyed and defied, so that, despite the laxity of her bosses, and the simple demands of her job, Gabriella often found herself tongue-tied with apologies, or else determined to stand on issues she alone perceived. Simply being late, which aroused the sad brows of Max or the sarcastic greeting of Stephen, was the situation that Gabriella handled with least grace. Tempted this morning to fake illness, she dialed the office number, which was engaged, replaced the phone and struggled for a while between guilt and defiance.

While she waited by the phone, the sound of rushing water reached her and she realized Claudio was still around, taking his shower and soon to appear. Her light-heartedness was immediate: remorse and hangover fled to the music of Claudio's immersion under the taps. She redialed the office number, told Stephen she would be there in forty minutes and moved toward the kitchen to make coffee for herself and her friend.

Gabriella filled the tin container with Claudio's mixture—half Medaglia d'Oro, half Bustelo—and set it in water over the flames, holding the image of Claudio as he took his sugar and stirred it so that the spoon barely scratched the bottom of the cup. She saw him as he kept his weight on one leg and leaned against the sink, inhaling a cigarette between sips, holding the cup and saucer out on the palm of his hand. Having coffee with Claudio, watching these same gestures, was one of the great pleasures of Gabriella's recent life. She knew Claudio would rather go without it than drink coffee with milk, coffee in a mug or non-espresso, and these facts, for no reason she could think of (since she herself would happily drink it straight from a pot, and often, given her late risings, had her coffee lukewarm), were cause for delight.

The pot hissed, then exploded. Gabriella turned down the gas, listened to the speed of bubbling, and set out two cups and saucers next to Claudio's brown sugar cubes. When it was ready Gabriella went off to tell Claudio what she had done.

"Sweetums, can't," Claudio shouted through the bathroom door. "Got to run." Gabriella stood still in front of the door and felt her disappointment blossom into outrage. Dismally, she returned to the kitchen, her office guilt returning, her mind racing to the proposition that Claudio's habits had now become hers and hers his, and that if it went on much longer, Gabriella would be without a job, and possibly a husband. By the time Claudio appeared from his shower, still warm and sweet-smelling, Gabriella was to all appearances unhappy to see him. So that as Claudio began his exit, having kissed the unresponsive mouth goodbye, it seemed to him that his decision to move out had been made, from both the Callaghers' point of view, not a moment too soon.

"Listen, sweetums," Claudio said as he hovered by the door, his small leather case in hand, the hand-pressed shirts visible in the zipless bag, "I've got to go back home for a few days, check the mail, pay some bills, see if the heat's coming on, you know." He dawdled, shifted his weight. The farewell made him uncomfortable; he was aware now he was springing it on her. At the same time he saw its effect. He reached upward to give a second kiss; this time consolatory.

Gabriella stood dumbfounded by so much loss. A small panic rose and was quickly censored: she was to be alone with Morgan. She hoped Kate would be in this evening.

"I've written Kate a note, asking her tonight for supper. Will you tell her?" Claudio asked.

"Sure," Gabriella said. "When are you coming back?" It sounded pathetic.

"Listen, I've got to go, I'll call you, okay?"

"I've got to go too," Gabriella said.

"You're going to be late for work," Claudio informed her.

"Go," Gabriella said.

Claudio opened the door slowly and put his case outside. "I'll call you," he said. "Will you be all right?"

"Of course," Gabriella said, and Claudio left, shutting the door gently behind him, in deference to her sorrow.

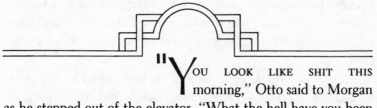

"Y OU LOOK LIKE SHIT THIS morning," Otto said to Morgan as he stepped out of the elevator. "What the hell have you been doing?"

The girl at the desk looked up, smiled. She was timid, respectful, a little in love with Morgan. It was her first job. Morgan moved past Otto and greeted her, "Sally, you couldn't see your way to making a little pot of coffee, could you? Otto, you want coffee?"

Otto came up behind them. "I've had my coffee. I've had my eight hours' sleep. Don't mess with the system, it won't mess with you."

"Black, Mr. Callagher?" Sally asked.

"Black," Morgan said.

"No kidding, Morgan, what have you been doing?"

"Jogging," Morgan said. Sally smiled.

"Yeah, sure," Otto said.

Morgan walked to his office, shut the door and sat down to read the papers and mail on the desk in front of him. If he could hang on till twelve, the office would gradually empty. By four the partners would be gone for their weekends. Thank God it was Friday.

Morgan returned the calls that had come for him earlier in the day, drank two cups of Sally's coffee, and then put his phone on hold and closed his eyes. He had read somewhere that ten minutes with your eyes closed was worth two hours' sleep. But the moment his lids touched, the floor of his head rocked to disco beat, and lights flashed between his ears.

This wasn't his life; he didn't live like this; he didn't think anyone could live like this. At that moment he thought he was dying. He opened his eyes; the room took a while to return; the music stopped. He lit a cigarette. He had to quit smoking. He was getting old. He was getting old this morning. He put his hand to the top of his head. The abundant frizz reassured him.

There was a modest tap at the door. Morgan removed his hand quickly from his head, fixed his expression and said, "Come in." His hand on the way down came in contact with the beginnings of a paunch, undoing the relief of the hair. It was Richard.

"Listen, Morgan." It was the voice of a man with a speech rehearsed. "I want to ask you to do me a favor which involves only a little dishonesty, but in a good cause." Richard waited for Morgan's curiosity to rise.

"How can I resist?" Morgan said wearily. Richard was looking well since leaving Kate, it had to be admitted. A month ago Morgan had gone, at Claudio's suggestion, to a nutritionist. "How's your marriage?" the man had asked him. "I've seen more patients spring back to life by getting out of bad setups than by all the megavitamins in California."

"Is this your usual prescription?" Morgan had demanded.

"I'm just saying what works," the man had said, writing out the dosages on a large pad. The pills had been too big to swallow. Morgan had gagged on the Cs. They were still in his sock drawer at home; even the bottles were too big for the bathroom cabinet.

Richard sat, paunchless, on Morgan's desk. "It is December," he said.

"Yes."

"Three weeks till Christmas."

"Yes."

Richard picked up Morgan's Odeon matches and put them down again. "I'm worried about Kate."

"Oh?"

Richard resumed the rehearsed tones: "I had an idea and I wonder if you'd think about it?"

"What?" Morgan relaxed into his slump again and waited.

"Liza's sister-in-law has a house in the country: wood beams, stone fireplaces, snowy hills, all that. They've offered it to us this year but we can't use it. We're going to California—to Liza's parents, actually." Richard waited for Morgan's remark, "Home to meet the folks, fast work," but Morgan said nothing. "Anyway, I thought it might be the kind of thing Kate would like—and you too, of course, and that . . ." The speech was going off; Richard began again. "What I wondered, Morgan . . . I can see it might be too late, and I don't want to interfere, I have no right, and it's only a suggestion . . ."

"What, for Christ's sake?" Morgan grabbed his pack of cigarettes and lit one.

"Well, look, what are you and Gabriella planning? I mean, if you're here and Kate's here and it's not a bore, maybe you might consider a little party in the country. I don't want to ask you to take care of her. Well, I do want to, but I can't. Anyway, I had a sort of fantasy of you all there, maybe with Claudio, Preston, all those friends."

Richard stopped now.

"Sleigh bells," Morgan continued, "snowball fights."

"Exactly," Richard said. "Christmas is a rough time. I, for one, am beginning to feel it already."

Morgan looked at Richard and drew on his cigarette, regretting his own last remark. "It's a great idea," he said, "but I've got to ask Gabriella and see what she has planned. Actually, I'm not sure she knows there's a Christmas this year."

"No," Richard said seriously, "but she will, and Kate will."

"Well, why not," Morgan said. "A big noisy Christmas." He tried to separate the words from the meaning.

"With Preston, Mickey, Gabriella . . ."

"I get the picture," Morgan said. "How big is this house?"

"Five or six bedrooms. It's very nice, Morgan. Liza's sister-in-law is terrific. They're going to Paris. I did say I'd offer it to you and they were pleased, burglars or something. Actually it was Liza's idea, too. But the point is that Kate would never accept this from either of us, whereas if you and Gabriella organized the whole thing . . . you wouldn't have to say whose house it was, Kate's never been there, there's nothing to give it away." Richard had the matches again and was flapping and unflapping the top. "Look, Morgan," he said, "I'd rather do this straight out, but just the idea of its being Liza's family's house on the big holiday would ruin it for her."

"I see that," Morgan said. He put out his cigarette. There were ten stubs in the ashtray.

"I'm very happy you say you'll think about it," Richard said, standing up.

"What day is Christmas?" Morgan asked.

"Saturday, but they give us Friday off, and there's a possibility of Monday too. That would be four days, enough time to get stuck into New England."

"I'll speak to Gabriella," Morgan said again.

"Thanks a lot. You're a good friend."

"I'll let you know."

"Thank you," Richard said again. "It means a lot."

"Well, no," Morgan said. "Thank you. It sounds terrific." For a while they both hovered.

"Well, thanks," Richard said quietly, and turned and left the room.

Morgan left his office shortly after Richard, and approached Sally. By her sympathetic smile he judged himself to be looking as seedy as when he'd arrived.

"I think it'd better be a working lunch," he said briskly, attempting to put an end to the expression with which she reflected his own misery. "Can you phone down for me?" He waited while Sally moved into action, still new to dictation, determined to get it right.

"One BLT on white toast, Russian dressing, and one, uh, Coke."

"Large or small?" Sally asked. She held her pen above the pad.

"Large," Morgan said.

"With lemon?" Sally suggested.

"All right."

She waited.

"That's it," Morgan said. "Thanks." Sally lay down the pen and pad and looked up the number of the deli in the small book in front of her. Then, her expression troubled, she swiveled her chair in Morgan's direction.

"Mr. Callagher."

Morgan turned on one heel; his speed made him nauseous. "What?"

"They have a minimum at lunchtime. Ten dollars."

"Then you have something," Morgan said. "Whatever you want." Big spender, he said to himself. Always one with the girls.

A hour later, ballasted by the BLT, sickened by the Coke (Morgan loathed Coca-Cola, but it was reputed to settle your stomach. Or perhaps by analogy with the drug Morgan had imagined it would set him up for the afternoon), he dialed Gabriella at her office. If, as he judged, she hadn't arrived much before noon, she was unlikely to be out to lunch. Perhaps she too was sitting nauseated over Coke and BLT.

"Gabriella," he said in his office voice.

"Morgan," Gabriella mocked him.

"I spoke to Richard this morning," he said more gently and explained Richard's proposal, trying as subtly as he could to indicate that while morally obliged to give the thing due consideration, it was his own preference to ignore it. But Gabiella said, "That's fantastic. How wonderful."

"I suppose so," Morgan said. Gabriella did not catch the tone.

"Five or six bedrooms?" she said. "That's you and me in one, Kate in in one, Claudio in one, Preston and whoever he brings . . ."

"Who's he bringing?"

"He's bound to have someone by Christmas. And Mickey and his German. Perfect."

"There might not be five bedrooms," Morgan said, "might be only single beds."

"The German may not come," Gabriella said. "Mickey can go in with Claudio. It'll all work out."

"We haven't even seen this house, Gabriella—it was only the vaguest, sketchiest suggestion."

"And we'll do it," Gabriella said. "Connecticut's New England, Morgan, that's your home country."

"What's that got to do with it?" Morgan said.

"You don't want us to go?"

"I didn't say that, but I think we could discuss it a little."

"We're always discussing things. Let's just do something for a change. What's the matter with it?"

"I guess I wanted to be with you this year."

"I'll be there," Gabriella said. "Anyway, we're always together." She said this affectionately.

"Alone, I meant," Morgan said.

"Think of Kate," Gabriella said.

"Think of you, you mean."

"All right, think of me."

There was a pause. Gabriella said, "Morgan, if you don't want to do it, just say so."

"Well, it's so sudden, it's going to be such a big production."

"You won't have to do a thing. I'll ring Kate and Claudio."

"Let me think about it."

"You don't want to spend Christmas in New York," Gabriella insisted, "it's too depressing."

"I suppose so," Morgan said. By now he was too tired to argue.

"Thanks, Morgan," Gabriella said kindly, "and thank Richard."

Morgan put the phone down and lowered his head onto folded arms. Even if the idea was for Kate, Morgan was not so sure that her being forced into proximity with him and Gabriella over the long Christmas weekend would do much to alleviate the pinch of the season. Still, the presence of the band (as Gabriella was beginning to call it) might water down their blatant coupledom —if indeed it still needed watering down. But it was true, Morgan realized, that he had not given Kate's Christmas much consideration. He supposed he'd thought she'd be going home, though as he remembered it now, Kate had not been home in fifteen years. And it really wouldn't be much fun for her to be dragged along for the evening meal, dry turkey, defrosted pumpkin pie, one glass of California Riesling, which was all that was available from his own parents. Gabriella's public version of it last year, repeated and embellished from December 26 until New Year's Day, had turned the thing from simple duty into high farce. It was true Morgan would prefer anything to another round of that.

An hour later, when Sally, on her own initiative, came by with black coffee, Morgan wrote a message for Richard and asked her to put it on his desk. After that he tried to forget everything but his work.

As the afternoon wore on, it seemed to Morgan that there were not many rewards for not having things his own way, except that, as they let him know in constant interruptions, other people were terribly pleased with him. Kate called first to thank him for the suggestion, and Richard stopped by to let him know how happy it had made him and Liza.

And Gabriella phoned. "Claudio's really excited," she said. "Mickey *is* coming with Heinz, and Preston is bringing a friend from Paris. Claudio's getting together a menu at restaurant discount. He suggested venison, but I said I'd ask you."

"Listen, Gabriella, I'm working."

"I won't be long. This is exciting. Mickey said oysters and goose, not turkey, but they're all willing to take your advice. Anyway, everyone says champagne, and Heinz, it turns out, has a cousin in wine imports."

"Who?" Morgan said.

"Heinz. We can get very cheap Moët. We can get a case per person. Preston said half a case, but—"

"This stuff will cost a fortune," Morgan said. "Who's supposed to pay?"

"They're all paying. Even Claudio's paying. It won't be more than a hundred dollars a head and probably less. Mickey says they'd spend twice that on seasonal depressions, anyway. But I did tell them we'd ask you first."

"Why can't we have a simple American Christmas, for Christ's sake, why does it have to be so fancy?"

"But it's their Christmas," Gabriella said, "and maybe their one shot at the country-house number. They don't have families, you know, or at least they choose not to. We can't make this drab and puritan just because we are."

"We are?"

"Well, rather drab and puritan."

"But all that champagne?"

"You drink milk then, darling, but they want to."

"Does Kate want all this hoopla?"

"Everyone does."

"Jesus . . . I'm not drab and puritan," Morgan said.

"No, the only straight in the world who'd be so nice. That's what Preston says."

"Thank Preston for me."

"That's what everyone says."

"Goodbye, Gabriella," Morgan said.

Morgan tried again to work but had to avoid Richard's eye all afternoon when, on frequent excuses, he came to aim his grateful glances. At five Claudio phoned to thank him and to consult on desserts. And in the end it would have seemed rather churlish for Morgan to refuse the role in which everyone wished to cast him.

O N A BLOCK NOT FAR FROM the once respectable town house that had been the home of Gabriella's great-great-grandparents, whose memories of Rhine castles had combined with those of other well-to-do immigrants to shape the architecture of this part of town, inspired its crenelated roofs and sweeping driveways, its fantastical window homages to the river—where among the pleasure boats and refuse barges, condoms and poisoned fishes, ghosts of the Lorelei still swam in neon reflections beneath the palisades—was Claudio's own castle dwelling: tiny rooms of a magic kingdom inside a graffitied river tenement, its former grandeur buried under decades of realtorial indifference, the response to the city's population shifts, and most recently, to the invasion, like a colonial revenge for the first Gothic theft, from the Caribbean.

The place was cheap, though only market rate considering the safety, hygiene and amenities of the building, but almost given away, according to Claudio, who had seen its potential three years ago, seized the offer from a startled janitor and begun the transformations, no more than Claudio's habitual practice of finding the silver in the dross and letting it shine.

Once safely out of the elevator and onto Claudio's landing— where Claudio himself washed the floors and kept a vase of straw flowers and pampas grasses properly arranged on a small polished table—once past the fire doors and inside Claudio's apartment, it was possible to see why Claudio lived where he lived, and according to certain of his friends, risked his life to do so.

It was all on a small scale, the whole thing being no bigger than six hundred square feet, divided into six unequal cubes of living room, bedroom, bathroom, kitchen, eating area and entrance hall, each part like one of Cornell's little boxes, a perfect miniature stage-set for magical performance. Along two sides of the larger frame into which these six boxes fitted, and in huge and spectacular contrast to the scale of Claudio's rooms, was the river, vast and magnificent from Claudio's sixteenth story, flooding in from the floor-to-ceiling windows and mirrored on the facing walls—so that the apartment seemed open to the elements, perilously hung in air—not only the moods and colors of the water, but reflected in that and arching above it, all the sky with its changing lights from dawn to sunset, in storm and snow, and between sky and water, though Claudio preferred not to think of it as such, a vast panoramic view of New Jersey.

It was, midair, nevertheless, an underwater kingdom, since Claudio had painted his rooms—lacquered and sanded them one coat a day over a ten-day period—a particular shade of green, gold-tinted, like a South American river, whose dark surface reflects between the overhanging jungle the diffused light of the sun. This green, exquisite though it was when absorbing the various colors of the day or when lit by tiny floor lamps and reflecting the night life from across the river, was actually, as Claudio informed you proudly, only the cheapest kind of porch paint: the whole job had cost him—walls and ceilings and the floors, where over the ordinary two-by-fours he had made a green-and-white checkerboard, as intricately patterned as the marbles of the Villa Borghese—no more than one hundred dollars.

In the living room there was little furniture, most of it street-rescued: one long pale sofa, two Bauhaus-type chairs, their curved arms reflecting metallically the low lights of the room, two small hand-lacquered tables covered by crystal ashtrays, silver cigarette boxes, packs of Gauloises, and one long, narrow glass-topped desk, positioned under one of the windows in such a way that you could watch, as you sat reading under the tall metal lamp, a river boat as it slowly crossed twice, once on the Hudson outside and once across the top of the desk, making elegant progress from glass pencil holder to Art Deco ashtray.

It was here that Claudio now sat, his back to the only heat of the apartment as it traveled the short distance between kitchen and living room from the open door of the gas oven. In the afternoon he had cleaned the apartment thoroughly, alarmed by the street soots that had seemed like field mice to have fled indoors from the cold, died and frozen on the floors and window sills. The gas had been on all day so that the place would be warm enough for Kate's arrival. Claudio had shopped for their dinner, made their salad, iced their wine. He had lit the night lights at the dimmer switches, set out the glass plates and red-handled cutlery on the round table that just fit inside the eating area, and was now writing out sample menus for the proposed Christmas weekend.

On a little pad in front of him he pressed down with his gold pencil:

Oysters for eight (8 dozen? 6?)
(cleaning?)

Goose with red cabbage (or too heavy?)

Chestnut stuffing

or Figs and Walnuts?

or Venison (speak to Kate)

purées; squashes; potatoes

Salads?

Dessert: Profiteroles, or too diff.?
Rum-fruit cake (ask Kate)

Cheeses: (Mickey to get Stilton from H. Bendel)
Wines: Heinz

Some of this could be gotten at restaurant discount, some could actually be stolen from the restaurant, e.g., chestnut purée, rum, etc.

At eight-fifteen the doorbell rang. Claudio crossed the entrance hall, stepping around the two-foot coral shell that sat on a green-lacquered Doric column, its rosy inside lit from a spot above it, so that the shell itself appeared to be the only light in the hallway, and opened the door for Kate, dressed in ski clothes and bearing three bottles of Chianti.

"I took you at your word about the cold," she said, "so forgive the synthetics." She kissed him.

"Look at this," she said. She made an appreciative two-step inside the tiny space and set down her bottles on the red-lacquered shelf that divided kitchen from living room. On a niche cut high between the large windows and spotlit from across the room was a vase of five carnations, red against the dark-green wall, and over the two chairs, laid out and half folded as though by a Pullman porter, were two blankets for Kate and Claudio.

"You've been buying flowers, and making dinner," Kate said. "And cleaning. Claudio, you *are* heaven."

Claudio smiled at her and bowed modestly. The pleasure of having Kate in his home, knowing he was going to cook for them, grew moment by moment. "Let me give you some wine," he said.

"It's only a kind of fueling, I'm afraid," Kate said, "I thought we'd need all that."

"We always seem to." Claudio brought out an Italian corkscrew and two goblets, carefully opened the wine and poured it into their glasses. "Cin-cin," he said to Kate. "Welcome back."

"It's lovely to see your home again, Claudio," Kate said. "I've missed you, or this."

"I know," Claudio said, "haven't we missed it? But you're always running around; I feel I haven't seen you for years. What have you been up to?"

"Only running around," Kate said.

"And how have you been feeling?" Claudio pushed off his loafers and placed a blanket over his feet.

"Up and down," Kate said. She drank her wine quickly to speed its effect inside the chilly room. Then she opened her ski jacket. It had been ages since anyone had cooked for her or looked after her properly. Watching Claudio, she felt the impact of all the weeks she'd been missing this. Simultaneously she envied Claudio because he was able to do for her what she longed to do for someone else: just that, cooking dinner for Richard, for Claudio, or for fourteen. Tonight she sensed she mustn't make too much of Claudio's invitation, spill over onto his tiny shoulders and scare him away. She drank her wine with the intention of taking the edge off her need, kept herself hard to a civilized manner and gently tested Claudio's capacity for her this evening.

"Gabriella described the house?" Claudio asked. He was careful not to mention Liza. Gabriella had said to say the thing was a windfall from Otto. But that was dangerous, could be checked.

"Wonderful, isn't it?" Kate said. "They're being terribly nice to me."

"Why shouldn't they be? They love you."

"Well, it must be a bore. I'm in their way."

"You're never in anyone's way. *I* was in the way, that's why I'm back."

"They'll miss you," Kate said. "How's the strike?"

"Mrs. Rodriguez says the heat's coming on Monday, but she's eternally optimistic. Personally, I hope it's after Christmas, I haven't got the rent anyway."

"All your nights out."

"Gabriella's. I can't keep it up."

Claudio refilled Kate's glass and looked at his watch. It had

47

stopped again; he would have to get it fixed for the fourth time that year. It was an antique LeCoultre; except for the repairs it had been a steal.

"Give me your watch a minute, Kate," Claudio said. "I just want to time the pasta, mine's not working."

He took Kate's watch and moved eight steps in to the kitchen, where she could still see him as he worked in the little space, avoiding the open door of the oven, adjusting the gas, pulling ingredients from the shelves. Claudio was a methodical cook, as Kate knew, so she did not speak to him while he worked but waited for him to settle out of the anxiety of his preparations.

"Bring a blanket to the table, Kate," Claudio said finally. "I'm going to close the oven for a while."

He seated Kate at the table opposite the window, lit the candles and placed her napkin with parodied professional flourish on her lap. "Now," he said. He grated a large piece of Parmesan over her plate, then sat down to watch while she tried it.

"Wonderful," Kate said, "what is it?"

"Tagliatelle with chicken livers and sherry. The pasta is made in a shop on Columbus. Is it good?" He tried his own. "Yes, it's good."

"Wonderful," Kate said again. "What a waste, Claudio."

"What?"

"You should be *cooking* at that restaurant."

"No thanks." .

"*I* miss the cooking."

"Why don't you do it? Invite people at Gabriella's." Claudio dealt with the problem in practical terms. A pleasure needed a little arranging. "Ask Gabriella," he said.

"I don't know. It's her house."

"Yes, but she's not exactly possessive. She doesn't cook much, does she?"

"They've been going out a lot," Kate said.

Claudio got up to get another bottle of wine. A phone rang and he picked it up. Claudio's apartment had phones in each of the tiny rooms, the gift of a former boyfriend, an ex-Bell employee who had managed to wire the house in one coked weekend so that not only was there a white phone next to the bed, under the kitchen cupboard, on the glass desk and in the bathroom—where Claudio often sat amid his bubbles, risking electrocution—but the calls registered to an unknown account in Nebraska. Claudio had not paid a phone bill in the three years the system had been there. Miraculously, the service had not been shut down.

Kate listened to Claudio accepting a party invitation and finished her wine. When he came back to the table, she was a little drunk. "I don't know how you do it," she said to him, smiling.

"What?" He uncorked the second bottle.

"This awful single life."

"What awful single life? That was a party."

"Well, I can't do it."

Claudio looked at her and said nothing.

"You've got to be my model now, Claudio," Kate said cheerfully. "Yes, you, darling, you've got to instruct me how to do it with elegance." She raised her glass to him and when he'd filled it, drank it down.

Claudio watched Kate and waited for the note of irony that would relieve him.

"When I was with Richard," Kate said, "well, Richard says now he was bored because we never talked. Sometimes I was a little bored, not bored but sort of unsurprised because it was always Richard coming home, really I was happy with him, that was the strangest part, because while I was happy with him, he was happy with Liza. Anyway, spoiled as I was with Richard's always being there. I thought occasionally I was a little bored because life was so easy, livable. Stupid, wasn't it? I used to think what I wanted was to feel things in their true state, unprotected by all that film of happiness. Now of course I've got it and everything *is* stronger, brighter, fiercer, just as I suspected. Except me of course," Kate said. "And I don't have the slightest notion how to live anymore. So, Claudio, tell me."

Claudio watched Kate's smile.

"How do I go on being single," she said, "without being humiliated?"

Kate tried to hold Claudio's attention, touching his hand. But Claudio said, "There's nothing humiliating about it."

"No, not for you, that's the thing I'm asking. You can be with people without expressing this awful desperation. Maybe you're not desperate."

"No, I'm not desperate," Claudio said.

"But I am desperate, and I spend all my energy trying to keep other people from seeing it."

Claudio looked away from Kate and poured wine into the glasses. "They won't last," he said, "these feelings."

"What I can't bear," Kate went on after a little while, but more quietly, "is what you seem to manage so easily, well, not you, darling, but in the clubs, all that traffic, all that asking and accepting and refusing, without any hurt feelings, or feelings at all, as far as I can see, just a great democratic get-together, just brotherhood."

"What's wrong with brotherhood?" Claudio tried feebly to joke with Kate.

"Because it isn't enough," Kate said, "not enough for girls."

"Then you've got to be brave enough to have your feelings hurt. Anyway, this is all bullshit, Kate—gays have feelings too you know, it's exactly the same."

"You mean everyone in the clubs is looking for the real thing?"

"Possibly."

"I don't believe it."

"Well." This was one of the lines that kept them apart, it was better to retrack. "Anyway, clubs isn't the whole story, you know that."

"I suppose. And I know it looks good from the outside, all that freedom, all that choice. Gabriella is totally enchanted with it. But just imagine if that was all there was in her life. A voyeur's nightmare."

"It's not all there is for you, Kate. For Christ's sake be patient, some three-piece-suit is waiting for you at some future dinner party. You're the last person who has to sleaze around bars. Don't be so melodramatic."

Claudio pushed the salad at her.

"You're wrong," Kate said simply. "No dinner-party Harry is going to take this. You see, even you can't manage."

"I can manage, Kate," Claudio said angrily. "Eat your salad."

And again, as so often recently, Kate changed the subject, apologized, joked badly while Claudio's good humor frayed. She had violated his surface calm, and she had spoken too seriously of what was underneath, and not even underneath for her; but it was *his* life and its limitations she complained of; *his* underworld; her analogies were rhetorical: he did not give her right to the pain.

They had their cheese and coffee and finished the second bottle of wine, but the elegance of the meal tottered. Kate knew that the premise of tête-à-tête was meant merely to set the style; and yet, here was the content, unadulterated. Hopelessly liberated by the drink, she began again. "What I want to know, Claudio," she said, unable herself now to look at him as she spoke, "is what you had to give up to make your peace with single life. What is the exchange?"

"But where do you get the notion that your life with Richard was the measure for everything else? You weren't so happy, it seemed to me, were you?"

"But this is worse."

"Because you're not used to it," Claudio said gently.

"I don't want to get used to it."

"Well, tough then."

"Tough?"

"Oh Christ, Kate, there are thousands of bozos out there waiting for you, just dying to enter into the little coupledom you believe to be where life begins. Do you have any idea how nauseating it looks from our perspective? The world divided into, practically patrolled by, hundreds of self-esteeming little twosomes?"

"I suppose so," Kate said.

"What you're saying amounts just about to what all those Moral Majority fascists say, that anything but married life is abnormal, perverse. I've never given up anything, exchanged anything, I've always been happy single, unbored, certainly never desperate on my own. Why should I be? But your condemning it for yourself in these terms means you must condemn it for me and for Preston and for all of us who live differently; you're really threatened by it."

"No, I love you. And you can do it, that's the difference. I can't."

"How do you know?"

"I just know."

"Well, Kate, as I say, tough. And as I say, not for very long. For Christ's sake, a little patience."

Claudio got up now and fussed about the table, clearing plates in order to move, as Kate knew perfectly well, from the position in which this argument had left them. When everything was cleared away, he went to sit next to Kate in the colder part of the room. She sat silently next to the Japanese prints, wrapped tightly in the blanket, her cheeks still flushed from the wine. Claudio, too, wrapped himself tightly in his blanket and tried to say something that would make them feel a little less sadly the cold air that surrounded them.

F OR GABRIELLA, ON THE
Saturday morning following
Claudio's departure, there was a strong sense of aftermath, of
waiting anxiously in space. She was used to Claudio's rattling, his
slow procedures, his twelve o'clock offer to get *pain au chocolat*
from the French bakery downstairs, his twelve-thirty plan for
them all to join Mickey and Preston for brunch in SoHo, his two
o'clock suggestion that they get in Chinese takeout, or his five
o'clock proposal that they all hop a cab for a Lana Turner double
bill on the other side of town. She was used to following the lead
of his organized indolence. Even Kate had learned from Claudio
to slow down, on Saturdays at least, to wander the house in her
blue kimono until the day presented itself, Claudio-made, guilt-
lessly self-indulgent. Even Morgan had taken up the rhythms of
their Saturdays, walking about the apartment listening to Verdi,
half-dressed, periodically returning to Gabriella, in bed among her
papers, to see whether they might make love.

But this morning Morgan had left early to take the car to a
garage in Queens; Gabriella was up, violently stripping sheets to
take with Claudio's to the laundromat downstairs; and Kate was
in the kitchen, polishing her boots over last Sunday's *New York
Times*. Apart from the sounds of this industry, the apartment was
silent.

Morgan's early departure seemed to Gabriella (as her stripping of sheets might have seemed to Morgan) a continuation of a scene begun last night, though a continuation in the guise of an ending. Since none of last night's fight had been more than masque and ritual, and since such indirection was alien to them, Gabriella and Morgan might have expected to spend this morning delving under the dumbshow. The present disjunction was pure evasion, therefore, providing time and warmth for bitterness to blossom in separation; and though Queens was far enough away for Morgan to return cleansed and renewed by an outside world, Gabriella was nonetheless dreading his return.

The bastard evening had begun badly, conceived in Gabriella's gratitude to Morgan about Christmas and her own remorse for her hungover day at work (on her way out she had apologized to Max for her poor performance and promised him better: Max had simply stared at her and returned to his crossword). Then she'd stood on the crowded bus all the way home, offering each seat as it appeared to people, older, heavier, more tired and then simply other than herself, until the hovering men implored her and those sitting in Gabriella-vacated places, miserably (since they had agreed to the assessment of older, heavier, more tired) cheered up, recognizing in her charity only eccentric high spirits.

Off the bus she'd thought of Morgan's favorite food and bought it: châteaubriand and Vosne-Romanée, the ingredients for *tarte au citron* and béarnaise sauce. She'd bought flowers and pink paper napkins, and as if this fare weren't already loaded with signals of gratitude, repentance and the least subtle sort of amorous declaration, Gabriella had put candles on the table and, tipping rhetoric into camp, Tchaikovsky on the stereo.

She had also, not altogether trusting Morgan to see these things as soon as he got in, put pine essence out on the bathtub and a clean towel on the chair so that even before Morgan could undress, he would be overwhelmed by evidence of her good intentions.

Of course the whole thing had misfired, which Gabriella should have foreseen the moment Morgan arrived, taking his newspaper in to the bath with him. And she should have forgotten the whole thing when after an hour Morgan came into the kitchen, towel-wrapped and pine-odored, having passed the candle- and flower-bearing table, to say that he felt a little queasy and thought he might go straight to bed.

At that point Gabriella had to choose between two images of herself: brave and reproachless and concerned for Morgan's health or vauntingly irritable, demanding at least acknowledgement of what she'd done.

Instead she'd read Morgan's "health" as part of a game, read herself as bound by its rules, gone off responsively to have the usual twenty-minute what is it/nothing/come on/nothing conversation until the terms were right for Morgan to say (as though irresponsibly and too-much provoked) that he was sick and tired of "this life" they were living; that Gabriella should leave him alone.

But Gabriella chose (or really could not choose, so caught were they) to triumph by pretending to surrender, offering to bring Morgan his dinner in bed. And once again, not quite trusting the power of her message to Morgan, set the hot plate on his stomach and the glass of wine under his nose (where one whiff would have told him it was something special and that he was a man who had wronged his wife). And Morgan at that point toyed with two images of himself: backing down and saying he'd had no idea of the trouble she'd gone to, or taking the plate and throwing it at her. Instead Morgan had risen from bed, gone naked to the table, set the plate down and the wine, set Gabriella's plate opposite his, poured her wine. He had even condescended to light the candles. They had then eaten their meal in total silence, broken only by a final sarcastic "Thanks" on Morgan's part and "Go to hell" on Gabriella's.

It had been too theatrical to do any damage, the theater itself only obliquely and safely expressing the real rage that Gabriella

sensed and then retreated from in explanations to herself of Mor
gan's fatigue, Morgan's jealousy, Morgan's problems at work. Bu
there were no problems at work, and no serious reasons for fatigue
or jealousy: what there was, was a hole somewhere, and thin ice
and this sort of danger signal, pretty legible despite the disguise

When the bed was stripped and the sheets had been thrown into
the corner, Gabriella found herself too perplexed and irritable to
make it up. Instead she wandered toward the sounds of the
buffing that came from the kitchen, punctuated by the little
whimpers and sighs that Kate made as she worked.

The light from the window set Kate's curls in a fuzzy brown
halo and fell on the long white leg that peered from beneath her
silk kimono. Her feet were bare and looked rather childish despite
the red polish on her toes. They seemed curiously flat this morning.

"Hello, Kate," Gabriella said in a voice that demanded a response.

Kate looked up at her friend, and breaking off her little hum-
ming noise, stopped polishing. "What's wrong with you?" she
asked.

"You going somewhere today?"

"Tonight," Kate said.

"Lucky girl, dates." Gabriella sat down on the kitchen chair.
"Anyone nice?" she asked her.

"Nope," Kate said. She had resumed the buffing. "No one nice
at all."

Gabriella watched Kate for a few minutes in silence. There was
great concentration going into that cleaning of boots: a little
buffing to the right, then a little to the left, a tilt into the window
light, a gaze and return to work. All the while Kate kept her body
rigid, moving only her arms and wrists, occasionally her head to
look at the light or speak to Gabriella. Kate's boots were lined up

against the wall. At the moment Kate had finished her third pair and was reaching for the fourth.

It was then that Gabriella noticed that the polish Kate had been using had slipped under the newspapers and was working its way in smears along the kitchen floor. If it had been Morgan there cleaning his shoes and making a mess, Gabriella would simply have said so, since her remarks—unless, as this morning, a previous fight hung in the air—would have retained a purity of information and been taken as referring to shoe polish and nothing else; or so Gabriella had always proceeded. But with Kate, the mention of mess bore with it a statement of relative power in that household, of the floor's being Gabriella's. Therefore, Gabriella said nothing while the brown wax bit deeper and grew larger under her eyes. Instead she concentrated on her talk with Kate, feeling the pulls of friendship against the pulls of property until finally, dispiritingly, friendship foundered and Gabriella said, by now without the least spontaneity, "Kate, sorry to mention it, but do you mind, the polish is going all over the floor."

And that was it, for Kate, interrupted in her contented concentration, made way for Gabriella's greater claim, lifted the paper, made the noise of horror and apology (so that Gabriella had now to say, inanely, "No, it's nothing; comes right up with a cloth") and stopped her polishing to clean the floor.

"Look, Kate," Gabriella insisted, "I'm sorry I said anything. You finish your boots, I'll do it for you."

"For Christ's sake, Gabriella, let me clean it up! It's my mess."

"All right."

It was gratifying to Gabriella that it took some time to get the polish off the floor, throw away the old papers and replace them with thicker ones.

"I'll make us some tea," she offered.

"All right," Kate said; slight irritation held in the voice.

"Have you had breakfast?" Gabriella asked, hostess being the more acceptable face of possessor.

"Just tea is fine," Kate said. No "Thank you" acknowledged Gabriella's position; but Kate was polishing again, and while the kettle boiled, Gabriella left her alone with her boots.

Her clumsiness with Kate confused her. Their relations seemed so uneasy compared to hers with Claudio, or Morgan's with Claudio, or most of all those between Claudio, Mickey and Preston. It seemed now to Gabriella that she'd never felt a bump or barb inside their friendship, nor felt any tension beneath its beaming surface, nor evasion of tension, nor any indication that there was anything in the realm of circumstance that could ever bring that friendship to an end. But what was most impressive was how much they simply took for granted what Kate and Gabriella failed to bring off.

There was a secret to such kinship. Gabriella envied it and wanted it with Kate; beyond that, she really wanted it with Morgan. Not this nervous waiting for his return, not the exhausting scrutiny of what had happened, what ought to happen. She wanted blankness, puppy trust, a bumpless harmony that she could simply lean into and count on.

Perhaps it was sex that made the difference, and the answer was to proceed as Claudio, Preston and Mickey, never making friends of tricks, never going to bed with a friend: strict categories for everyone. Morgan, though, was Gabriella's lover *and* friend, and that, perhaps was the explosive combination. Or was it, rather, no combination at all, and was Morgan always *either* lover or friend, and never, in the same passionate breath, the two at once? And yet the two at once had once been their ideal: to be equal, really the same, and to be passionate. And perhaps that was what wasn't possible. Perhaps the sex itself, however innocently and fraternally the bodies came to bed, ensured that they leave it with one more powerful than the other.

But even supposing it were the nature of sex that separated Gabriella and Morgan, why couldn't Gabriella and Kate, who'd known each other as long and seen each other as frequently, have the kind of closeness that Mickey, Preston and Claudio had? Was it because they didn't cruise together that they didn't bond? No wolves, no pack? Had they been culturally separated by the expected competition for men, were they thus too much on the same footing? Or the reverse, were they not on the same footing at all, as Gabriella's floor and polish number had just indicated, and as was indicated more seriously by the fact that Gabriella was married and Kate was just now, and quite miserably, not?

Gabriella returned to the kitchen to make the tea, glancing nervously over to Kate as the image of Mickey, Preston and Claudio, lined up at a bar, all handsome, all drinking, all laughing, rose to reproach her. Perhaps their friendship had its security in the understanding that nothing so gauchely earnest as a real question would impose itself on that barroom amity which they rightly held precious. That was probably one secret, because for Gabriella the silent understandings just weren't there, neither for her and Morgan, nor for her and Kate. The direct lines seemed the only way. As she gave Kate her tea, she asked, "Are you all right here, Kate?"

"Yes. I won't be another minute and then I'll get out of your way."

"You're not *in* my way. I mean generally. Is it all right?"

"What?"

"Life."

"Of course not."

Gabriella sighed. "But you must enjoy your freedom a little, Kate."

Kate looked up and for a few seconds stared at Gabriella. "Grass just looks greener," she said eventually.

"But you are free," Gabriella ventured again.

"Am I? Well, then, so this is freedom." Kate went on again with her boots while Gabriella tried for something else. But then Morgan's key sounded in the door and Gabriella found herself waiting for him to come in and end their doomed intimacy.

Morgan, seeing the two women talking quietly in the kitchen, and at noon still in their bathrobes, decided not to intrude. He said good morning as he passed them but did not stop. And Kate, feeling that Morgan had not come in because she was there, stopped polishing, collected her five pairs of boots and rose, like a Seventh Avenue Kali. "Thanks for the tea," she said to Gabriella. "See you later."

Abandoned, Gabriella followed Morgan into the bedroom.

"How are you?" she asked him. She was a little aware that her failure to contact Kate made her less unwilling to confront Morgan.

"All right," Morgan answered her. "You going to stay like that all day?"

"How was the car?"

"Horribly expensive. Probably would have been cheaper in Manhattan. I'll have to trek out there again Thursday."

"Poor Morgan," Gabriella said, unconvincingly.

"What's this mess in here?" Morgan asked her.

"Look, Morgan, just because you had a rotten train ride—"

"Come on, Gabriella, it's twelve o'clock. You could get dressed. What are these sheets doing here? Why isn't the bed made?" Here it was, a little contact.

"I'm going to take them down. Why don't you have some tea?"

"What do I want tea for? It's lunchtime."

Gabriella went off to the bathroom. With Claudio gone, civilized languor slid into squalor. She did see how it looked from Morgan's point of view. She got dressed quickly and made the bed, and found Morgan in the kitchen, heating a can of tomato soup.

"Is that what you want?" Gabriella said.

"That's what there is. Is there anything else?"

"I was going to go out."

"When exactly?"

"Come on, Morgan, cool down. It's Saturday."

"This is how we live weekdays, too."

"All right. It will stop."

"We can't afford it. That was two hundred dollars last week."

"Well, it will stop."

"And it's getting to be an ordeal. I can't just coast at the office any longer. And you—what's going on at the agency? Do you even show up these days?"

"You know I do."

Morgan tipped the soup into a bowl and ate it with a small spoon, leaning carefully over the sink: a pathetic tableau.

"You want me to get you something from the deli?" Gabriella asked him.

"No, no more going out."

"The deli's not going out."

"No more idiotic expenditures."

"Four dollars for a roast beef on rye?"

"Twenty dollars for a bottle of wine, God knows what for the steak. It's finished. We'll have this idiotic Christmas and then it's back to normal life."

"Which is what exactly?"

"As we used to live," Morgan said, drinking his soup now straight from the bowl, "before all this."

"All what?" Gabriella challenged him.

"Before the fag invasion."

IT WAS WITH THIS TERM THAT Morgan announced the beginning of a new phase in his dealings with Gabriella. The first time he used it, Gabriella dismissed it as mere irritation; then, as Morgan continued, she saw his words as counterprovocation to her own soft phrases: "the band" or, in higher affection, "la bande." Later she saw in Morgan's attempt to dissociate himself from her world with them, and in particular their Christmas plans, a new kind of cowardice with respect to her, since under the barbs of the words: "pansies," "fags," virulent and aggressive as they were, was an evasion of head-on discussion. And, too cowardly herself to challenge him, to provoke a scene that would ruin their Christmas and possibly bring to an end her association with the group, Gabriella allowed him to say such things as a safety valve, she told herself, a self-protecting flinch. The new company had arrived so suddenly, and Morgan was, after all, a slow adapter. And perhaps Morgan's menaced shorthand was no more offensive to her than were to him the terms by which Gabriella named a harmonious circle to which she as yet only superficially belonged.

In any case, it wasn't often that Morgan exploded in this way; nor did it seem in the least to reflect a change in Morgan's liking Claudio or his ease in being with him, nor the frequency of their outings. What it did affect was Gabriella's freedom to talk to

Morgan about her happiness: that now became a private, separate matter. For a while before Christmas they not only ceased to go to discos (an economy that suited everyone, anyway) but ceased to speak to each other about a subject that grew increasingly important to them both.

For both of them, the reticence was menacing. In the past it had been their procedure to scrutinize each other's responses: to people, to books, to meals, to cities. It was their great pleasure and later their great pride that they seldom disagreed about such things. This made travel with Morgan pure pleasure for Gabriella, made visits to art galleries and movies reliably happy: the bond and identity of their tastes were sure. And what they didn't have in common (Morgan's Greek and Latin, his fondness for beer and seersucker, her skiing, her love of ballet, a great many former friends) had either been isolated from the shared life and treated like private vice (Morgan read his Ovid in the bath; Gabriella sneaked off occasionally to Stowe) or else had been abandoned, weeded out of their lives to provide the illusion, at least, of harmony.

Not that they hadn't fought, they fought all the time, but like gardeners embroiled with an overgrown hedge, they had talked for hours to straighten out the tangle, prune the wild branches so that the simple living plant of their agreement would show itself, green and healthy, if somewhat thin.

And these entanglings—public, tiresome, but constant, based, as Gabriella occasionally now suspected on a terror of dissimilarity —were what Claudio had so often found "impressive."

But in the new silence that grew between Morgan and herself, the old method of talk began to appear to Gabriella as something fraudulent; like an ancient language whose vocabulary no longer bore reference to the material world or sensibilities of its modern-day users, its apparent richness was misleading. It began to seem to Gabriella that this impressive language of theirs might be not only dead but actually deadening. For Morgan and she, by discussing every new event in their lives, whether film or friendship (and to this the notable exception had been Claudio), simply rendered each new thing harmless, deprived of any power to change, for good or ill, what had by now been worked into a comfortable and proven means of survival.

It was hard now not to see the fear behind this mechanism, to wonder whether those fringe disputes—over kohl and relatives and household economies—were not there simply to keep away the real dispute, whatever it was, the thing that, honestly appraised, might blow their "great marriage" to smithereens. Different for them than for Kate and Richard, Gabriella thought: it would not be a lover that would come between them but a new reading, a revelation that the structure of their married life was and had been—perhaps for many years—rotten, hollow and—it would surprise them, they of the proclaimed candor in all things—entirely dishonest.

A little of this Gabriella knew, but it was knowledge she resisted by filling her consciousness with other things, and increasing the objects of her apparent honesty. She had developed a kind of arrogant truth to herself, for example, about what she would and would not agree to. Except in one baffling area over which she and Morgan had their most felt and pointed disputes—namely, Gabriella's career, about which she seemed to the work-adoring Morgan extraordinarily indifferent. At thirty-two she had a job so irrelevant to her interests and capabilities, which she performed with such obvious apathy, that it was by now almost an embarrassment—not to her, but to Morgan. It was here, according to Morgan, that Gabriella deformed herself most while apparently holding out on him: the perverse manner by which she sometimes sought to ensure truth to herself. And yet Gabriella did not change jobs or make a move to, as Morgan put it, "take herself seriously" for two reasons: first, she was only now beginning to feel the existence of this real self, and second, she guessed that her own vulnerability in this matter of work suited them both: Morgan because it gave him a kind of hold over her, and Gabriella because his dominance brought with it Morgan's obligation *(noblesse oblige)* to let her do in all other (because to him less important) spheres whatever it was she thought she wanted. This was another of their trade-offs: her "authenticity" in every area but work, for his ownership of her, a pact disguised under his expressed irritation with her indifference to the serious demands of the world.

Their marriage had always involved such sacrifices: other people, conflicting interests, their honesty, and freedom. But always the sacrifices had seemed to be in a good cause: ensuring that each would always be there to save the other. It was a marriage of only children, self-spoiled, self-proclaimed orphans who in their fear of separation tried to make each other identical twins. And that was where the deadlock came from. Now as the orphans grew or longed to grow into adult selves, the necessary redefinitions of power threatened the first frightened pact, the defensive egalitarianism. Occasionally a huge loneliness loomed up before each of them, a glimpse of the time when they would part and go their separate ways. For even Gabriella suspected that authenticity was something not to be arrived at while thus yoked to Morgan; and even Morgan could see that he could not find his own place in the world until he left the enchanted castle of his life with Gabriella. Yet neither could say so yet, and each dissembled, bargained and clung to the other and disguised the clinging in the gestures and language of freely chosen unity.

And still they were so close, after all those years of proximity. Yet Gabriella had made a space for Claudio. Or perhaps Claudio, seeing the hole between them, had found his nest there ready-made. Perhaps under Morgan's contemptuous phrasing lay his recognition that Gabriella's love of her "band" derived from the failure of the marriage of identical twins to provide anything but mirrors. It wasn't as a man that Morgan was threatened by Gabriella's "band," though his words were crudely sexist; it was as a playmate: he simply did not wish to be left alone in the nursery.

So now Gabriella, out of pity for the threatened child in Morgan, and out of cowardice, let him have his sarcasms, gave up the dancing, arranged their Christmas without him. And Morgan, feeling safe to still see the child in her—both in these concessions and in her pleasures—let her have her willfulness, wrapped, as he thought, in his protection, and kept her safe from the outside world.

I T WAS GETTING LATE FOR Gabriella to be heading back to work after this long lunch break. Even if she left now by cab, she would not arrive much before three-thirty. But still, faintly bored as she was, she could not move. In the past few hours the four of them had slowly worked their way over the secondhand shops along upper Broadway, searching for cheap presents. Since twelve o'clock they had fingered their way through countless pairs of faded satin knickers (with Kate in mind), through piles of army surplus, through rows of limp and greasy post-war neckties; had peered through the cigar smoke of bored shop proprietors into cracked glass cases for treasures—a tie clip, a cigarette holder, a chipped enameled eggcup—that would serve on Christmas morning as tokens of their precious friendship.

A warm, acrid waft rose from the bale of garments, shirts mostly, collarless, buttonless, on which Gabriella perched, not so charmed this third hour by the parading of Mickey in the jacket of a Catskills bandleader, of Preston in a tuxedo from the thirties.

They, on the other hand, were used to this patient search through the dregs of other people's wardrobes. It was thus, for example, that Claudio regularly outfitted himself, after sporadic methodical crawls from one moth-spurned rack of clothing to another, and so successfully that Gabriella when she first knew him had imagined him to be what he intended to suggest, some princely bachelor with a private income and a family tailor. As for Mickey and Preston, they wore clothes which had they been available on Madison Avenue would have cost them more than they earned in a month. But it was painstaking work, not just weeding through the schlock, holding up each piece to the light for tea stains and cigarette burns, trying it on, haggling over the price; but more exhausting was the projecting of self so garbed out of the rag shop and (via the dry cleaners) into the future cocktail lounge or gallery opening, the imagined turning in profile and assessment of future public effects. Yet all of this was art and science to Claudio, allowing him to script his identity every morning, announce his aspirations, keep his enemies at bay. There was independence and joy in it but there was also, Gabriella thought, some of the fear that lies under camouflage and in the desire to please—a sense that to step out in the wrong shoes was to invite destruction.

But if not recklessness, there was a kind of freedom here, it seemed to Gabriella. Preston, an accountant, and Mickey, a book designer with a university press, had, like Morgan and Richard, jobs that might have predicated their clothes and prescribed their haircuts. But they'd dealt with those potential constraints long ago. Like Claudio they worked to finance their lives, and not as Morgan and Richard did, for the pleasure of the process, or as Otto in order to be dutiful threads of the social fabric. They neither subordinated their identities to their work nor incorporated what they did in their sense of self. Neither Calvinist nor bohemian in attitude, the three of them lived instead in the spaces between earning and spending; and though such spaces (as for Preston, who worked long hours in pursuit of some future freer time) might be small enough, it was there, unrestricted, that they cavorted, in forbidden places and at odd hours, among night people and underground men. Gabriella, used to Morgan's world of early risers and briefcase-carriers or Max's pleasure-denying, muse-directed *literati*, found it hard not to feel the bravado of this, and at times, inside the fatuity, the heroism.

That word might have seemed peculiar, attached just now to Claudio as he held under the light, peering as though at some priceless jade carving, a pathetic thin green tie, over which he moaned and clucked softly, on the threshold of purchase. Yet it *was* heroic somehow to live as though life were no more than this; impressive to be able to say, casually, stoically, that the things which the world values—monogamy, mortgages, family, "job satisfaction" and social approval—are worth no more than this was: the ability to recognize the splendor of just such a green tie.

Nevertheless, she did not join them. Apart from the occasional testing of headgear, holding up of drawers, expressions of approval or outrage, Gabriella remained outside these goings on. Her Christmas presents when they were bought would be duller, more expensive, got with less pleasure; they would be *her* tributes to Claudio, Mickey and Preston, to them not as apparitional phenomena with blue eyes or heights to be matched, but as other phenomena, soul-burdened, at least personality-burdened. She would buy books, records, concert tickets: things pleasure-directed but by no means gay.

Gifts, pleasures, gestures, everything in Gabriella's life had to signify. Not for her this life of unscrutinized moments, acceptance of surfaces, but more like the leaning and whining and constant demand for what was underneath and what was going to last. Her friends, in refusing the conventional anxieties, seemed to her not only nobly above the fray but rather pure, admirable in the way they took their pleasures where the world pitched its leavings. The independence of the hedonism was manifest, likewise, in the love life of these three, not just the ability to find the diamonds in the rough trade, but it was clear, too, in the general admiration, so unlike what motivated heterosexual bonds, of mobility and passage. In Gabriella's experience, partnering had always ended with someone being possessed and someone else possessing: men possessed women, and women, by agreeing to be possessed, secured possession of their men. But gay life seemed to function rather along the lines of the celebrated anarchist Dutch white bicycle: a vehicle for communal transport, ridden for joy or quickly abandoned; in either case, altruistically shared among the brethren.

Gabriella admired, and felt as something no longer available to her, the fraternal nature of her friends, liked to watch how close they were, how naturally they functioned as bodies, never bumping in that small space of the shop, touching each other easily, like children of a family where there is plenty to go around.

As now, this afternoon, Gabriella loved to feel herself closely held inside their friendship or perhaps merely sprayed in the overspill of friendliness, touched without constraint, patted, kissed, without their least fear of her misreading. Best, she liked to watch them in their greetings, or when bidding each other goodbye, no matter after what exuberance or hilarity, when they became suddenly delicate, and with their chaste, serious kisses, rather like the apostolic figures on the walls of Giotto's famous chapel.

Actually, it *was* rather more like a religion than a childishness, the innocence of Claudio and company being something acquired in adulthood and espoused as a way of dealing with a rigid and disappointing world. Real childhood, as Gabriella thought about it, was unlikely to make one so at ease or loving. Her own had hardly existed; she'd been thrown as soon as she could talk into the world of her mother's bohemian friends with *their* talk of sex and money and the trials of relationships. And Morgan's childhood, far more conventional, had made him even less fit for this sort of trusting. *He'd* been horribly lonely. His parents, both busy teachers at a New England college, and not able to face the further impediment to academic peace by the addition of humans to the household, had tried to relieve his isolation with various pets. These easy to look after, but to Morgan charmless, were generally sent away after a few months, and then Morgan too, at the age of thirteen, was packed off to prep school, where, his parents told themselves, he would be provided with lifelong friends, as well as the tools for advancement. But these two aims seem to have conflicted, for Morgan found at school, in the rigid grading system and weekly prize givings, a disruptive rule of competition, to which his parents added the weight of their own ambition for him. Morgan won prizes and had "friends" at school, but since he was never allowed to forget that he was meant to strive against them in the academic and official (more esteemed) areas of school life, the real, egalitarian bonds were never made.

At Yale the same pressures applied, aggravated by the added competition for women, and the need, in those early days of the Vietnam war, to avoid being drafted by not falling behind in one's grades—an issue, then viewed, if somewhat exaggeratedly (since the cannon fodder actually came from elsewhere, much further down in the academic hierarchies) as a matter of life and death.

For Morgan, the separations continued after Yale with Gabriella, in the cheerful dismissal of friends not suitable to the coupledom, in the stratification of life at work. And in the end it could be said that Morgan's expensive education, in having failed to provide him with correct and abundant friendships, had for that very reason proven a useful training for life. Loneliness or, at best, a despairing two set against the world, companioned by the shadows of other twosomes, had been the official offering.

But Gabriella's new friends were free, it seemed to her, to spurn the prevailing choices: the stereotypic male wisdom of a private life subordinated to the egocenter of work, and the cliché female model, where the objects and values of the world fly out from the still center of Romantic Love, like an exploding diagram of Matthew Arnold's "Dover Beach." Theirs was free to be a separate formulation: work was less important than love, and love could manifest itself in community and friendship.

So Gabriella fantasized, grew envious and depressed, inside the

71

dusty shop. Set against the gnarled coupledom of herself with Morgan, or Kate's broken-hearted sense of herself as a crippled fragment of a former one, was the picture Gabriella made of these loving friends, admitted into their Giotto heaven one by one as each "came out" and professed the faith, free to touch and kiss like angels, while the sad work of the world went on beneath them, obeying its lunch hours, accumulating its commendations, celebrating its correctness in joyless dinner parties and doomed marriages. This Gabriella thought as she now slipped off her bale and made her way to the back of the shop, to take her not quite apostolic leave and return to her not yet abandonable place of work.

MORGAN'S HAVING AGREED TO Richard's proposal for Christmas thawed a friendship frozen ever since Kate had accepted shelter in the Callagher apartment. Richard's gratitude to Morgan had declared itself in an invitation to dinner, which, since Morgan had been allowed into the secret of Richard's remorse, might now take place in Richard's present home, the loft where Liza lived and painted. In the week before Christmas, the four of them sat together there, brought indirectly by Kate, but bent on exorcism of Kate's ghost.

Gabriella did not know Liza well, had seen her only briefly, at Kate's parties or in the street, a tall, pink, bony apparition, with paint-spattered cropped hair, and an unbuttoned coat, an expression of hasty friendliness in her greeting, the manner of someone eternally on her way, late, elsewhere. It occurred to Gabriella now, watching Liza on this evening, that it was her constant movement that had attracted Richard, challenged him to get in its way and slow it down. Leaving Kate, he had destroyed the calm with which she had customarily functioned, handed her the hellish baton with which she now raced. Perhaps Richard liked his women speeding past him, or perhaps, more simply, liked to be the one to adjust their speed, keeping the controls in his own pocket. But Liza, it seemed to Gabriella, was not yet entirely his. There was a kind of waiting quality about him.

Liza refused to be judged. She flashed about her a strange sexy cheerfulness, covering the resented inspection with bits of "business": drinks, ashtrays, removal of cats. Her loft had its own recalcitrance, with its rolls of canvas and tubes of acrylic left in the places where her guests had to walk; with its palette knife for cutting the cheese and the thumbprints of dried paint on the glasses. There was an air of abandon, too, about the meal, served partly hot, partly cold, the chops congealing in grease and curled at the edges, the spuds bare and boiled, presented in a handleless pot, from which the table was protected—unnecessarily, since the heat had vanished long before the meal—by a sauce-encrusted potholder. And yet there was more than bohemian mannerism in all this, a request that the meeting take place on some level other than food and décor and the demonstration of harmonious surroundings.

Richard's own position was neither apologetic nor flaunting, as it might have been had he intended to say to them, See how I've freed myself from all those senseless dinner parties, all that matching china and *cordon bleu*. He ate his unwashed salad and circulated the Barolo with as much dignity as he had ever radiated at any of Kate's banquets. Inside the self-possession Gabriella could see how pleased he was to have Morgan in his home again, talking about corruption and law, viewing the women out of the corner of his eye, seeing them together and content, as though, for all the upheaval, the old times were once more blessedly upon him.

For a while Liza's talk with Gabriella moved from one inoffensive topic to the next, as if the neutrality of their conversation could make its own apology for Richard and herself having stepped so violently aside from the mores of the world. Liza refused to stand on their act as a great clean swathe of true feeling; she took no romantic stance but made her speech wrap their doings in the dreariest cover of daily life, simultaneously asking for acceptance in that world of the undramatically married by

74

mimicking its tones and confidences while yet refusing to acknowledge the recent breach of its law. Yet all around them in
the vast loft, as the two couples warmed themselves with wine and
canned lichees, were signs of Liza's greater belief, in the large,
dark impastoed portraits of men she'd known, portraits of herself
in states of lunacy, ecstasy, depictions of her and them making
love, so crudely violent as to describe the whole thing, at least to
Gabriella's eye, as so much carnage.

When they had spoken earlier, about the part of California
where Liza and Richard were to spend Christmas, Liza had said,
hastily, "It's wonderful that you and Kate are going to use the
house," and Gabriella, too slow-witted at that point, had not
thanked Liza for the house and had missed her chance to show
her understanding of what had been meant by Liza's gesture.
After that, they had not mentioned Kate again, Liza perhaps
interpreting Gabriella's reticence as a refusal to discuss Kate with
her. But now, breaking off a description of recent gallery shows,
and in the same voice of "by the way," touching lightly, less to
catch attention than to demonstrate companionship, Liza said to
Gabriella, "Is Kate all right?" And Gabriella, more pleased to be
thus touched by Liza than to consider the question, had replied
in the same casual voice and not quite honorably, "Fine."

Liza took a cigarette from her pack and lit it before engaging
Gabriella's glance. "I do miss her," she said. "And I hate having
to play the 'other woman.' I wish she'd accept the thing and come
over to see us."

"But she's still too hurt by it," Gabriella said. "It might happen
later." Richard looked toward Liza, and understood that they
were now talking about his wife. He turned uneasily back to his
conversation with Morgan, who for his part simply hoped that
Gabriella would be careful.

"Well, it's not that exciting, is it?"

Gabriella hung for a moment on Liza's choice of words.

"I suppose," she said inanely, "it's pretty exciting for Kate."

"Well, if she'd see us, she'd see it wasn't that exciting."

"I think," Gabriella said, "she's rather upset that she can't sit here unexcited with Richard herself. I don't think she thinks of you two in constant flames."

Neither of them knew whether they were really going to talk; the strange ironic vocabulary sat in their way. But thanks to its oddity, Gabriella had lost the overwhelming sense of Liza's life and was able to imagine Kate again. She said that it was hard for Kate to have lost her husband.

"Well, he's not dead," Liza answered. "She can come and see him, she can even sleep with him if she wants." She looked up at Richard, not certain whether he was still listening, and then suddenly dropped her tone of exasperation. "She just can't be sure about him anymore, but then, she never should have been. I'm not sure. Are you so certain about Morgan?"

"Of course." Gabriella didn't mean "of course" and it provoked Liza. "Well, that's just your being asleep," she said. "Kate's sureness about Richard had nothing to do with what *he* was actually feeling, not just about me: his being alive. Don't you think that all that binding in sureness takes too much away? If I let myself be sure Richard's always going to stay with me, it's a kind of blackmail, and then if he wants to leave, he'll be crippled by guilt. He's hopeless now because of Kate; he's made his move and he can't act on it. Look at him, he's paralyzed. And he's so horribly grateful you've both come here and blessed our union." Liza looked at Gabriella and saw her confusion as it wavered into hurt. "And I am, too," she said, defeated. "I am pathetically grateful you've come and blessed our union."

What Liza described did not appear to Gabriella to be precisely that. Liza presented herself as a being not yet caught or not yet completely tied and tamed, while Richard at his end of the table did look like a man no longer free but bound by his actions—by his past with Kate and the constant sense of what it was that had been done to her. Yet Gabriella had the sense that it was Liza who

76

was subjecting herself to Richard, out of love entering into his cage, his unhappiness, his habits. Though Richard sat at Liza's table under the portraits of her past lovers, looked down upon by line-up and declarations of sexual abandon, sat ill-fed and deprived of customary comforts, it did not seem to be Richard who had joined Liza's free life, but she who was surrendering slowly and accepting his.

"How's Claudio, Gabriella?" Richard addressed her, taking her attention from Liza, at whom he glanced briefly. Gabriella sensed the glance as a challenge as Liza repeated, "Yes, how is he? I haven't seen him for ages." The light-hearted phrasing hardly concealed the reason for Liza and Claudio's separation; that hung momentarily in the air above them.

"He's fine," Gabriella said. "We were all out ten days ago."

"Where do you go now," Liza asked, "which nights, where?"

"Do you want to join them, Liza?" Richard asked her, "Are you longing to step out?" He smiled cheerfully in her direction.

"You know I am," Liza answered him. "I just don't want to run into Kate, that's all. So which nights do you go, and where?"

Richard got up now and walked to the back of the loft, ostensibly to get more wine, but Liza named his gesture. "Please don't walk away every time I say Kate's name, will you. It's so damn rude."

Richard continued on his way and then brought them the wine. "Can I give you some more?" he asked Morgan.

"Thank you." Morgan looked nervously at Gabriella, unsure whether she was now expected to take Liza's part or whether he alone had been assigned an uncomfortable allegiance.

"Actually, I'm not at all sorry to have stopped going," Richard said. He filled Gabriella's glass. "You'll see," he said to her, "the thing's a nine-day wonder, you'll get bored after a while." Then to Morgan he said, "I'm not sure we're not the wrong sex for it, or age or profession. How do you manage to work at all? You must be in better shape than I am."

"Unfortunately not," Morgan replied. "It's the beginning of the end for us, too. I can't do both."

"Well, we'll go," Liza said to Gabriella, "shall we?"

"All right," Gabriella said. She waited for Morgan's contradiction. But it was Richard who said, "Some of us have to work."

"I work," Liza said. "Anyway, work and play should all be one thing, you've got it wrong."

"We can't all be painters," Richard repeated. "Someone's got to do something else, if only to pay for the canvas."

Liza poured wine into her glass and into Gabriella's.

"No one's ever paid for my canvas except my father," she said, "and he made his money doing what he likes. I've no guilt about that, Richard. And it's a little ugly to insist everyone pay his own way."

"I never suggested you didn't or should, I merely reminded you that you were on your own time, unlike Morgan and myself, or Gabriella."

"Gabriella seems to be on her own time," Morgan said, and then, sorry to be seen siding with Richard against his wife, said no more.

Gabriella rescued him. "I should do something else," she offered, "but I feel too lazy to look, or perhaps Morgan's right, too tired."

The phone went in the loft, Liza leaped to get it. When she came back she was visibly happier, someone with her own life, apart from all the minefield and mire about her. In the meantime, listening to Liza's laughter on the phone, no one had spoken. The Callaghers sat uncomfortably with the question of Gabriella's work between them. Richard, unable to deal with their marital strains as well as his own, drank in silence.

"Anyway," Liza said to Gabriella as she sat down. "I do want to come. If there's a night I could. It doesn't have to involve Richard, unless you want to come"—she smiled at him—"I need to move a little. Especially in the winter, don't you think?" she asked Gabriella. "You get frozen."

"You'll be in California soon," Morgan said. "You can swim."

"Yes." Liza smiled. She did look like someone who was going to be free to swim soon. It was everyone around her now who seemed frozen.

"All right, you and I will go, with Claudio and company," Gabriella said; she, too, wanted to be free.

"And tell Kate," Liza said in a low voice to Gabriella, "not to be so much in mourning about Richard. Tell her to remember hard what it was like. Tell her how this evening is, for example."

"Why," Gabriella said cautiously, "it's lovely to be here."

"Try to make Kate remember what it was like to *have* it," Liza insisted. "It really isn't the opposite of the pain of not having it. It has its own pain."

"But you're happy with Richard?" Gabriella said.

"Very," Liza said flatly. "And Kate can be happy too, that's all I say. She shouldn't think that with Richard gone everything's been taken from her. There's a lot she can be pleased not to have again. I mean, it's only the fact of loss that makes what was lost seem so precious. Tell her to really imagine having what she had again. I don't mean Richard, I mean being part of a couple."

"Please, Liza," Richard said softly. They all waited now.

"We ought to go," Morgan said.

Liza stood up to let them depart, watching Richard convey to his friends that it was not at all necessary for them to go. Gabriella got her coat and then came back toward the group, toward Liza particularly, but unable to say more than what is conventionally said, and thanks to Kate's presence in their home, unable conventionally to return the dinner invitation. Instead they offered each other wishes for Christmas while Gabriella tried to will Liza into inviting them again so that she could be armed with Liza's future friendship against the anticipated gloom of her return home with Morgan.

But Liza, herself anticipating the imminent silence with which she would be left with Richard, was unable to offer Gabriella anything but "Glad you could come," a phrase far too short to keep them unembarrassedly occupied by the door, where Richard and Morgan seemed to take forever with their parting and fussing with coats, handshakes and repeated phrases of thanks and reminders of data from their shared office life.

And just as Gabriella had predicted, as soon as the fire doors of the loft were bolted behind them, she felt herself once more enclosed in intimacy and opposition with Morgan. And on the other side of the thick metal doors, a similar chill, a similar sense of loss, as Liza scraped the grease from the plates and Richard collected the empty wine bottles and set them under the sink.

RICHARD STOOD STAUNCHLY IN his double-breasted gray suit, blue cuffs and amber cuff links, and tried to calculate how much longer he would need to stay where he was to do his duty by the office Christmas party. The thing had been going properly since six o'clock, though long before that, perfumed secretaries had giggled in and out of the boardroom with bottles of booze, trays of glasses, tiny cut sandwiches under green cellophane wrap. The tree, no longer sharing its glory with the front receptionist, had been moved into the large room with the food, and stood guard over a pile of garish parcels. All the directors' chairs, leather-surrounded ashtrays and note pads had been removed from the board room. Only the founders' portraits and the large map of Long Island Sound remained unfestively on the walls.

Richard stood by the door and tried in this second hour of the party to look merry. He tried not to think about the transactions that had been interrupted by Olivia's announcement that work on Christmas-party night was not allowed, nor about Liza and their trip tomorrow to the Coast. Above all, he tried not to think about Kate and how she would be feeling on the weekend. He wondered if he'd been right not to buy Kate a Christmas present. He'd wanted her to have a lime-green silk slip he'd seen on Madison Avenue. He would have enjoyed being in the shop, asking the beehived, corseted Russian saleslady for a size ten, watching her put it in the box, wrap it elaborately, hand it to him ceremoniously. He would have enjoyed paying for the thing with his credit card and exiting, like any other Christmas husband in the glow of the Russian's approval, with the package under his arm. But he'd resisted all this because he hadn't wanted Kate to think the gesture came from an overspill of his own well-being, or to be misled about his own perfect happiness this Christmas. Neither had he been able to feel sure about his present for Liza, and was once again anxious about what he'd got her, the gesso candlesticks, pretty but not very intimate. It was annoying not to feel confident about her reactions. For years he'd known them perfectly, when she was Kate's friend. Then he'd fallen in love with her and she'd suddenly become mysterious. The loss of his familiarity with her had been part of the greater devastation.

Richard rocked on his heels and looked around the room for Morgan. To his left a burst of horrified laughter followed Harry Staines's appearance as the office Santa, rather makeshift in a red flannel blazer padded with several still-visible sweaters that pulled his buttons dangerously. Over the gap where his lapels parted, Harry's chin trailed wads of surgical cotton. Actually, Harry presented rather a horrifying figure under the light, with the Scotch tape shining over his mouth, the dead white beard setting off his pocked orange skin. And instead of sitting quietly on the dais provided for him, Harry was darting around the room, provoking squeals among the women like the chief goblin at a children's Halloween party.

Richard moved from the doorway and approached a group of partners watching Harry with fixed attention.

"He's going to get a heart attack," Sherwood said. They all had paper cups of whiskey except Sherwood, a jogger and teetotaler.

"Nah, keeps him young. Only exercise he gets, old Harry," O'Rourke said. Willett smiled and emptied his cup. "Hello, Richard, do you have a drink?"

Richard held it up for their inspection. Sherwood's habits were, as he knew, barely tolerable to the older men. But Sherwood was a grandson of a founder; he could do more or less as he liked.

At the other end of the room Harry appeared to be, as predicted, totally winded. He now sat on his Santa's chair with Barbara Calmann perched nervously on one knee. While she waited, a long moment of embarrassment held in that corner of the room as Harry sat and puffed, grotesquely immobile all of a · sudden. From time to time Barbara tried to rise, but Harry's arm restrained her.

"He's going to keel over." Sherwood's voice had a nasty, sportscaster's excitement.

"He'll be fine," Willett said. He was Harry's age.

Stephanie Reese, Harry's secretary for twenty years, now walked—tall, spare, unhurried—across the room, a white shopping bag full of presents in either hand. When she got to Harry she smiled encouragingly at Barbara, like a Red Cross matron with a panicking junior, and said something deferential but bracing to her boss. Harry sat up, and still holding Barbara with one arm to his knee, dipped the other hand into the bag. He read what was written on a green package. "Janice Krewsky," he said loudly, almost soberly. "Janice, where's Janice? Come to Santa, darling."

Janice, not more than eighteen and only recently hired, approached Harry nervously. She wore flat shoes and a red dress. Long straight hair hung down her back. She might have been twelve. Harry, looking at her, suddenly halted in his dealings with Barbara, who squirmed as she tried to get off Harry's knee. Someone near them cried out, "Barbara, don't hog Santa, give Janice a shot." And then all around the room, voices shouted a version of the same instruction, in relief that the situation once more had its guidelines.

Obeying the orders, Harry relaxed his grip and Barbara slid off, heading for the drinks table. But Janice stood there, frozen in front of him, unable to mount.

Harry looked at the girl and all his own confidence vanished.

He almost begged her to sit on his knee. "Just for a little second, honey," he said. Janice, her face now beginning to match her dress, turned and backed toward the leg that Harry held out and away from his torso. With the girl finally astride, Harry, grateful to have got so far, forgot his lines as Santa and simply handed Janice the present so that she would be able to move quickly, clutching her package like a relay racer, now on the verge of tears.

The party continued and Santa held. Not until eight-thirty did Richard catch sight of Morgan, looking anything but festive. Momentarily Richard forgot to ask about Kate. "What's wrong with you?" he said.

"Nothing. Why? Just having a good time."

"Oh, is that all? We should be able to leave soon."

"When is your flight?"

"Tomorrow afternoon. It was the best Liza could do. She's had to wait for some color slides for a gallery that says it's interested. I doubt it, though; it's all talk and bad checks in Liza's world. However, the sun will be nice. And snow for you, it looks like," Richard said. "When are you all leaving?"

"Whenever the party gets organized tomorrow."

"Kate's going?"

"Of course—that was the idea, wasn't it?"

"I keep thinking she might change her mind at the last minute."

"Don't worry about Kate, Richard, she'll have fun; she'll survive."

"You mean Christmas?"

"And everything else; she's a tough girl."

"I know, but I don't want her to get any tougher."

"Meaning?"

"I don't want her to develop that shell."

"You want everything at once, don't you?"

"Yes."

They stood for a while, the two of them, both flanneled, pink, gloomy, holding their Dixie cups.

All around them were other men in polished shoes and silk ties, likewise holding Dixie cups. The shouting from the earlier part of the evening had done its work and subsided. At present there was a low hum of people wishing one another well.

"Actually I hate this season," Morgan said, "I always did. It was very depressing for my parents until they were old enough to be told."

"I'm afraid I'm still pulled by it," Richard said. "Even the Salvation Army band makes me mournful. That's why Liza and I are going to California. Short of a trip to Haifa, it seemed the farthest away from Christmas we could get."

"There'll be reindeer at the airport," Morgan said, "and fake snow. Be prepared."

Otto came over to where Richard and Morgan were standing and greeted them with a salute of his paper cup. "Not exactly Chivas Regal," he said, "but it seems to work." He drank it down and stood with them, smiling benignly.

"When are you moving?" Richard asked him.

"Are you moving?" Morgan said.

"Yeah. This is going to be our last Christmas in town. To tell you the truth, I couldn't be happier about it."

"Where are you going? You're not leaving us here, I hope."

"Not Topknoll, McDermott; the city. Casey and I found a terrific place in Connecticut. One hour by car, longer by train of course, but a real country feel. Didn't I tell you, Morgan? We finalized last month. A hundred and fifty years old, old trees, big back acres, room to breathe; Casey's been in the wallpaper shops since Thanksgiving. We were hoping to be in there in time for Christmas but it didn't work out. Still, next year, and we'll get to see it in the snow."

"Say, that's great," Morgan said, "but a big move."

"Sure," Otto said, beaming again.

"You're going to miss New York," Richard said. "I bet you're back this time next year."

"Not a chance." Otto stood away from them and contemplated his audience from the ends of his heels. Then, swinging forward and adjusting his jacket, he told them, "My feeling is, we should have left this damn place sooner. We're too old for it. New York is for youngsters, men on the way up, women on the make. It just doesn't make sense for people who aren't single. I mean, if you can afford to leave. I'm not talking about the blacks, they have to stay. For anyone else—no offense, you guys—this place is Never Never Land, you know *Peter Pan*. It's all there in the ads here, you've just got to read the ads to know what this place is about: every goddamn product filtered through the image of some young female executive—they're all executives now, as though every bimbo's got a steel-trap brain overnight thanks to hours of consciousness raising. No disrespect . . ." Otto tipped an imaginary hat in the direction of one of the lady partners, who was dressed, as it happened, in a parodic version of Otto, in a three-piece flannel suit and high-heeled brogues. Otto, noticing this for the first time, paused and laughed. "It looks better on her, though. I admit it."

"You'll be back," Richard said again.

"And the pitch that's not for the girls here is aimed at the boys, boys with mustaches and shaved heads, boys with blue eyes and tight crotches. The city, my friends, has been taken over. Look, have either of you tried to get an apartment lately bigger than a breadbox? The real estate just isn't aimed at the two-people let alone four-people market. And where are the schools? In my neighborhood I only see midget drug dealers. The place just isn't for families anymore. Look, Richard, if you and Kate had stayed together, you'd feel like Casey and me. But you're single again, so the place looks normal. And you, Morgan"—he touched Morgan on the arm—"as soon as you and Gabriella figure out you're no longer eighteen, as soon as you two realize you're going to have kids, which is why you got married, and you look around and see that the executive women aren't having kids and the fags aren't, you're going to see that the only place where your kids are going to meet other kids is outside of New York City. I'm not talking about black kids. Those are going to stay around to remind everyone what kids still look like."

"What are you so excited about?" Otto's secretary asked as she approached her boss.

"And when are you getting married?" Otto asked, slipping his arm around her waist. "You know Stacey," he said to his companions.

"Sure," Stacey said, and in answer to Otto's question, "As soon as anyone asks me, you know that." She blushed a little, uncertain that the irony had been clear, and because Otto's arm felt rather awkward against her.

"Nice old-fashioned girl," Otto said. "Aren't you, Stace?"

"Sure," Stacey said.

"Well, I wish you luck with your move," Morgan said to Otto. "I was brought up in the country and kind of miss it. But I'm not yet ripe for retirement."

"Maturity," Otto corrected him. "You're thirty-two, right? Same age as me."

"Right," Morgan said.

"And how old is Gabriella?"

"The same."

"Well, that's it. We're even a little late for all this. You wait, any minute you two are going to get broody and start looking at bassinets. First it will be kittens and puppies, then it will be real estate. Finally you'll move and start reproducing, it happens to all of us."

"Sounds disgusting," Stacey said. Richard and Morgan laughed.

"It does sound disgusting," Richard said.

"You laugh," Otto said, "but nature's out there waiting to pounce. You've got maybe two or three years of that singles sprinting left, then it's all over."

"Over?" Morgan said. "Why? What happens then?"

"You'll become an old swinger, dressing in tight clothes and sniffing out young girls, and not seeing that real life everywhere but New York City has just passed you by."

"Gee, that's pretty depressing," Stacey said. She removed Otto's arm by a jolt of her hip. "I guess I better get a move on. I think I'll go home and set my hair or something, try to catch a man."

"You can't bluff it, Stace," Otto called after her, "your boss knows whereof he speaks. Dance now, kiddo, you've got five years before the suburbs."

"Oh Jesus," Stacey said and went off.

"Nice kid," Richard said. "Well, I'm going too. Have a great holiday, Otto; say hello to Casey. Morgan, will you tell Kate I'm going to phone her on Sunday—say you gave me the phone number—and have a great time yourselves."

"Thanks, Richard. You and Liza too. Let's get together after Christmas."

Richard said goodbye again and walked through the remainder of the party toward the door.

"Are you going to be with Kate this Christmas?" Otto asked Morgan. "That's right—she's staying with you, isn't she? That was pretty tough on her. How's she doing?"

"Pretty well," Morgan said, dreading what was coming.

"Still, she sort of asked for it," Otto said, "all that fairy court, and her the fairy queen. You couldn't expect Richard to go on taking that."

"I don't think it was as simple as that," Morgan said, hoping Otto would let the matter drop.

"Has to be rough watching your wife become a fag hag," Otto said. "No wonder he ran away from home."

"Listen, Otto," Morgan said, "I've got to go too. I said I wouldn't stay too late; I've got to help Gabriella with the packing for tomorrow."

"Don't you get pussy-whipped now," Otto said, laughing. Morgan looked at him, but Otto radiated benign merriment. "Say hello to Gabriella," he said. "Listen, we haven't seen you guys for ages. Why don't you come around before we leave. We'll do some steaks, smoke some dope. What do you say?"

"Sounds great," Morgan said. "We'd love to. Say hi to Casey and have a good Christmas."

"You guys too," Otto said. He looked around the room to see who was left and then stood where he was, eyes twinkling.

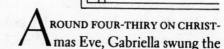

AROUND FOUR-THIRY ON CHRIST-mas Eve, Gabriella swung the baize door over the noise of the Chinese cooks tearing feathers from the goose. They had ripped out handfuls while she was in the kitchen making tea for herself and Claudio, first the rough greasy back feathers, the two of them working in tandem as she pottered unfamiliarly among the shelves finding sugar, honey, bread for toast. The cooks had arrived that morning with the goose in the backseat of Mickey's rented station wagon. "May I present," Mickey had said, as Heinz stood behind him, giggling, "the ultimate in Chinese takeout: Sam and Kao. They do parties and don't give a shit about Christmas."

"Oh," Gabriella had said.

"Fabulous," Claudio had said, "they'll do the oysters."

"Right," Mickey had gone on proudly, "and the goose." "Listen," Mickey had said to Gabriella when Claudio took them off to find extra beds, "I can see you're a little surprised. First of all, they work like dogs; secondly, they only cost twenty-five dollars a day; sixty dollars for the weekend. Also—this is the best part—they don't eat anything."

"What do you mean, they don't eat anything," Morgan asked. "What the hell do they do?"

"They eat the garbage."

"They what?"

"They make little wholesome soups and things out of what's left on the plates. I've seen them at several parties, it's all very ecological. They clean off the plates into the pots and add water, stir, and in ten minutes what was French or American becomes Chinese. They bring their own rice and chopsticks. And they're very clean. Listen, once you start using them, you'll never understand how you made out before. Besides, I can't return them."

"No, I see that," Gabriella had said as Morgan went off in a silent rage. "Well, aren't you brilliant?"

Now, in the afternoon, as Gabriella moved around the kitchen she had tried to be friendly, to make up for everyone else's treatment of the Chinese, particularly Morgan's, whose way of dealing with the situation apart from constant sarcasm was to pretend they didn't exist, to avoid every place they might be encountered. But the sight of their operations, of that brutally balding bird, had interfered with Gabriella's ease as mistress of the house. In any case, the cooks preferred to ignore her, returning blank faces to her ingratiating smiles, interested only in the rapid stripping of of the bird, baring more and more of its pathetic pink torso. As Gabriella left the kitchen, tea tray in hand, they had reached the soft underfeathers, the short, light down that flew about the room in swirls and attached itself to their woolly clothing and alighted on their heads and hands. Inside this nursery cloud, Gabriella saw the big red feet of the bird, and in its snowy, lolling head, the eyes clamped shut.

On the floor of the living room Claudio was stretched out under the tree, bought and decorated with cans of silver spray that afternoon. His feet were almost inside the fire that Morgan had made for them before he'd set out on his walk across the hills. Outside the windows the sky was a dark gray. At floor level, currents of cold air blew the smells of pine and metal paint across the oak boards. The house felt empty, despite the activity in the kitchen, despite the sleeping men and Kate, upstairs.

"Tea," Gabriella said. She stretched with her foot toward the low firestool, pulled it close and set the tray on it. Claudio remained where he was, as though asleep.

"Do you want some tea, Claudio?" Gabriella asked him.

"Hmm?" Claudio stirred, turned his head slowly, opened his eyes briefly and regarded the tray on his right. "What *kind* of tea is it?" he said.

"Just tea." Gabriella said. "Earl Grey."

"Any lemon?"

"Just have it with milk, Claudio, please. Do me a favor. I'm not going back into Mott Street."

"Oh, toast!" He sat up. "Toast and honey. What kind of honey is that?" He picked up a piece of toast and applied his nose to it. "Ordinary," he said and put it back on the plate. "You'd think in the country someone would keep bees."

Gabriella held her tea in one hand and ate her toast and honey. Claudio watched for a while before joining her. "Have you ever had bee extract?" he asked. "It does incredible things to the skin. You get it in capsules. After ten days you're radiant. I can't imagine why I stopped. God, this is awful."

"Just eat it," Gabriella said, "or don't eat it. The bee extract was part of your hippie life, wasn't it? I can't picture you as a hippie."

"Oh, sure," Claudio said, "long hair, beads, drugs in the fridge, the whole bag." He snapped his fingers and made a peace sign at her.

"Unconvincing," Gabriella said, "and you were a gay militant once, weren't you?"

"Yeah, but I never bashed any straights." Claudio held the little plate under his chin.

"You've been a lot of things," Gabriella said.

"Sweetums, think how old I am." He put his plate back on the tray and lay down again on the floor.

"Which life was best?" Gabriella pushed the tray away from both of them and collapsed toward Claudio.

"This is best," Claudio said. Gabriella leaned over and gave Claudio a sticky kiss on the mouth.

"Thank you," Claudio said. He removed a perfectly ironed handkerchief from his pocket and dabbed at his mouth.

"Was your childhood fun?" Gabriella asked.

"You've got to be joking—in Ohio?"

"Why not?"

"It just wasn't."

"And when did you come out?"

"Sweetums, I was always out."

"Always? As a baby?"

"Of course."

"How did you know?" Gabriella persisted.

"It's just a thing you know."

"Maybe you never went through puberty," Gabriella said, looking up at the ceiling.

"Oh, I went through puberty, all right." Claudio gave a loud, long excluding laugh.

"Did you tell your parents you were gay?"

"No, I just left home at sixteen, came to New York, where people didn't have to be told, or not that way: sat down in the kitchen and given brandy."

"You don't mind my asking these things, do you?"

"Ask away," Claudio said; he moved around toward Gabriella and lay his head between her hip and navel, adjusting her body like a series of cushions. Together they formed a wide V, warmed between them by the fire, their outer edges cooled by the pine drafts inside the room. "Is that all right?" Claudio asked her when he had made himself comfortable. "Perfect," Gabriella answered. They held hands for a while, Claudio keeping Gabriella's slightly sticky fingers carefully away from his Argyll sweater.

"What I want to know, Claudio—"

"Yes . . ." Claudio made a noise of mock wariness, perhaps not so mock.

"—is what do you get out of it, besides the sex, I mean? Don't you ever want to live with just one person?"

"Sometimes."

"Well, are you going about it the right way? I mean, five times a day; no one can look good if there's always someone else around the corner."

"That's Preston's life, that five times a day. I haven't been laid in weeks. It's driving me crazy."

"Well, you can get it, Claudio, can't you, in the bars, etcetera."

"Sure, but that's not exactly the point. I mean, the thing requires a little charm, otherwise . . ."

"Otherwise, masturbation will do."

"Exactly."

"But you're out there looking for Mr. Right?"

"Not exactly Mr. Right, sweetums, Mr. Wrong more like. But actually *I*'m getting harder to put up with, set in my ways. And there isn't all that much point, after all."

"You mean marriage?" Gabriella asked. "Well, you could always go into business or something, there are other things to produce besides families."

"Open an antique shop, I presume you mean. Of course I'm frightened of dying alone, if that's where this is going. But what do you want me to do about it? Apart from getting a dog. And besides, I like my freedom. I do like my freedom."

"I don't have any freedom," Gabriella said.

"Crap."

"All right."

"Crap. Morgan's incredible for a husband. You don't know how lucky you are. Apart from Richard, Morgan is the first husband of a friend who's not been threatened by my being gay. You've got a wonderful marriage, Gabriella. Don't be an idiot."

"I suppose so."

"I love Morgan, you know, Gabriella. He's incredibly important to me."

"Yes, but you've just said why. For you, he's a first, an unantagonized husband."

"Actually, I would almost go so far as to say I was in love with Morgan—in love with you both. If you want to know, I'd go to bed with both of you if I could."

"Gosh," Gabriella said. "You mean together, or separately?"

"Sweetums," Claudio said, "I think I've got you worried."

"Actually," Gabriella said, "I don't feel like that at all. I feel perfectly peaceful with you, as though we were both the same, sexually, hermaphrodites. With Morgan, I used to feel we were each two halves, and I felt terribly incomplete when he was away. But with you, I feel like a whole person made of male and female halves, which is how I suppose I think of you. I don't know if that is how we are, but that is how it feels, complete and peaceful."

"There doesn't seem to be much room for Morgan in that description."

"I suppose not."

"Also it sounds rather like two castrati."

"Yes, it does," Gabriella said, "except the odd thing is that at college once, before Morgan, I had that with someone. He was wonderful, very beautiful, and it wasn't at all like castrati. It was wonderful sex and wonderful peace at the same time. It was all even rather religious, like a descent of a Holy Ghost when we were together, another person. In fact, we did use to sense it approaching when we were lying together. We would say, amazed, irreverent, 'Here it comes again.' We used to call it our third person. We were terribly in love. I never felt that third person again, with anyone."

"Why would you leave that peace and Holy Ghost for anyone else?"

"I've never known. I left him for Morgan; perhaps I had an instinct against perfection. After all, there's nowhere you can go from there. And maybe I needed not to be hermaphrodite, but only female. Morgan was certainly terribly 'male' when I first met him: angry, rough."

"Butch." Claudio put on his Mae West voice.

"Yes, butch," Gabriella said. "But the other was miraculous, now that I remember it, perfect equality. And now sometimes with Morgan I feel only the polarities, and the huge distance between us. There's so much struggle, and very little coming together."

"But that seems to be what you want. You seem happy. Our perfect couple."

"So you keep saying," Gabriella said.

In the doorway now Mickey stood, looking down on Claudio and Gabriella. Behind him Heinz giggled, and Hubert, Preston's Frenchman, smiled the fixed, nervous smile of a houseguest a million miles behind the intimacy of the other occupants. *"Allô,"* he said, "can I do somesing, make somesing for you?"

Gabriella looked toward the door where the three men were, all of them handsome, elegant, a kind of paradise really, except you couldn't do much with it except look, like an old lecher at a school playground. "Did you have tea?" Gabriella raised her head from her arm and played at hostess.

"Sorry?"

"We have this." Mickey raised an opened bottle of Moët. "I could get some glasses, or shall we pass the bottle?"

"Glasses, please," Claudio said. "You're such a slob, Mickey."

Hubert approached the two bodies and sat down nearest the heads, on his heels. Gabriella smiled up at him and noted the muscles of his thighs as they shaped his jeans. "Hello, Hubert," she said. She called him You-Bear, refusing to Americanize him into the unlikely Hugh-Bert as Claudio and Mickey did. "Are you hungry? You missed lunch, I'm afraid, and dinner's not until ten."

"Preston made me a sandwich." He smiled. "I am very well, thank you." He looked around him, and at Claudio, beaming. "You are having a serious conversation which we are interrupting."

"Not at all," Gabriella said, now up on one elbow, welcoming.

"Yes, we were," Claudio said, "but join us. We were talking about male and female and hermaphrodite, also marriage."

"Ah."

Heinz giggled. Mickey returned with the glasses; a few goose feathers clung to his hair. "Hubert was married," he said.

"Really?"

"I am *still* married," Hubert insisted. "What do you mean?"

"Oh yes, still married," Mickey said. "He puts it on his *curriculum vitae* here to get a job."

"Yes, I put it after formal education and army service, it is very similar."

"That bad, eh?" Claudio smiled at him.

"Not at all, we are *very* good friends."

"Ah." Claudio, confused, remained silent.

Kate appeared in the doorway, cautiously, Bambi.

"Here we are," Gabriella said. "Come and listen, we are talking about Hubert's marriage." To Hubert she said, "Kate has been married too."

"Really?" Hubert said politely.

"I know it's hard to believe," Kate said.

"Not as hard as with Hubert," Mickey said. "Tell us."

"Well, is it so surprising? I grew up in ze town where she grew up, and we always went to ze same parties, and then we married."

"Were you gay when you married?" Gabriella asked.

"I'm sorry?"

"*Pédé—pédéraste,*" Gabriella said.

"*Je ne suis pas pédéraste!*" Hubert said.

"Perhaps that's not the word. I thought it was."

"Gabriella's a little high," Claudio explained. "I think she wants to know if you were always gay."

"Or were you turned off women, by your marriage, say," Gabriella said.

Kate took some champagne and tried to engage Heinz in diversionary conversation.

"No, you must believe me," Hubert said, "my wife is *wan-*derful. It was she who became a lesbian, and suggested zen I become also *gai.*"

"How French," Gabriella said. "You mean it was all ideologically arrived at?"

"Of course!" Hubert smiled at Gabriella, but braced himself slightly. Here was the famous American directness.

"Late sixties?" Gabriella went on, "the era of polymorphous perverse?"

"Early seventies; exactly, at ze Sorbonne." Hubert smiled again.

Gabriella laughed, Kate and Mickey watched nervously. Heinz did not giggle. "So," Gabriella went on, "now that we're in the boring old nest-building eighties you can switch back and be straight again. You see, Claudio, it can be a choice."

"But I can't," Hubert insisted. "I am *gai.*"

"Wrong again, Gabriella," Claudio laughed.

Hubert turned and addressed Kate. "Besides," he said, "my wife is—what is it in English? . . ." Kate's eyes widened, the audience hung on his words. "Cleetoral," Hubert said at last.

"You know," Hubert said, seeming now to address Kate alone, "how some women are cleetoral"—he waited as Kate nodded apprehensively—"and some are vaginal?" Hubert pronounced this oddly, like "vegetal."

Kate nodded again slowly.

"Well, my wife," he said, "is cleetoral."

"Oh . . ." That was Claudio. No one else said a word.

Mickey poured champagne into the glasses. Claudio lit a Gauloise. Hubert sat back on his heels, a man who has given a successful accounting. Kate said, "I think I am going to see about dinner."

Mickey said, "What do you mean, Hugh-Bert, 'clitoral'?"

"I mean, she likes sex of ze surface, not deep, wizout penetration; in effect, she likes girls."

"Did you know about this, Gabriella?" Claudio asked.

"Well"—Gabriella tried to reassert herself—"it's supposed to be the great myth, you know, the vaginal orgasm, it's supposed to all be clitoral."

"But, not at all"—Hubert was now authoritarian, *Troisième République*.

"Oh?" Claudio waited, drawing noisily on his cigarette, removing tobacco flakes from the tip of his pink tongue.

"Surface sex," Mickey repeated.

"Exactly." Hubert was pleased. His English was becoming versatile.

"You mean all the little buttons," Gabriella said, "nipples and so on? But it's masturbatory."

"Exactly," Hubert said again. "My wife did not like being— how do you say?—possessed, by the cook."

"By the cook?" Gabriella said.

"Bite—ze man's cook."

"Ah."

"She wanted not to be possessed; she wanted to be the one who is possessing. That is a logical position, after all, don't you find?"

"Yes, I see," Gabriella said, not quite seeing. Claudio, Gabriella and Mickey regarded each other for a few moments, and then Mickey began to laugh.

"What is it?" Hubert asked.

"Cock, not cook," Mickey said.

"Kahk," Hubert said.

"You sound like you're choking," Mickey said.

"Sometimes you do choke," Gabriella said.

"Gabriella!" Claudio sat up.

"It's your influence," she said.

"Do you like to be possessed?" Hubert asked Gabriella. If this was the style of talk here, he would oblige.

"Hugh-Bert!" Claudio said.

"You don't ask ladies such questions," Mickey said.

"Well, You-Bear," Gabriella said, intending to reassure him by thus pronouncing his name. "I do sometimes, but I also take your wife's point; there are times when you would like to possess and not be possessed."

"Bullshit," Claudio said suddenly, "it's the women who possess and the men who get possessed, entering into the vaults and dying there, poetically and so on speaking. Men surrender to women, don't they? I mean, just physiologically."

"Yes, but traditionally it's the women who capitulate, swoon and are 'taken.' "

"And the men who have to sleep it off."

"How do you know all this, anyway, Claudio?" Gabriella asked him. "I thought you'd never been with women."

"Well, it's not so different," Claudio said, "I keep telling you. It simply depends, in every case, who likes what."

"Who fucks and who gets fucked," Gabriella said.

"Gabriella," Claudio said, "if you're going to speak like this, you won't be allowed to talk with us about our mysteries."

"Without hermaphrodites," Gabriella insisted, "there is no sexual equality possible."

"But the lack of sexual equality is precisely what good sex is about," Mickey said. "That's where the fun is."

"That is not the French position," Hubert said.

"That is not the feminist position," Gabriella said.

"Well, there are a lot of positions," Claudio said.

"Where's Morgan?" Gabriella asked suddenly. It was dark outside, nearly six.

"He's back," Mickey said, "we met him in the hall an hour ago." Mickey had become suddenly formal speaking of Morgan. He seemed to be a kind of shadow upon them, and for a while no one spoke. Even Hubert sensed some of the awkwardness in the room with the arrived notion of Gabriella's husband; he shifted uncomfortably.

"You see," Gabriella said to Claudio, "a new kind of third person."

"What?" Claudio had forgotten the earlier reference; but he, too, expressed a dignified guiltiness, rose to his knees and prodded the fire.

"Well," said Gabriella, wishing to name and thus destroy the source of their discomfort, "I ought to go and see how he is."

Claudio understood that the tone of her voice was a betrayal of his friend Morgan, feared that their talk had been a betrayal as well, and wondered at the implications of Morgan's long absence from all of them that afternoon.

Gabriella found Morgan stretched out on the double bed with one arm over his eyes. He had been reading and the bedside lamp was on, but now he seemed to be asleep.

"Morgan"—Gabriella spoke softly—"are you all right?"

Morgan lifted his arm and looked down the length of his body toward his wife.

"Tired," he said.

Gabriella sat at the foot of the bed and began to remove her husband's shoes. They were heavy walking boots. Between the rubber ridges of the soles little bits of frozen earth and crumbs of leaves had stuck. "How was your walk?"

"Good. It might well snow, as predicted. How was your talk?"

"Good. Did you know You-Bear was married?"

"Who is You-Bear?"

"The Frenchman. His wife is a lesbian."

"How chic."

"That's what I said." Gabriella lifted the heavy shoes from

Morgan's feet and warmed his toes in her fingers. "You're cold," she said. "Why don't you take a hot bath?"

"I'm all right. Come and lie with me."

Gabriella lay down next to Morgan on the high bed, her head in the crook of his arm. "I don't get the impression you're having a wonderful time," she said. She could smell him, his skin odors mixed with something from the cold outside, a slightly chilled waft of Morgan. "You smell healthy," she said.

Morgan stroked his wife's arm with his left hand. "I wish it were just the two of us here," he said. "I don't like all these people."

"That's not very Christmas-spirited of you," Gabriella said. "We have each other all the time. They have no one, usually, or different ones. Anyway, you love Claudio, you love Kate."

"How is Kate?"

"I think she's all right. Except she's got a cold. She and Preston and Mickey have made an amazing dessert for tonight. You know it's black tie."

"Oh Christ, this is so pretentious."

"It's not, it's nice." Gabriella felt them on the verge of argument. She wished not to step over. "Will you kiss me?" she asked.

Morgan kissed her and began to undress her while Gabriella watched herself accede simply in order to avoid struggle. Then, as Morgan made love to her, she let herself remain unengaged, except on the surface, where her sensation was. Noticing herself detached from her husband, she wondered whether this was what Hubert meant by surface sex. From time to time Morgan questioned her with a look or pause, and Gabriella responded, but she did not make love to him, she simply let him make love to her.

Instead Gabriella thought about the boy she had loved in her first year at college. It had been more complicated than what she had described to Claudio. Gabriella had been seeing someone else first, dates at movies, books shared at lectures, until he had introduced her to his best friend. Thereafter for two weeks the three of them had gone about together as an inseparable trio. After classes in the afternoons Gabriella used to lie with them on the narrow college bed, listening to the noise in the halls as people came in from the playing fields, took showers, banged doors. Those three, weirdly still behind the locked door, would remain poised inside the silence, mystified by their own peace. Gabriella had been a gift from the one boy to his friend, binding the boys to each other and her to both of them. Suspended on that perfect balance for two weeks, they had remained, sexless and free, living together as much as university life would then allow, until it began to happen that, lying between the two men, Gabriella came to notice a difference in herself, how her right side lay peaceful and dead, in friendship, with the first boy, and grew disturbed and alive on the left. Torn in two, she watched how her chemistry separated them. The division had been wordlessly understood; the men resumed their friendship and Gabriella and the other became lovers.

It seemed odd in memory now to Gabriella, as she lay quite out of contact with her husband, how those three eighteen-year-olds had simply fallen into a state of grace, where for hours at a time they would lie entranced by each other's skin and eyes, bonding through the eyes like mothers and infants, or ducks, not needing even to touch each other for perfect knowledge and intimacy. No one had ever told Gabriella about this peculiar form of love; she had thought of it later as a puppy love, close to childhood, a transitional stage before the real thing; but she remembered it now as a precious unearthly space inside of which will, desire, had suddenly risen like a serpent to expel Gabriella into the wilderness of sexual love.

AROUND NINE-THIRTY THE HOUSE came to life again, sex-lightened, a little weary. In the upstairs bathrooms, showers and baths had been running for the last hour. Kate, dressed in long red silks, and Claudio, black-tied, were in the kitchen when Gabriella arrived, rosy from Morgan and festive.

"It's getting exciting," she said. "Did you sleep?"

Behind them, ungreeted, the invisible Chinese cooks opened oysters with lethal speed onto a large ironstone platter. And on to this, Claudio, his stomach protected by a white tea towel, arranged at a slow pace, like a small matador, ornamental seaweed and slices of lemon.

"Not very well," Kate said. "This lousy cold." She drank from a large glass of champagne, which she raised a little ironically to Gabriella, the unpartnered to the partnered on Christmas Eve. "Home remedies," she said.

"Yes, drink up, sweetums," Claudio said from his creative daze. "We've got another case to kill by tomorrow."

"It's a rough night for you," Gabriella said to Kate. "I'm sorry."

"Not that rough." Kate made a gesture at the bounty inside the kitchen, the bottles of champagne, the paraphernalia for the goose roasting in the oven. But her cheer failed her and she lowered her hand. "Have a drink," she said to Gabriella.

"Thanks, let me set the table," Gabriella answered, penitent for her own happiness, and eager just then to be away from Kate and her courage.

Preston came down the stairs as Gabriella put out the glasses on the big table, dapper, bouncy, handsome in his thirties black. The cut and color of his clothes made him taller and darker, and for a second Gabriella forgot that she knew him, and caught her breath. There was a lot of kissing in that house, after the shortest absences, on the smallest excuses. Out of habit, Preston approached Gabriella and kissed her, near the mouth. She caught his eye when he kissed her, and he smiled. "Can I help?" he said, and the slight flash of desire died inside the courtesy. Gabriella adjusted. "Sure," she said, and then, not content to surrender the new sensation, "You're rather beautiful tonight, Preston." Preston returned white teeth in a dark smile, a second kiss, and for Gabriella a brief prolongation of ambivalence.

Mickey came down the stairs, small and blond and energetic, and behind him, the unusually elegant Heinz. Again kisses, but angelic kisses, for all that male beauty and all that recent copulation, in the house. Gabriella stood in her evening clothes and regarded.

The Chinese served the oysters at ten-thirty, first to Kate, then to Gabriella and Claudio, and lastly to Morgan, as though they'd comprehended some descending order of femininity. Morgan sat at his place a little worn out, less from Gabriella than from the evening still ahead of him, uncomfortable in his dark-blue velvet, a concession to the costume regulations of the party, yet hopelessly out of date. He'd last worn the suit in the early seventies when a tiny dandyism had blossomed briefly among his set. He'd lost the bow tie that was meant to be worn with the blue, and sat now in one of Claudio's, an incongruous white cotton number. He felt himself, familiarly recently, ridiculous.

Actually the problem with his clothing was that it was not dated enough. The prevailing look was thirties movie sheen and fifties. Heinz had his hair slicked back and parted down the middle like the villain in a Ronald Colman film. Hubert's trousers were leg-tight, his jacket reached mid-thigh, making Hubert, at odds with his demeanor, a Greaser from the fifties, or perhaps, the *Cahiers du cinéma* fan raised on James Dean and Troy Donahue.

Morgan sipped his champagne and wondered if he was going to get an ulcer. Champagne had been turning his stomach sour all weekend. He hated it and had always been thankful it classed itself among the luxuries where a little went a symbolic long way. Never in his life had he had to drink it in such quantities, playing at Noël Coward or Winston Churchill. Churchill's deep voice had probably come from the appalling indulgence, the constant repression of belches. Fortunately they were going to change the wine for the goose. An ominous claret stood open on the sideboard.

Morgan regarded his wife aglow in the candlelight at the end of the table. She looked extraordinarily beautiful and alive this evening. Alive, as though pulling energy from everyone in the room, drawing on it as she breathed. Perhaps it was the sex. At school someone had told him that women genuinely flourished on sperm, coming to life like vampires, having drained the men. That would certainly explain their different states. The old Samson and Delilah fears. Each gender had its peculiar postcoital resentments. Gabriella spoke of her own capitulation as though orgasm were some kind of moral collapse. Yet their sex had evidently fueled her; she was practically flying. And flirting, here, for all the good it would do her.

Morgan waited and made appropriate noises as the goose was brought in and publicly dismembered. There was a great deal of oohing and then the steady noise of people eating. The bird seemed unwholesomely fatty to Morgan. Workouts at the gym three times a week, and then all this. Slowly the goose went down with the chestnuts, cabbage, jellies, purées. Morgan glanced at his watch: the midnight feast.

At the other end of the table Mickey and Kate were arguing,

Kate uncomfortably. Mickey, however, bound on left and right by friends foreign to gay life in New York, was eager to make his point. From time to time he would shout over to Claudio. "It was a very different scene in the fifties, isn't that right, Claudio? It was dangerous. The only gays tolerated then were the Cuban fairies on the West Side, and only because they serviced the cops. Anyone without a handbag seen with another guy, right up to the mid-sixties, was liable to get busted. Isn't that right, Claudio?"

"Well, you've conquered now," Kate said. "New York is yours."

"But for how long? Look at the Born Again fascists, look at the Central Park murders, the anti-gay violence is only just below the surface. One swing of fashion and we'll all be driven back under-cover. In the fifties, being a gay was like being a Jew in Berlin."

"Oh, come on," Gabriella said, "that's too much."

"Fuck it, I'm telling you."

"New York pah-ranoia," Hubert said disdainfully.

"I think it is a bit," said Kate. "Anyway, don't get so excited, Mickey, you're among friends."

"Yeah, but for how long?" Mickey said bitterly. "You've only taken us up because it's okay. Imagine this scene in 1955. You're kidding. Isn't that right, Claudio?"

"I don't see why you're on the attack," Claudio said. "Relax, Mickey. Kate, can you pass the walnut stuffing." He exaggerated his languor.

"How many gays did you know five years ago?" Mickey de-manded of Kate.

"I don't know," she said. "I've never thought about it." She hid behind her cold and blew her nose.

"How many?" Mickey insisted.

"Ease up," Preston said. "Why are you attacking Kate?"

"Listen," Kate said; there were tears in her eyes. "I don't know why you're getting at me, but as the only person actively engaged in what can be called the straight marketplace, it seems to me that not only have gays nothing to be worried about, but heterosexual women have everything to be worried about because our potential partners are deserting the ranks like flies, and there isn't too damn much that's left."

"Fruit flies," Gabriella said. Only Claudio, pulled in two, laughed.

But Gabriella went on. "Just think, Morgan," she said. "One of the last, like Davy Crockett at the Alamo." She leaned over to touch him; he moved away. It was just about all right for her to joke, if she was careful. At the moment there was no animosity flying in her direction. As for himself, the humiliation of the blue velvet was one thing, but a verbal lynching by gay vigilantes was another.

"People are people," he said unconvincingly. Claudio, however, tried to make the most of it, got up and kissed him on the cheek. "Bravo, Morgan," he said. "Now shut up, Mickey, and eat your stilton."

"Yeah, shut up," said Heinz.

"I wish to propose a toast," Gabriella said. She caught Kate's eye, still tearful, and held it. "To all my dear friends," Gabriella said.

"To Gabriella's friends," Preston mocked.

"To Gabriella's friends," the table toasted, and drank down.

Gabriella looked at Morgan and stood again. "And to the last and best of an endangered species," she said and raised her glass at him.

"Here, here," said the table.

Gabriella pushed her luck: Morgan was obliged to drink.

By the time the Christmas pudding, and brandy sauce, and the twelve-layer chocolate-rum-cream concoction, had arrived at the table, Mickey, Claudio and Kate were chatting in the old way, affably about nothing. That was the norm within the group, hours of topicless conversation, more a kind of laying on of hands than of thoughts. Morgan wondered why Mickey's sharp memories had surfaced just then, why only tonight he had let anger get through. Perhaps it was a measure of trust of them newly pronounced, or perhaps Christmas was the villain, all that familylessness shoved annually up one's nose. Again, briefly, Morgan wondered whether he and Gabriella ought to start a family now. But in New York? Otto was probably right. The suburbs? Instant death. And this Morgan supposed was better: an adult family, self-chosen, or at least wife-chosen.

"I want my presents," Claudio said.

"Tomorrow morning."

"Now, now is Christmas, midnight, way past. Merry Christmas."

"Merry Christmas!" The table guests, candlelit and beaming, kissed one another as in a scene from medieval life. Even Kate in the moment of well-wishing seemed to Morgan genuinely happy. Perhaps Gabriella was right about the gay wisdom, life as a series of points like these, angelic algebra versus Morgan's solid geometry.

"Merry Christmas, my darling," Gabriella said to Morgan when she came to his part of the table. "Merry Christmas, my darling," she said to Claudio. Morgan would have had her distinguish between them, despite Gabriella's great joy then, and Claudio's, and what should in proper spirit have been his, that she did not.

"Presents," Claudio shouted again. "Presents!"

I T WAS NOT EXACTLY CURRIER &
Ives, though there was the pond
in front of them in the pink winterlight of that three o'clock on
Christmas Day. They were going home tomorrow morning, and
thus had a full evening before them, but the day was somehow
mournful, in that light, in that cold, with its sense of things
drawing to a close. On the ice, the not quite etchable figures of
Claudio in Austrian hunting gear, Preston and Heinz in drainpipe
jeans, and Mickey in tartan plaid, moved woodenly over the
bumps and frozen mud clots of Liza's sister's artificial pond. On
a nearby tree stump Morgan sat in hostly courtesy discussing
French films with Hubert. On the other side of the pond, nearer
the house, Gabriella and Kate were talking on the hood of the
station wagon, whose doors had been left open so that the radio
sounds could travel and guide the movements of the skaters. But
the mix of rock and Christmas carols died on the open air. The
stillness was broken only by Claudio's laughter as again and again
he came to grief with his turns.

"A touch sadistic, your presents to the boys," Kate said.

"I suppose so. I wanted to see Claudio on ice. It was worth it."

"Whoops, down again."

"He really doesn't care."

"You didn't buy Morgan skates."

"He's got some in the city. He can use Preston's today if he likes, they're the same size. I think he's happier sitting it out. Actually, he was sick all morning. I don't think he's very well."

"Poor Morgan. Why was he sick?"

"The goose, he says. He threw everything up at about five A.M. Oysters, goose, chestnuts, pudding, everything."

"What a waste."

"I know. How was Richard?"

Kate sat up to deal with the question. Richard had phoned her at eleven, but no one in the house had mentioned it. Kate had taken her call privately and then gone back to bed.

"He's all right. Said he had sunstroke. Tried to make it sound less than paradisical—for my sake, I think. He's like that, very considerate, and not always truthful. I suppose he's actually very happy. And there's a side of me that longs for him to be happy, and even worries that he's not."

"Let's turn this thing off," Gabriella said, "no one's hearing it but us. I'm freezing."

They moved inside the car, on to the icy plastic seats, and shut the doors. Within minutes the windows had fogged up and they were unable to see outside.

"But the other side of me," Kate went on, "wants Richard to be miserable, realize I'm a wonderful person, take account of what has happened between us. Everyone deals with everything so damn well."

"Yes," Gabriella said, "you certainly do."

"Except for the memory of all those other Christmases. And then the last year and a half spent trying to get me pregnant."

"I didn't know that."

"Didn't you? Well, we did. Horrible, all that scheduled sex and thermometers by the bedside, all those regular monthly disappointments and feelings of failure. Richard's face all the time and those pious OB/GYNs with baby pictures all over their walls and that sanctimonious air of 'We're going to make a little mother of you, lady.' It was all hideous and degrading. Now I feel a bit like one of the wives of Henry the Eighth, axed for infertility. I hope Liza gives him what he wants."

"Oh, Kate, I didn't know," Gabriella said.

"Well, I do feel like such a failure."

"Of course not. God, you're so lucky you didn't have a child; think of the child now, if you'd been divorced."

"It's okay. I was brought up without my father. If you'd ever met my father, you'd know how grateful I should be for easy divorce laws."

"But think of your life now with a child."

"I wouldn't be so lonely. I'd have something to hold and talk to."

"Oh, Kate, is it so bad? Sometimes I envy you your freedom; sometimes I think it's the right way to live."

"But I'm not free; I'm tied to my loneliness."

"It'll pass, Kate."

"Into what? Anyway, I don't want to talk about it. I don't want to spoil your Christmas; you're having so much fun."

"I wish you were."

"I am," Kate said, "inside the other thing."

There was a shout now and a lot of laughter from the pond. Kate and Gabriella got out of the car to look. It was Morgan, whom Claudio had persuaded to join them, on Preston's skates. Morgan was demonstrating, quite modestly, backward skating and small jumps, not very well, but he seemed pleased with their rapt attention.

Preston came up to the women. "It's not easy on this pond; he's pretty good."

"Let's make some hot chocolate and bring it out," Kate said. "Isn't that the tradition?"

"There may not be any."

"Hot champagne?"

"How revolting." The three of them went toward the house, slowly, Preston limping slightly because the new skates had rubbed his ankles and because his toes had frozen during his slow travel over the ice. Around them the bare trees bent in the slight wind. The moon had been out for hours.

"It's sad to go," said Kate.

"Very sad," Preston said.

From behind them came the sudden noise of the station wagon, doors banged, then a prolonged crunching of gears.

"Claudio's driving," Kate said. They turned to see, but it was too dark now to make out the figures across the road. Hubert rushed up to them.

"Morgan slipped on ze ice," Hubert said. "Claudio's taking him to hospital."

"Hospital?" Gabriella said.

"Christ, Claudio will never find it," Kate said, "Let me go."

"Too late," Gabriella said. "He's gone. What happened?"

"I don't know," Hubert said, "but don't worry. He fell on a jump."

"Oh Christ," Gabriella said.

"It's ze ankle," Hubert said. "He can't move it. Better to get it checked."

"Oh Christ," Gabriella said.

"Poor Morgan," Kate said.

"Poor Morgan," Hubert repeated.

"I hope Claudio can find the hospital," Preston said.

O N CHRISTMAS NIGHT KATE went to bed before the others, before Morgan's return at ten with a broken ankle as Claudio had reported by telephone from the ski-accident–packed emergency room of the hospital. They had spent the evening in the kitchen with the cooks, eating leftovers and drinking champagne and brandy. Kate had drunk too much of both and had stumbled off early, tired of using her cold as an excuse for her misery, tired of other people's kindness that measured the distance between herself and them.

Now she lay turning inside the old bed, pulling herself from the dip in the mattress, made, as it now seemed to her, by centuries of sexual erosion. Everything inside the room was black and still; she was awake and dead sober. This always happened to her and she always forgot: a moderate amount of alcohol knocked her into sleep and kept her there, but too much set the system on overtime and burned itself out by four. Kate switched on the bedside lamp and looked at her watch. Not even two: prematurely beached, and without soft edges now to her grief. She was going to be awake for the rest of the night, that was certain. Sooner or later she would have to think of Richard. At the moment she felt only the nearness of those thoughts inside the room, their small rank presence. Kate had filled her days with meetings, extra work, drinks, brunches, just to make it impossible that there would ever be time when she was alone and trapped and vulnerable. She could deal with thoughts of Richard when they came to her on her way down the subway steps, inside a moving cab. In transit, she almost welcomed them. "Come on," she might say, like a busy dentist, "I can just fit you in if it's not too serious." Here, flat out, the alcoholic poisons washing through her body, at two o'clock in a silent house, there was no point resisting. "All right Richard," she might have said, "let's get it over with."

Kate tried to think of it logically, as though it were a puzzle whose pieces could be moved, until she saw clearly why it was that after six years Richard had just got up and left, leaving her in this broken state. But in the end none of the particulars of herself and Liza seemed to mean anything. The mystery could not be dealt with in terms of fixed quantities: Liza was more of this, she less of that. It made Richard the accountant, herself the liability. What had happened had to be seen in terms of time and changes, such as war, plagues, the invention of movable type, events that simply happen and then demand the adjustment of those to whom they have happened. But villages and individuals don't ever adjust to wars and plagues and revolutionizing inventions, they simply endure them and go on producing new people, for whom the upheavals will be not that, but simply part of reality as given, something not necessary to adjust to.

Kate insisted on surviving. If it were possible, like someone shifting place in bed, to simply accommodate the fact that Richard, who once adored her, was no longer there, she was willing to move over and do so. Kate had lost Richard. Kate had lost her home. Kate had lost Liza. There were three shifts. And there was another: Kate was frightened about herself, about losing control and bidding goodbye to her former accountability.

Kate reached for the book on the table, put it flat against the top sheet and hung on with both hands. Then she tried to read, but the air made her hands cold and her tears blurred her vision. She thought of going downstairs for more brandy but knew she would only lie there with the stuff burning her stomach and head, leaving her sober enough to project herself five years hence as an alcoholic.

And as a strange new corrupt creature. In the past few weeks she'd sensed a frightening willingness to distort herself, disguise her nature, in order to get through dinners or into bed with men who then addressed someone other than Kate, the girl she felt herself obliged to present to them. And sex was becoming for Kate just a bargain made to get someone to touch her, to break down her ice-cold terror of herself suddenly alone. As Kate saw herself getting more alone, more cold, more crazy as the weeks carried her further and further from Richard's warmth, she knew she was losing her lovableness, her containment, and was coming apart, never to be whole again.

She began to cry slowly for the loss of Richard and Liza, but most of all of herself, getting broken daily while she, Kate, had to watch. And to this loss she added the loss of all her old selves, herself at five, herself at eleven when she'd known everything and never been afraid, at seventeen, the age of the first breaking and entering in the form of love, and for the young bride Kate, and now for this Kate, who was going to have to begin to learn how to live alone.

She lay in bed and listened to herself crying in long, violent sobs that shook her body. She turned off the light, turned herself into the pillows and cried there, voluptuously onto the shoulder of the darkness. As she lay there, her chest heaving, her breath coming in short stabs, it seemed to her that the sound was coming back to her, through the neighboring wall. She lifted her head and listened. Clearly she had woken someone and he was mocking her. Who else could be crying in such total desolation?

She stopped a little, tried to get her breath and listened again to her echo. It breathed in spasms, like her own. Then it cried out and Kate recognized the voice of Preston, not mocking her at all, but noisily making love. He cried out again. It stopped her dead in her grief. It made her smile.

With a series of long sighs and then one contented musical sigh, they were finally silent next door. Then Kate sighed, and forgave herself, and went to sleep.

MORGAN'S BROKEN ANKLE hurt him for the first few days in the city; after that it merely weighed him down and provided him with an excuse not to accompany Gabriella to the clubs. In his customary affable way he encouraged her to go without him—and then began to resent her going. In the spaces between his self-abnegating charm, his bad temper flourished, and Gabriella found herself caught inside the message of Morgan's growing ambivalence.

For several nights, among them a television-sodden and champagne-free New Year's Eve, Gabriella felt herself homebound; after that she followed the dictates of her double will: not to be with Morgan and to run off and join her band.

On these nights out Kate accompanied her less and less, in ever more open pursuit of the "real thing." In Kate's mind the band was part of all she was struggling to avoid, beginning to be not very distinguishable from nights out with the girls. She felt under new pressure after Christmas, felt her time precious, her health precarious. She was drinking less, smoking less and running harder —away, she hoped, from whatever it was that was catching up.

For a while during the first weeks of January, Gabriella had the band to herself; that is, Claudio, Mickey and Preston, the last two having lost their tricks after the New Year, in Mickey's case at a New Year's party where Heinz had simply vanished into the crowd, resurfacing ten days later, postally, from Jamaica. And Hubert had gone back to Paris, where, he said, a job at the Centre Pompidou had suddenly materialized, and as he implied, a new commitment to the correct life. For their losses, neither Mickey nor Preston seemed to feel any pain. In fact, thus lightened, they resumed their prowls together, accompanied by Gabriella, happy to be hunting in a pack, at first amused and then totally at ease with the she-wolf among them. With Gabriella as witness, they grew rather proud of themselves and their world, guided her through its accessible corners with a loving, ostentatious hand, like important fathers bringing children to the office, to test the carpets, see the city views and be spoiled by Daddy's secretary.

There was a club where women were allowed on Sundays only, and there eventually Gabriella's curiosity and the band's generosity brought her, down a long dark passage, past a bull-necked bouncer, toward the bar and floor show, a small affair: one bikini-clad black man rippling his torso and queening his hips in time to the music along the shelf of the bar. Around him, a tougher crowd than Gabriella had seen elsewhere, turned sullen faces upward, drank beer, smoked, said nothing. Except for the black queen parading above their heads to a number that went on and on, it was deadly quiet. Gabriella tried to relax into the music, but the eerie waiting crowd checked her. Mickey bought a bottle of wine for them and they drank this until the queen got down, his body wet from his exertions, a dead smile on his face. No one applauded. Two or three followed with their eyes as he exited toward the back, oddly ridiculous at ground level, wet, and naked except where a tiny suit covered the powerful buttocks, like a figure emerging from the sea.

When the disco music resumed, the crowd broke up into its dance shapes. In the corners of the dance area, Gabriella saw rows of men watching from shadows of smoke and noise, like the crowds at a cock ring. Menaced by her own undesirability here, she felt something stronger than rejection, almost the force of a hand that pushes one aside on its way elsewhere; she felt corpse-like, stepped over. Mickey took her arm. "Do you like it?"

"Great."

"Do you think Morgan would like to come when he's better?"

Gabriella searched his face for the irony; but there was none. "Sure," she said.

Mickey, Preston and Claudio made a shelter around her, pleased she liked this place where they often came. On the dance floor two men fucked as they danced. The one in front had his jeans and belt undone, showing hair and a small triangle of white where it shone against his tan. Of the man behind him, Gabriella saw the cock and the thrusting, and a strange lost intensity on his face.

"Shall we take her downstairs for a second?"

"I don't think we can."

"Come on." Preston took her, carried her wine. Mickey and Claudio remained where they were, drinking, looking, cruising. Though it was Sunday, Gabriella appeared to be the only woman there. But with Preston she felt safe, and oddly restored to her own sexual nature. A bartender said "Hello, beautiful" and meant her.

Preston held Gabriella's arm and guided her past the groups of men watching the dancers, through a corridor lined with empty wine bottles, down some steps into a dark area lit only by the flicker of images on an overhead screen. Gabriella took her wine again as Preston let go of her arm and watched her identify the sounds and shapes in the darkness. On the screen gigantic mouth met gigantic cock, then disappeared. Cock approached and receded from camera, connected with mouth or with hand, went up and down, blasted, like a melancholy performing animal with few tricks. In the darkness Gabriella could just make out the eight or so pairs of men, grunting, banging each other against the walls. The noises as they hit her were disconnected, cruel, the sounds of killing, not loving. This was no angelic band, and for a moment she was without illusion, defenseless.

"What the fuck's she doing down here?"

"Come on," Preston said to her.

"Get her out of here or I'll break your heads." Someone pushed through the darkness, massive, leather-clad, chained, dome-shaven. Gabriella reached for Preston and fled with him toward the light.

Upstairs, Claudio and Mickey greeted them. "Hi!" They smiled blandly, two tame ducks paddling a sunny pond.

"Hi."

"What's wrong with you two?"

"The fucking room got a little rough."

"Curiosity's going to kill our cat."

"Enough," said Gabriella. She was shaking still. "Let's leave."

They went on somewhere else, a better mix, benign with pink lights and soft mirrors. Gabriella quickly let the images of the Tunnel's fuck room depart and returned happily with Claudio, Mickey, Preston, to the surface of things, the wafts of cologne and the cuts of clothing, the price of a pair of shoes, to babble and notice orchestrated by the sound of ice inside their glasses. Gay again, gay life. Yet she wondered how the two sides of this thing mixed for them, wondered whether they were simply innocents playing with the trappings of menace, but protected in their childishness, like Mowgli, from all that ferocious part of it.

But she could not hold on to what she had just seen. It did not fit with anything she knew or valued in her friends; and because it did not fit she simply turned her back on it.

Here it was all so attractive, a group of people pursuing their pleasures, down-and-out hedonists whose clothes parodied the work ethic of the world outside, the thick boots, leather and denim boilersuits in which they danced through the hours that the truckers and meatpackers worked for real in streets outside.

And Gabriella was made so welcome—except in the underground, the sexual bowels of the thing. She would stay on the
surface. There she could share in the pursuit of pleasure, among
the faces radiant from dancing and the thump of the music. In
the midst of them, secure once more, she thought unfairly of
Morgan, dragging his plaster foot from room to room, his face
tense from missed appointments, duties unperformed. She
thought of Morgan's use of the word "ought": "We ought to do
something about the Kaplans"; "We ought to see that play";
"We ought to think about the summer"—that "ought" damning
the occasion before it started. And then there was "We ought to
think about what is happening to us."

But here Gabriella thought there was only the moment and the
gentle assistance of its pleasures: "Do you want a drink? Do you
want to dance? Do you want to stay?" Gabriella wanted this noise,
this happiness, this group of people, and with it, the awareness
that this was happening to her and to them at this very moment.

She felt gratitude, an overwhelming affection for them, as they
stood smiling, drinking their noisy drinks, their bodies touching
hers, their smells of leather and lotions reaching her, their friendship reaching her and giving its blessing. She kissed them now,
all three of them, along their sweaty necks, but they didn't know
what she meant. They simply kissed her back. "I do love you,"
she said.

"And we love you."

"No, no," Gabriella insisted, "I do love you."

"We know, we know."

"No, no."

They pummeled it into a joke.

Preston took her hand and led her to the dance floor. As they
danced, Gabriella found herself touching him, though the dance
decorum forbade it. Yet she could not keep her hands from him.

She felt an overwhelming love. She would express it. She wanted to hug Preston. She wanted. It didn't matter, she was high on it.

"Free yourself," the music screamed.

Gabriella listened to the disco music and heard its discrete parts: the jittering, tinkle surface, flashing, charming, and the underbeat, constant drumming, the two layers together shimmer and constancy, like eternally offered joy, unending Christmas. Gabriella danced and touched Preston, and now Preston responded. Inside the music Gabriella tried to express her transformation to him; she felt herself addressing him through the music, frustrated by her ineptness in this language, unsure that Preston got any message other than her own delight in herself. "Come to bed with me," Gabriella shouted.

Preston pulled back, looked at her, then grabbed her and danced with her tightly. "With pleasure," he said as they moved together.

Avoiding Mickey and Claudio dancing with boys on the other side of the room, they slipped out of the club onto the street.

Preston hailed a cab. Gabriella watched him, tall, damp from dancing, his warm breath signaling his warm life to her through the cold air. Inside the cab, she pressed her face onto his wet shirt and body. She had never been so forward! But not forward, backward—she could hardly keep pace with the feelings that dragged her irresistibly to mingle with Preston.

"I adore you, Preston," Gabriella said.

"I adore you," he said. Gabriella, inside her own warmth, felt only the slightest chill from his response, her own words given back to her, not Preston's words. She was too far gone to be warned. They got out; Preston paid the cab and they went up, three long filthy flights above the flower shop where his small loft was. Gabriella saw none of the squalor, enjoying her deep breaths as she climbed, exalted inside Preston's room while he fiddled with the lights and offered her coffee. Coffee! Gabriella laughed and drew him down, on to his rumpled floor mattress.

"Wait, wait, just a minute."

Gabriella let him go, put her arms under her head Maja-like, not yet *desnuda*, and waited.

Preston fussed: went to the bathroom, pulled her off the bed, remade it, put her back, gave her wine, took some, removed his jacket, all without looking at her or speaking to her except to say, "Here, just a sec," "Up we go," and so on; and yet Gabriella held, an Aeolian harp, poised for the wind.

When Preston was altogether ready, he got them both naked into bed, lay on his side and addressed her. He touched her hair and kissed her lightly. He said, "I'm glad you want to sleep with me. I'm flattered."

"Flattered? Oh, Preston, how awful. Don't *you* feel it?"

"Of course," Preston kissed her again. Then he said, "I want to make you sweat. I want to hear you scream."

And yet, even hearing these parodies of movie lines, Gabriella was not warned, but kissed Preston back and tried to caress him.

"You know, Preston," she said, stroking his arm. Preston stroked back, but almost as though not to let her take the lead, to keep his hand in. "We don't have to make love if you don't want to. I could hold you."

"Of course I want to," Preston said with dignity. "Do you think I'm crazy?" He resumed his strokes.

"Gay," Gabriella said, still.

"I adore women," Preston said. He held her.

Gabriella took him at his word and returned to her float in space. There, with Preston far behind, she blossomed, melted and began to think peculiarly but distinctly of Christ, imagining she understood how you could arrive on earth with your self transformed by love, informed by it, pumping it out to men and women alike, knowing that it was divinely given, offer it, and not care that the offer was spurned, how it might have been enough simply to know that feeling of absolute, divinely given, hopelessly offered love.

They made love. And Gabriella saw that it was not very good, because Preston was not there with her. But she did not say that. And Preston rather surprised her with his own verdict that it had been wonderful. It seemed to Gabriella that Preston really had thought it was wonderful, for he had that male pride about the whole thing—that was the giveaway. And she, Gabriella, was left with her own love offered, spurned, intact.

After a while Preston smoked a cigarette.

"You were made for men, Gabriella," Preston said seriously. He ran his hand over the long descent from shoulder to waist, up along the brow of the hip.

"You like women's bodies?" Gabriella was asking in a detached fashion, not flirting.

"Evidently," Preston said.

"I can't help feeling you're searching for a man's body and then finding mine, and that it must be a shock, if only to your hand, to find breasts and belly and hips and all that, and then, down there, nothing."

"Nothing is not what I found."

Gabriella waited.

"Let me put it this way," Preston said, enjoying, at long last, signs of Gabriella's embarrassment. "Your insides feel a lot better than a man's. It was made for that, after all, got the design award. The asshole, excuse my language, doesn't even place. Not for nothing was it called the asshole. Still, mutual masturbation is no fun."

"Well, that's all right; you like the main thing about women."

" 'The main thing,' so sweet, Gabriella, so coy all of a sudden —where's my tough adventurer?"

"Not here."

"Anyway," Preston said, leaning over Gabriella to drop his cigarette in the ashtray, "I've had women before. I told you, I like them. I like you especially. I like your cunt."

"Thank you."

"You're welcome."

"Thank you."

"Oh, come on, sweetie. 'Cunt' is not such a terrible word."

"Only from you, for some reason. I would think for a gay, cunt was the enemy."

"Nah, if anything, it's the straight dick."

"Sounds like a detective."

"Behaves like a detective."

Gabriella was not sure she liked the direction of this conversation. It was rather away from the divinity she had felt, a little too corporeal and a lot less expressive. But Preston went on, "And breasts are marvelous things. Look at that? Whatever is it for?"

"Oh, Preston, you know what it's for."

"But not that amazing line, that's all extra. And look at that," he said, slapping her ass, turning her over.

"I think I'm leaving," Gabriella said. "I feel like meat offered to a skeptical hausfrau; also, I'm not really needed in this conversation: you could go on without me."

"Don't be silly." Preston drew her back to him. "You talk to me."

"Well, if you like women, Preston, why do you like men? Is it greed, is it narcissism? Your mother, or what?"

"Certainly my mother liked men, but I don't think that was it. Yes, there's greed and narcissism in it. Dickie looked like a small version of me, and I sometimes wanted to be like that, small, fast; my better self.

"What happened with Dickie?"

"Good sex, good company. But he wanted love."

"Well, of course"—Gabriella was appalled—"doesn't everyone?"

"Not unless you believe in it."

"But what's to believe, Preston? It's a feeling, a conviction."

"Yes, like lust."

"No, not at all like lust!"

"Yes, it gets satisfied and it goes."

"God, it's not like that. Haven't you ever been in love?"

"Of course. For about two weeks. Never longer than that; after that I want out."

" 'Want out'? Why?"

"Because I'm bored."

"Because you're invited more like, because someone is asking you to stop there."

"Do you want love, Gabriella?"

"Of course, all the rest is just sex."

"Ah. You want love from me, Gabriella? How much love do you want? Do you want to leave Morgan and live with me?"

"No, I want to love you both, I want to love all of you, Mickey, Claudio . . ."

"That's what I said to Dickie."

"Oh."

"He didn't think it was a good answer."

"Well, maybe he's right."

Preston got out of bed and put on his clothes. "Come on, I'll get you a cab. Morgan's going to be frantic."

"Morgan's going to be asleep."

"I don't want to fuck the serious side of your life around."

"Very considerate."

"Oh, I forgot that part." Preston came back and kissed Gabriella.

"What?"

"That part of being with women, the sulking."

"I'm not sulking."

"Good. Then let's go."

"I better have a quick bath."

"Oh yeah, that too, I forgot." Preston bent to give Gabriella another kiss. His mind, Gabriella could see, was already elsewhere. She had forgotten *that* part, the spoils of division. She felt suddenly nervous about this acting of hers on the spur of the moment, as though she had thrown something precious away, jeopardized it for what she called "sex" and that she was going to come away with nothing.

The affair with Preston was too narrow a conduit to express Gabriella's feeling of gratitude for the life she was leading. Yet she went on with it, stuck with this primitive language that was neither understood by Preston nor directly addressed to Claudio or Mickey. These two saw Gabriella's rapture at the clubs, and though pleasantly flattered, felt she was simply inside a novelty of which she, if not the mysteriously tolerant Morgan, was bound to tire. Preston, stuck the odd night with Gabriella's passions, of which he understood little, grew perceptibly uncomfortable with the thing, with the necessary deception, and the division it made between himself and his friends. To Claudio's invitations that he join them on their cruises, Preston would make a weary demurral. "I'm fixed up," he'd say. Claudio, provoked by the uncharacteristic mystery, felt and expressed a continual irritation.

Claudio also worried about his friends and their marriage. It seemed to him that Gabriella was not as careful as she should have been with her precious relationship. Not that Claudio understood the dynamics of their volatile union. On occasion, siding with one or the other in their arguments, he had been crushed between them. After that, he maintained a wary position on the outer ring and continued a fretful but silent watch.

As for Gabriella and Morgan, they were held in a new dark tension, a refusal to bring what was below the surface up for inspection, as though both of them, individually, had some inkling of the danger. Though they went on with their lives and their shared jokes and gossip, it seemed to Gabriella that the good humor was gone, replaced by a faked jollity that hovered lightly over mistrust. Gabriella went out with her band three or four nights a week; other nights she sat dutifully with Morgan through dull and anxious suppers or watching television, feeling his resentment inside their strange silence with each other. Passively, Gabriella watched the anger growing in Morgan, saw how that and their reticence slowly pried them apart. She saw it inside the new way in which Morgan made love to her at night, his strange absence there in bed as though in response to her strange absence on nights out with the band and her stranger absence when they were together. Morgan expressed his rage only when he touched Gabriella, his manner in sharp contrast now to the instinctive thoughtless caressing of Preston. He was rough with her, bruising her when they made love and kissing her with his whole head as though he meant to butt her into submission.

So she fled back to Preston and his sweet confusion, almost embarrassment, with the degree of Gabriella's tenderness for him. She could see him striving for delicacy when getting her out of his bed late at night; she could watch the temptation that flew across his eyes—dull inside the lights of the disco—to suggest that tonight, perhaps, they go home early. And she noticed with a tender amusement that soon became sadness how if she suggested going home alone, he always agreed, always careful first to convey courteous disappointment. Gabriella knew that her love for Preston lay heavily on his hands, and as the winter weeks succeeded, began to languish for lack of his support; yet she went on with it, driven more and more by Morgan's own new roughness, into the soft, apologizing tenderness of Preston's, faked as she knew, and doomed to an early death.

One night, lying on the crumpled wine-stained black bedding in Preston's room, after they had been making love with, as ever, a great deal of noise from Preston and none from Gabriella, she asked him, "You don't much want to go on with this, do you?"

"Of course." A tiny pained line lifted the corner of his mouth.

"I don't think you do. I think you are getting a little bored with it—or with me." Gabriella turned toward him and watched his eyes carefully. Preston said nothing. In the silence he reached for his cigarettes. Gabriella lit one for him but went on, "Shall we stop?"

"Whatever you like."

"But what do *you* like, Preston? Don't you miss the boys?"

"I don't have to miss the boys," he said quietly. "I get all the boys I want." He smiled, again, a small embarrassed smile.

"What, now?" Gabriella sat up.

"Yes," he said.

"Don't you take anything seriously?"

"Of course. I take us seriously."

"But—"

"Look, Gabriella, this is me. I'm just like this. I've told you, I've never been in love longer than two weeks. Anyway, I don't think it's a possibility. What do you want, Gabriella, you want to marry me and have children?"

"Children? I want us to love each other."

"Well, we've done that, Gabriella. It doesn't take us very far."

"We haven't done that. We haven't even started. You haven't let your guard down for me to get through."

"It's not my guard. You've had all of me, all there is. It's just like that for me. I'm sorry."

"But why?" Gabriella could see the confession hurt Preston's pride, but she needed to hear.

"Why?" Preston said. "Why don't you have children with Morgan? Why do you stop where you stop? Why don't you take *that* relationship to its conclusion?"

"Which is?"

"I don't know—children, isn't it? Why do you two keep hanging on in the initial stages?"

"Like us, you mean?" Gabriella said. "I don't know what's happening between Morgan and me, but it doesn't look like it's going in the direction of children."

"Maybe that's because of me," Preston said.

"No," Gabriella said, smiling.

"It seems to me," Preston said, "that you're not taking me very seriously, either, eh? Or perhaps Morgan."

Gabriella said nothing, but got out of bed and into Preston's grime-ringed bath. He remained where he was next door, saying nothing.

When she was dressed again, she headed toward the door. Preston sat up under the sheet. "Look, Gabriella," he said sadly, "you go away and think what you want. I've told you what I can do. I can see it may not be enough. But I am not going to run away with you, and you are not going to run away with me. This is more or less it."

"What you see is what you get?" Gabriella challenged him.

"Will you call me?"

"I'll call you," Gabriella said from the top of the stairs.

KATE FORGAVE RICHARD DAILY. Often in her room in the Callagher house, she would wake to the sound of herself crying, or finding her face wet with tears, would hear herself saying, "It's all right, Richard," again and again, in a sleep-born chant of forgiveness. Exalted by her own compassion, Kate would then lie under the blankets until another consciousness came to mix with her great nobility toward her husband, and this would take her up and set her down gently in a world she commanded less well.

Kate cried easily these days. On the bus that took her to work, its rubber-ribbed floors black and wet from the melting city slush, she found herself chilled among the furs, her broken heart springing to her eyes and welling over like the seasonal incontinence, ice into water, numbness into grief. Then she would get off and wander among the big shops of Fifth Avenue until she found her place of work, and there the saving frenzy that let her forget, whole mornings at a time, the acts of self-healing that otherwise engaged her.

In the midst of these wet/dry cycles, she would sometimes speak to Richard, gauging each successful dealing with his voice as a measure of her progress back into the world of the ordinarily numb, or at least ordinarily un-weeping. She could even joke with Richard these days, by phone. In his presence a joke would hurt too much, lifting as it did the curtain of his formality, reminding her of the softness that had once transformed his face when they made love. Now, coaxing out this private former Richard, and hearing it laugh, Kate would feel the need to send it back, hurt, because it had hurt her, into its hole.

They made attempts to meet again, hoping each time that they would find themselves suddenly at ease, in painless camaraderie, with the transition achieved, as if by magic. One day they met for lunch. Richard had chosen formally, expensively, the restaurant in the St. Regis, to celebrate, as it seemed to Kate, as Kate hoped too, the end of their sad era. Under the vast varnished mural of Old King Cole, they drank each other's health, unstiffened, amazed themselves with the simple pleasantness of the occasion. But the good feelings caught Kate unaware, or perhaps the wine; the cautious good manners that had survived the whiskey sours to become a gentle engaging tenderness, had survived the first course to become a loving tap from a worldly-wise lady to her former spouse, had, by the end of the meal, spilled over into a teasing, flirtatious, strained manner, part bravado, part despair, and had at last crashed headlong into panic, into the plea, drunken, charmless, as clear as a child's howl that Richard take Kate upstairs in the hotel and make love to her.

"No, Kate," Richard said, in a low voice, in dignity and shame. And Kate winced.

Late that afternoon Richard telephoned her at work; inside his kindness, understanding, his happy safety at that distance, she heard his anger at her sabotage of their civilized lunch, his bitterness that she had yet again confronted him with her own Richard-generated pain.

Such failures assured her of her own weak state; but her new compassion for Richard was a self-preserving sidestep that let her escape her sense of herself as his victim. "Richard," Kate would say to herself on her way home from work, headed for an evening which now less and less engaged her optimism, barely aroused her curiosity, "I forgive you everything; it is life I cannot forgive." By which she thought she meant time. It was a sudden sense of time that had made her leap drunkenly at Richard before the end of the meal. And it was time that had altered their feelings, so imperceptibly as to have allowed her to give those feelings marble names like "love" and "certainty," and therefrom to construct a palace, inside of which only years later, according to Richard, they had found themselves to have been imprisoned.

And then Kate would come home to the Callagher house and find those two engaged in what she considered the mad, destructive testing and tapping of *their* palace walls, as though determined to show each other, mostly Gabriella showing Morgan, that the foundation was not likewise marble; and this done not just in the face of *their* enemy time, but in the pursuit of another hollow abstraction, freedom, and whatever it was that Gabriella meant by gaiety.

In the space left by Gabriella's pursuit of such things was Morgan's querulous sadness, and like a relative by the deathbed, the uncharacteristically mournful figure of Claudio. On winter evenings, in the hours before Kate's joyless rushing off, Claudio's worried chaperoning of Gabriella at the gay clubs, Morgan's sour return to law briefs, they made an uncomfortable foursome, united by a bottle of wine and a recitation of the day's events, and more and more by a growing realization that something bad was happening, separately, to all of them.

On these evenings Kate noticed a small change in Morgan's relation to Claudio. From time to time she caught them in a tiny conspiratorial snideness about Gabriella. Once, she thought, they offered her a part of it, when Gabriella was gone from the room and Morgan said to Kate, "I'm afraid Gabriella's going to burn our supper, she's in such a hurry to be out of here." Claudio had contributed. "I'm too old," he said. "I can't keep up with her anymore." They had both looked then toward Kate. But Kate had said, "You must miss her, Morgan. Why don't you say so?"

But in truth, Morgan was beginning to realize that he enjoyed his wife's absences, his freedom from her past demands for entertainment. Freedom, really, from the loneliness demanded by their union. Richard apart, Gabriella had never liked Morgan's friends from the office; it had been part of their closeness, those little, affectionate, annihilating jokes at the expense of Morgan's colleagues, of anyone external to their shared life. With Gabriella now going her own way part of the week, Morgan began to contemplate a revival of his own life, as much to fill the center where Gabriella had emptied it as to answer her disloyalty with his own. As yet Morgan had done nothing, apart from transferring some old names to a new address book, and one rather depressing lunch with Otto. In the meantime Claudio filled a gap, in the increasingly longer and longer stretches before he went off with Gabriella to the clubs.

Claudio began to seem to Morgan a civilizing influence, a man who neither competed in the subtle manner of the crowd at work, nor flaunted the gains of a career under the dismal evidence of a horribly embraced middle age, as had been the case with such college playmates as Gabriella's tolerance and his own curiosity had allowed. And Claudio's being a man, a creature capable of self-containment, made a difference to Morgan just then, pressed as he was at work, and harassed at home. He was neither willful and spoiled like Gabriella, nor, like Kate, washing about her the hourly evidence of her distress. At night sometimes Morgan would hear Kate crying and feel inside him a secret rage, as though that wail proclaimed *him* inadequate, useless and in some vague way guilty by virtue of his gender.

Morgan liked the fact that Claudio was so willing a companion to him, willing to discuss whatever Morgan wished to discuss— films, books, politics—pleased to get up and fetch the drinks or change the records, the way Gabriella simply was not, Morgan's plaster foot notwithstanding. "You'll get fat if you let everyone look after you," she would say, or "Here you are, O master—anything else?" as though some philosophy of marriage and not the absurd Christmas injury had kept him off his feet.

He was aware he enjoyed Claudio's admiration of him. Claudio was so open about it and so sweet, praising a haircut or a pair of socks. Men at work hardly did that sort of thing; in fact, only one's mother did that sort of thing. Now, occasionally, Morgan found himself choosing a shirt or tie with Claudio in mind, anticipating a little crook of the brow and Claudio's "I haven't seen that before, have I?" And that was all, no secret flowering of Narcissus, Morgan thought, just a little awareness of the tastes of his companion, and the pleasant, secure, Gabriella-proof desire, to please.

Of course Claudio felt the change in Morgan's attitude and began to warm to it; but as his pride in their friendship grew, he began to share Morgan's resentment of his wife's outings in the clubs, because they deprived him, as Gabriella's companion, of Morgan's company and implied—for Claudio was not yet certain that Morgan understood the great double love that made up Claudio's impartiality in that marriage—that in matters of pleasure and its pursuit Claudio was entirely on Gabriella's side.

Now when Kate suggested to Morgan that he simply tell his wife he missed her and wanted her to stay at home, Claudio leapt to agree, repeating the excuse of his age and income, gaining in Morgan's esteem from his apparent altruism. Morgan (half recognizing his own pleased freedom from his wife) said he wouldn't dream of interfering with Gabriella. But Kate, fresh inside her conviction that marriages must be saved, insisted. Gabriella came back from the kitchen to find these three indeed conspiring. "Morgan is beginning to miss you," Kate told her. "Claudio's not young enough to keep up with you anymore," Claudio told her. Morgan kept his silence, and was startled to hear his wife's reply. "It is getting a little boring, isn't it?" she said, an unconscious repetition of her remark to Preston, the affair with whom she thus brought to an easy and discussion-free end.

But Gabriella did not quite relish altogether giving up the clubs. They were important to her in counterweight to the truths she picked up at home, about Kate's relationship to Richard both past and present, and about hers with Morgan. Balancing these gloomy realities was the evidence the clubs gave her that life, on the other side of this door, was a great pleasure and that simply to be alive and be Gabriella, with other live beings around her, was, contrary to what she learned at home, a great blessing.

Sometimes still, at the clubs with Claudio and Mickey, or watching Preston at a distance—up close, the embarrassment of their abortive affair wrecked the peaceful contact between them —Gabriella felt a happy softening of herself, a sense that it was so easy to be happy, to feel this love, platonic, parental, fraternal, of her fellow beings. It needed only a slow lowering of shoulders, a surrendering of defenses, and there it was, so accessible, her love of other people.

The clubs changed Gabriella's attitude to parties. Before, she'd seen only the rapacity and guardedness, how contact seemed to be something carefully priced (power, repute, beauty) and then measured out, nothing freely given for the simple pleasure of the salute, one pilgrim to another. But the anonymity of the crowds at the clubs, the speed and noise, the principle of change: change of partners, change of energies, change of light that picked up and isolated a profile, a sequined shoe, a leer, a neck on a shoulder, a slow roll of a pair of hips, orchestrating an aesthetic of glimpses and exteriors, and not the calculation of other people as things of value, power, importance—all this had changed her. Where once Gabriella had seen only a shallow gathering or defending of conquests, among faces that had been like slamming doors, returning her empty-handed to her isolation, where once she, too, had divided others into the known and the nobodies, as though anyone who took up space on any floor could be nobody, and had made others invisible, as others made her, now Gabriella knew that behind each mask of the unfamiliar was someone real and present, and that it was possible to go to a party of strangers and come away having found souls inside the suits, having pulled them into her own pool of sunshine, having touched in the precious fleeting tango.

Gabriella went to parties frequently now, to Claudio's friends' apartments, to art openings, in New York there were always parties somewhere. She went without Morgan and to places where she knew no one, and she was delighted to find herself no longer alone.

At the beginning of February, Richard had a birthday party in Liza's loft, and here Gabriella knew a lot of people, drank a lot of champagne and admired the beautiful clothes. She wore a long pink silk caftan, pearl-and-bead–encrusted, stiff with antique embroidery and what the junk shop salesman had assured her was an Arab chieftain's dried blood inside the lining. It was a sexless garment, regal and ceremonial. Gabriella was proud of it and felt an odd urge, beyond display and admiration, to share it with someone else. Caught up in the peculiar sensation, a little drunk, she approached Richard, himself tall and beautiful in his satin lapels, silk shirt and jeweled cuff links. For a while they admired each other's dress and then, at Gabriella's suggestion, went into the bedroom and rather chastely exchanged clothes. There was some cannibalism in Gabriella's pleasure, Richard's smell adhering to the silk, a little transvestite thrill: she looked good in Richard's shoulders and tie; it was an erotic and unerotic tribute she paid. Others caught on. Liza changed clothes with Claudio, whose trousers were too short for her; then with another, smaller girl. (Claudio's pale silk clothing traveled the most in that room, from one small female back to another.) Almost everyone at the party chose a partner and moved, into the bedroom area of the loft or the bathroom, or simply behind the screened-off kitchen, treading warily over Liza's acrylics, shedding bras and belts. The room was alive with the noise of zipping and praise. All sexless, communal and heroically childish. Morgan stood off in a corner and watched, his plaster foot exempting him from the goings on. But Otto joined in, without the least self-consciousness, drinking down his champagne inside Liza's blue-sequined dress, his red chest hair blossoming over the bosom, his back bulging a little spottily from the unfastenable zip, diamond pendants dripping from his heavy, mournful lobes.

Beyond the self-admiration, the peculiar thing was that no one commented on what they were doing, no one resisted, no one named it, and no one took it any further than it went already. The thing was properly and mysteriously understood, as self-enclosed, innocent and celebratory.

Morgan's gloomy watchfulness could not restrain Gabriella publicly. Though she gave up the clubs under his pressure, she clung to her gaiety. Yet he weighed on it, and she tried to escape. Preston Gabriella had abandoned easily; Morgan was harder. She conspired in his friendship with Claudio in order to help him shift a little away from her. More and more, as it had been before Christmas, the three of them found themselves together in a perfect balance, Claudio ballasted by their love of him; they, through him, more lightly laid upon each other.

Claudio no longer dared to speak to Gabriella and Morgan about their "impressive marriage." Partly, he sensed that what might be keeping it buoyant was his own cheerful presence. For once he no longer felt obliged to have excuses for staying there, sensing that he had now become part of a structure, which without him might easily crumble. He felt himself spongelike, bland, but usefully so, absorbing tensions and hostilities he'd not felt before with the Callaghers, but which he now vaguely remembered from his own infancy, when, similarly, he'd been pulled from his cloudlike innocence and dropped into his parents' latent sexual hell.

And Morgan sensed it too, the inoculation that Claudio was providing against the pain of his marriage. He realized how it tired him, the leash of loving Gabriella. But he refused to be her jailer, and he could not yet challenge her. He tried to slip back into the relief of the world of work, and before smashing his fraudulent home life, think first what freedom he wanted and whether it was possible for him or right.

Gabriella, too, flailed inside the anxious union, longing to break out but not yet break away where there was no safe footing. Her brief push through Preston's sweet welcoming had convinced her there might be nothing on the other side. And against that nothing, would she really risk losing Morgan? Gabriella felt a horrible heaviness about herself and her insistence on love with Preston. She had no right to her evangelical demands, to her sense of betrayal, particularly given that Romantic Love had been the departure point of her present hellish life at home.

All three were held by the strange sexual tension, paralyzed by ambivalence and the jarring of desires and dissatisfactions that surfaced only when they were drunk, in small fights or lewd proposals.

One evening when they were together, sitting late at a SoHo restaurant, Claudio began to comment on the waiter, a dark good-looking Italian in his early thirties. As though on order, Gabriella tried to flirt with him, ostensibly to bring him nearer Claudio's line of vision, but in truth, to watch for the possibility of provocation in Morgan. For it seemed to her that jealousy lay dormant in this new truce of theirs, and that if she could see it rise, it would announce itself as a kind of last hope for them. She did not know that she was already thinking in such terms, that such hope as she had daily for them could be described as "last." Her sense of their marriage would have included neither desperation nor strain. They were on an adventure, that was all, where their familiar marital barque would carry them, safely, as it always had before.

Claudio, too drunk or too taken up by his desire for the waiter to sense what was going on between his friends, sat back, drank slowly and watched Gabriella at work. Morgan sat similarly silent while Gabriella, feeling his alertness, performed. Twice she caught and held the waiter's eye as he moved across the emptying restaurant room. When he went back and forth to clear their table she smiled at him fully, obviously. To her first smile, the Italian responded; thereafter he concentrated on what he was doing and avoided her gaze. But when he brought their bill, Gabriella spoke to him. "Have a drink with us," she said. The sound of these words in her own ear, so proficient, so like a man, made her joyful. She was thrilled by her daring, felt a small malicious triumph that she was making Morgan uneasy, and an altruistic and predatory pleasure that she was able, like a mother eagle, to hunt for Claudio.

"A drink?" the Italian repeated. Manhood was challenged; it was the lady who spoke, the two gentlemen who watched for his answer. "It's late," he said simply. But he did not leave the table. He brought his thighs, jean-clad, against the top of it, and leaned a little toward them. Gabriella smiled at him again, as though to fix his attention on her alone, to make him ignore what might confuse him, the gender of her two other companions.

"Won't they let you join us here?" she asked, her smile now challenging him, like her words, his position as waiter against hers as customer, and inside that, his power as a man against hers as a woman.

"Perhaps," he said, "if it weren't so late."

"We could go elsewhere," Gabriella said. They all of them now played for time, particularly Claudio, like an awkward suitor, not knowing when best to cut in. The drink had slowed him. Gabriella could feel him tempted to clear his throat. And Morgan, too, would have liked to assert himself, to end her control of the situation.

But Gabriella, triumphant, held on. "Let's go somewhere," she said familiarly now to the waiter, as though his agreement were a thing too obvious to wait upon. "Where shall we go?"

The thighs moved back the slightest bit, just a faint muscular retraction. But Claudio saw it and sped up. "That's a nice idea," he said smokily, languorously, his own vocal roll over onto the boy.

The waiter looked at Claudio and shifted, moved from challenged heterosexual to propositioned male, moved, but not away. He looked now at Morgan, to confirm that he, too, was gay. But Morgan's dark brooding belonged not to a cruising predator but to a sulking husband. Again, the waiter backed off, confused. "It's late," he repeated.

"It's late," Morgan said. Only Gabriella would have heard the anger in his voice. To that anger, she responded. "Oh, come on, how late do you both think it is? It can't be past one. That's not late." She smiled again at the waiter, and as if to show him he was outnumbered, added, "Is it, Claudio?"

The name gave her a clue to the next move. "My name is Gabriella."

The waiter looked about him now in the restaurant, to see who was watching, for signs that he was still at work, for time before answering.

"Luca," he said. "Italian for Luke."

"Claudio is Italian for Claud," Gabriella said, "and Gabriella is Italian for Gabriel."

"No," said the waiter, laughing now, "Gabriella is Italian for Gabriella, Gabrielle is Italian for Gabriel. And you?" He turned to Morgan, but Morgan wasn't playing this game, and the waiter's smile died.

"Morgan is American for Morgan," Gabriella said. It was almost insulting. She added quickly, "You call him Morgana, Luca, to Italianize him."

Luca smiled again and looked at Morgan. Morgan had begun to rise. Gabriella saw his anger now, as did Claudio.

"All right, another time," Claudio said quickly. "We'll come earlier. Do you work weekends?"

"No." Shop talk ensued. Two waiters. Gabriella caught Morgan's eye while Claudio and Luca exchanged numbers. Morgan said nothing at all.

In the cab on the way home Gabriella held herself buoyant, still carried by her own daring. But as they approached their address she saw how Morgan's silent disapproval was so much stronger than her happiness, and she knew that he would break her spirit. She did not want to go home with him, not even with Claudio there, because he could no longer protect them against what was coming. And it seemed to her that they were trapped in it, Morgan's anger and weight against her spirit of freedom, or perhaps her spirit of revenge that masqueraded as joy.

IN THE END IT WAS THE WEATHER that got them, in early March, as the exhaustion set in, as for most New Yorkers, seemingly suspended forever between the warmth of Christmas and the first signs of spring, only a couple of presidential holidays and the odd Valentine between them and depression. As each new thaw uncovered another layer of old snow and excrement, and promised nothing but a two-day respite of wet feet and slush before the ice began again, it seemed to all of them, the Callaghers, Claudio, Kate, that the seasonal record had got stuck, that nature had forgotten how to proceed.

Inside the stasis, each one thought of escapes, four days in the Caribbean, divorce, hard work, change of life. Morgan, among the slipping elderly and overbundled young, limped with his bad foot from home to office and office to home, trying to reserve his energies for his job. He had made up his mind to deal with his complicated home life by lying dormant inside it. Such blooming as he did, he reserved for lunches, now more frequent with Richard, and on occasion Otto, with whom it was his guilty pleasure to listen to complaints about married life.

"She spends all week and more than I make in those phony antique shops," Otto told Morgan. As soon as they'd got the house, he said, Casey had lost all interest in him, drove him out with every new roll of wallpaper. And no one had warned him what hell the pregnancy was going to be, the vomiting, the complaints, the refusing to have sex.

"My life," he said to Morgan, in a phrase that hit home, "is beginning to feel like someone else's. Short of her miscarriage or my bankruptcy, I don't see any way it's going to get better. Once the breeding's started, you're in it for life." He stared morosely at Morgan. "People like us are, anyway. The reins of this thing just aren't mine anymore," Otto said. "If I were you, I'd think hard."

"Are you suggesting I get out while I can?" Morgan said with a laugh.

Otto waved to the waiter to bring them the check. "I'm not suggesting anything. But how's your sex life been lately?"

Morgan's sex life lay in bed with her third flu of the season, letting her temperature rise because her spirit could not. In its melodramatic fashion, her body made a theater for her emotions, swelling her joints, preventing her swallowing, rocking her on a nauseating sea.

Gabriella's disappointment in the outcome of her affair with Preston had lain low for a while, then shaped itself into anger at his inadequacy, his spurning of her gift. But long before it came to the surface of her thoughts—where it would have to be checked: she, a married woman, had no right to demand anything more solid from her gay lover, particularly given that the light weight of the gay world had attracted her to him in the first place —the anger had turned against herself, in the fishhook of depression.

In depression, Gabriella languished, resisting expressions of rage, against Morgan, too, because she could not risk open battle with him. Her depression slopped naturally into flu. Though she loathed the masochism in these periodic retreats from her life, was impatient with her own dormancy, she recognized the impossibility of any other action and retreated to bed.

Kate's move, less self-destructive than Gabriella's—but then, as Gabriella had always insisted, Kate was a freer agent than herself —was flight. She arranged her escape via work, to the California branch of her company, where, though she dragged her New York past behind her, no one would have the bad manners to ask about it. California was to be Kate's tabula rasa; she might even herself be new at the other end of the American continent, matching the unfamiliar terrain with her own unfamiliarity. Or so she hoped; her present driven state was beginning to seem nothing so transient as a phase, more like a structure, as real and solid as a rat's wheel. Besides, her pain was leaking drastically, and she was ashamed of her suffering; she needed to escape visibility.

Kate's goodbye party was a drab affair, hardly a party at all by Gabriella's recent standards. In a peculiar reversal of their Christmas roles, Gabriella forced the cheerfulness and ignored her flu; Kate played joyful belle. But instead of the gay chorus (of whom only Claudio was present), Kate's farewells were bidden by a small team from work: four women in tight skirts and high heels, one pampered boss and seven or eight friends, all that remained of those years of dinner parties, the breathless social life, a mere handful it seemed to Gabriella, hardly enough to fill one page of Kate's name-jammed address book. *"Partir, c'est mourir un peu,"* Gabriella quoted, *"mais mourir, c'est partir trop."* In New York, she thought, *"partir, c'est mourir tout à fait."*

Claudio seemed to be the only one saddened by Kate's departure. For the rest, it was perfectly all right for her to slip from their lives. People were replaceable and properly replaced; the party was simply the ritual that let Kate go away. Her guests drank their drinks, kissed her, promised to write, and left by nine. Kate, feeling something was wrong with her flight plan, sensing herself left and not leaving, wandered among the broken canapés and

146

empty wine bottles in Gabriella's kitchen and remembered how from the deck of his moving ship, Sam Goldwyn had shouted to his friends on the pier below, "Bon voyage!"

At dinner, Claudio and the Callaghers made a great fuss over Kate, embraced and sighed, and predicted their grief. The following evening Gabriella went to bed early; Morgan and Claudio went out to a film. The night after that, it was strange how little any of them noticed that Kate was gone.

Richard noticed that Kate was gone, and watched the walls of his guilt about her recede. He became almost breezy, a former self.

"That foot's been exhausting you," he said to Morgan over lunch a week later, "and Kate's been exhausting me. Nothing to do with her, of course; that's just the way it's worked. Liza wants to take a holiday; Gabriella's had all this flu. Why don't we get out?"

"We?" Morgan asked him.

"The four of us," Richard said cheerfully. "Why not? We'll take two weeks now instead of four later; I can get the time off, what about you?"

"I suppose I could," Morgan replied cautiously. "I've been clearing my desk at a pretty good pace. When? And more to the point, where?"

Liza telephoned Gabriella at the office.

"How's the flu?" she asked her.

"How did you know?"

"Morgan talks to Richard, Richard talks to me; now that Kate's gone we might end up talking to each other."

Gabriella looked over to Max. He was on his own phone, booking a feminist poet into a lecture hall in Oklahoma. "Ideological," Gabriella heard him saying, "but human."

"The flu's better," Gabriella said, "but the batteries are still flat. How about you?"

"Disgusting," Liza said happily. "I need a vacation. You want to come? Can you leave your job for a couple of weeks?"

"She'll need expenses," Gabriella heard Max arguing, "and a little entertainment. You can't expect her to scrounge off Germaine Greer like the last one."

"I could leave it longer than that," Gabriella said. "In fact if Morgan would let me, I'd leave forever."

"If Morgan would let you?" Liza repeated.

"Look, Tulsa's the center of Women's Studies in this country; Melanie is a very respected figure down there."

"I mean if I could face him."

"Well, face him," Liza said. "Quit your job and come to Mexico with us."

"It doesn't matter whether you like it or not," Max was saying, "she's not writing for us."

"Mexico?" Gabriella asked.

"It's got to be hot, and I can't stand all those steel bands and rum cocktails in the Caribbean. Anyway, I know someone—"

"Liza, you always know someone. I don't think Morgan will agree."

"He's the one who needs it most."

"True. What is it?"

"A tiny white villa in Acapulco. I know what Acapulco sounds like, but this is isolated, it has a swimming pool and a view of the Pacific, one part-time cook, one cleaner, and it's only fifty dollars a day. We could swing it if you two came. Anyway, it would be nicer if you two came."

"Wouldn't you rather be alone with Richard?"

"What a question! If I did, I wouldn't ask you."

"Half the world is women," Max said, "more even."

"I'd love to come. I'll have to work on Max and Morgan."

"Work on them, be cunning."

Gabriella put the phone down and looked at Max.

"Did you book her?" Gabriella asked him.

"Sure."

"Can I have two weeks off?"

"Sure," Max said.

"It's for a vacation," Gabriella said.

"Sure," Max said again, "you need one."

Gabriella got home at eight to find Morgan alone in the living room, listening to Wagner and reading work from the office.

"Claudio not here?" she asked.

"It's Tuesday."

"So it is."

Morgan turned around and looked blankly at his wife. "You look exhausted, been working hard?"

Gabriella gauged the sarcasm. "Not very," she said.

"No." Morgan returned to his reading.

"Are you working tonight?" Gabriella asked him.

"No." Morgan turned toward her again. "What are your plans?"

"We could eat in; there's something under foil in the fridge."

"Sounds like something dead," Morgan said.

Gabriella lay in her bath and postponed her evening with her husband. She felt strange antagonisms about his being in the next-door room, as if his presence had grown with the absence of the other two. She also felt frightened of proposing Liza's Mexican trip, and tired in advance for the arguing. He might not be able to get off, though. But there was also a dread for her, beyond the dread of the evening, that were they to go, Liza and Richard's union would be forced upon them, making their own togetherness, shaky and brittle as it had become since Christmas, appear even more feeble and dishonest. Did they want that? To suffer while the other two sported, to fake the holiday? And all those nights with two people who have the joys of bed before them, and they with only its sad confrontations and evasions?

Two weeks was a long time in one place; they would be forced to acknowledge the existence of love, and its absence, by the proximity of a loving couple. But she and Morgan did love each other, of course; it was the proverbial bad patch. Maybe a holiday was exactly what was needed. Maybe Mexico would do the trick.

But what exactly would the trick consist of? Giving up Gabriella's more or less free and chaste life for more marital intimacy. She was frightened of it; it would take away too much.

But then, she would quite like to go to Mexico and be with Liza and Richard. Why must her marriage continually come before her friendships? No, they would go, she and Morgan would fight and have bad sex and see the ruins. She would have the pleasure, between *their* amorous hours, of Richard and Liza's companionship.

Gabriella got out of her bath, slowly, figuring out a way to bring the trip off, and yet rebelling against that role with Morgan, with whom she was always so open, of calculating wife, conniving female. She could hear that terrible whining "Morgan???" and his "Umn??" Had she been single, she would have been able just to go.

It might be the trip that precedes divorce. They might even get divorced in Mexico. They could do the whole package together, first the misfired honeymoon, then the divorce. But where was this notion of divorce coming from? Gabriella asked herself suddenly. For how long had Gabriella been so sure, or so bitter? Her voice sounded tragic to her ears, and tired, too old to be her own.

They ate their cold supper coldly, all Morgan's warmth going into his reassurance that the aging moussaka was fine, and that he didn't mind drinking beer with it.

"How's work?" Gabriella asked to change the subject.

"Hard—how's work with you?"

"As usual," Gabriella said. She was grateful now she hadn't had to quit. If in the end she didn't have the vacation, Max wouldn't care. Max never cared about anything.

"I spoke to Liza today," Gabriella said. "She and Richard are going to Mexico. She suggested we come."

"Richard told me," Morgan said.

"Oh? . . . Do you want some more?"

"No, thanks."

"Not very good, is it?"

"It won't kill us."

"Well, what did you say to Richard?" Gabriella asked and waited.

"Do you want to go?"

"I would," Gabriella said, "but can you get off?"

"Probably," Morgan said. "If you let me work for the next two weeks—I mean, weekends and so on. You really want to go?"

Gabriella was up now. "Yes, I want to see that museum."

"The museum's in Mexico City; the flight goes direct to Acapulco."

"Oh, but if we're going all that way," Gabriella said, "and the pyramids, and the Riveras, and Trotsky's house . . ."

"That's a lot for one change of planes," Morgan said.

But Gabriella was out in front again, happy. "We could go perhaps for a few days and then meet Richard and Liza by the sea. It would be lovely, Morgan, don't you think?"

"Maybe," Morgan said grudgingly. "It would just be us," he added.

"Of course," Gabriella said.

They were silent. Once again Gabriella's gaiety had menaced Morgan's gloom, and Morgan's gloom had depressed Morgan, because he did not want to be that way either, yet it was the only way he could keep his hand heavy on his wife. He would have liked to have it all open; his nature craved clarity. And yet here it was as always between them, truths twisted by games, humiliating poses: Gabriella having to hide her desires and distort her happy nature, Morgan having to watch her do it, demanding that sacrifice because something in him sensed that what she wanted was wrong, wrongly arrived at.

"We'll go," Morgan said, "whatever you like."

"But I want you to like it," Gabriella broke through.

"Then I'll like it," Morgan said. He kissed her hand. She took away his plate.

GABRIELLA SAT IN HER SEAT ON the rain-battered AeroMexico flight and felt dreadful; dreadful because anything less than a view of full sunshine and cotton clouds out of a plane window told her the thing she was in was as fragile as a kite and might tip her into the unknown at the least kink of fate or Mexican engineering, and dreadful because she was going into another unknown with Morgan where it was her obligation, and his, to have a good time. They both knew that if they couldn't bring that off, their failure would have its consequence. The thing was beginning to seem less a vacation than a last stand against the coming dissolution of everything.

Morgan drank from his twist-off bottle of white wine and read his paperback on Mexican history, his shelter against the cold space between them. The leftover antagonisms, shelved in the rush to the airport, checking in and eyeing of other passengers, rather prematurely and garishly dressed in tropical gear, overtaken by the nerves about getting into planes, strapping in, gripping hard through takeoff, were now settling for Gabriella as the engines droned and the plastic creaked, into anxiety about the next few days, mingling with irritations from the past few weeks, the struggle that this holiday, for all its good intentions, had finally become.

The main problem had been Claudio. For several days Gabriella and Morgan simply forgot about him in their plans and discussions with Richard and Liza. Then when it was all settled, Gabriella remembered and fell into secrecy. It was this that oppressed her, as day by day she felt how long Claudio had been abandoning his magic nest to prop up theirs and how much they both had relied on him. In the end she'd simply told him, disingenuously suggesting he come too while counting on his not having the cash.

"Do you really want me to come?" Claudio asked. His eyes were so bright, his smile so open that Gabriella had no choice but to reassure him.

"It might be expensive," she said cautiously, but Claudio's expression forced her to add, "We could lend you the airfare anyway."

In the evening, while Gabriella figured out how best to break it to Morgan, and then to Richard and Liza, she overheard the ecstatic rise of Claudio's voice as he engaged Morgan on the subject of cheap Mexican pottery and enamel *santos*. Five minutes later Morgan appeared in the kitchen.

"Why the hell did you ask Claudio?"

"I didn't ask exactly, but we had to mention it sometime."

"Jesus, are we expected to take him everywhere?"

"No, of course not. Tell him you don't want him to come."

"On what grounds exactly?" Morgan had said. "He practically lives here, anyway. Our adopted son. How could you get us into this? How am I supposed to square it with Richard and Liza?"

"I'll do it," Gabriella said.

"Jesus," Morgan said again. "This is totally ridiculous. Why don't we ask the whole fag contingent as well?"

"I don't see them anymore. You know that. Claudio is your friend too," Gabriella insisted.

"He's not our fucking chaperon."

"He has been," Gabriella had said, "with your assent as much as mine."

"He's been our sickness," Morgan said brutally.

It had been far easier to fix it with Liza. "The more the merrier," she said. "Richard likes him, I like him, you two love him, what's the problem?" So now Claudio was going with Liza and Richard on the charter plane that went directly to Acapulco. And three days later Gabriella and Morgan were to join them. In the meantime, for five days they were going to be alone.

Gabriella looked over now to Morgan as he read.

"Is it interesting?" she asked him.

"Very."

She looked outside again at the rained-upon wings of the Mexican plane and gripped her armrests while they landed.

The first thing that reached them as they got off the plane was the heat, solid, bright, disorienting. It changed the sensation of clothes on skin, so that the gabardine jacket in which Gabriella had frozen on her way to JFK now hung rough and heavy on her shoulders and held back the air and light. Around her the Mexicans wore colorful, light clothes. No border-crossing, untolerated immigrants, but possessors, next to whom Gabriella felt herself and Morgan intrusive, winter-woolly, clumsy. As she and Morgan shifted slowly through customs, she watched the Mexicans moving through the clean wide spaces of the airport. Beyond them, through the high airport windows, she saw a patch of heat-vibrating tarmac, bougainvillaea, palm. She felt prematurely tired.

The crowd from the plane moved slowly under posters advertising penalties for drug traffic, through customs, and toward large buses waiting in the heat outside. Inside the airport, around the souvenir shops Gabriella saw the homeward-bound Americans, tanned, camera-hung, in polyester and serapes. Gabriella hoped that under all the presented Mexico she would be able to get a sense of the place, that there might be for them a little bit of Mexico left.

At the Avis stand they hired a car from a familiar car-rental lady, only discernibly local, with more facial hair and a squatter build than her American counterpart, but the manner similarly brisk and friendly. They were not yet, except for the heat, in Mexico.

Inside the tiny car Morgan and Gabriella let down all the windows, took off their jackets and consulted the street maps. The place names evoked nothing to her: Chapultepec, Alameda, it was all to come. Morgan started the car and pulled past the buses filling with tourists, the bus bellies sagging with the weight of all that anticipated consumption, menopausal and marital eagerness, large hopes and empty spaces where the sights and sounds of the coming vacation were to lodge.

They drove in their car toward a modern city, strangely dust-covered, it seemed to Gabriella, dramatically noisy. Gabriella looked at the passing streets and at the Mexicans, occasionally at Morgan's face as he concentrated on the driving. She felt her dread again, reading his tenseness, and her own fatigue. She would leave him in his mood; they would become more cheerful at the hotel.

For an hour they drove through heavy traffic and constant noise, looking for streets where good hotels might be. There didn't seem to be any good hotels, only American hotels with Mexican names and Mexican reception, sullen hospitality and no rooms. They tried the hotels on the main strip, tangling in the flow of traffic, pulling out, waiting to turn into a line of angry small cars, shouted and whistled at. They tried the more elegant back streets, where the hotels differed from those of the main drag only in size and muster of enthusiasm at the front desk. Outside in the car Morgan, his shirt wet under his arms and over his back where the car seat stuck, nursed his headache over the plastic wheel. Gabriella stood in the heat next to the car and waited. "What shall we do?" she said. "They're all the same. Shall we give up and go to the Hilton?"

"If you can get us there," Morgan said.

Forty minutes later, while Morgan parked the car, Gabriella

looked at the shops of the Hilton lobby which told her she was in Mexico City. In front of posters of Aztec headgear were plumes of birds, silver bracelets and Claudio's cheap pottery. Only here in the hotel it would not even be cheap. A bulletin board announced daytrips to Taxco and Cuernavaca, weekends in Acapulco, mornings among the pyramids.

Morgan came back with the bags. A small hurried bellhop took these and rode with them in the elevator to the twenty-ninth floor. Morgan looked terrible. Gabriella thought they must all look terrible to the Mexicans, these yards and yards of Yankees, sleeping on the linen, dirtying the ashtrays, fouling the bathrooms; and then, after the sweaty arrivals and the huge expenditures, the pathetic, inconsequential departures.

On the twenty-ninth floor they walked down a long corridor between dozens of rooms full of people wanting to see Mexico City. The bellhop unlocked the door, put their bags on the luggage rack and drew the curtains from a large window. There, below them, the city sat, panoramic, lit for night. It could have been New York.

"Beautiful," Gabriella said.

Morgan paid the Mexican and shut himself in the bathroom.

Gabriella took off her shoes and lay down on the bed with a guidebook. As she read she listened to the sounds of Morgan's splashing. Not much energy coming from that quarter. She closed her eyes and breathed deeply. She would not waste the night, she would not let Morgan waste it for her.

"Are you exhausted, my darling?" she said around the bathroom door.

Morgan faced her, stretched out in his blue soapy water, the plastic sachet ripped open and discarded by the side of the tub. Morgan among his bubbles was grim and dark. "Totally," he said.

"We'll go out somewhere near then," Gabriella said. She picked up the pile of sweat-damp clothes, the heavy shoes.

"I'm not driving again on these streets."

"We'll find somewhere to walk to," Gabriella said. "I'm sorry about the driving."

"This place is ridiculously expensive."

"And not very pretty. But we tried. I'm sure there must be somewhere beautiful from the twenties, some famous place."

"Oh, I'm sure, and we'll hear all about it from Mickey or Preston or Claudio when we get back."

"You are tired," Gabriella said, herself tired again. "Have a quick nap while I take my bath. I won't be long."

Morgan sloshed out of the water, wrapped himself in two towels and lay under the air conditioning along the bed. Gabriella covered him with the hotel bedspread and took the sodden towels. She knew they were both watching her fake the wifely solicitude. She knew Morgan was pushing her humoring, holding on to the small humiliations.

Gabriella got into her bath and tried to rid herself of the resentment that was creeping already into this new cohabitation. The place was not Mexico yet; it was thuddingly still home.

Morgan lay on the other side of the bathroom wall and tried to close his eyes against the light overhead. He didn't much want to go out, but he was hungry. He wondered whether he could get Gabriella to have sex with him after dinner and judged it unlikely. He almost never now thought of those years when they made love twice daily, more often, whatever the circumstances. Those weren't years, though, they were months; after that, the love-making had been gentler. After the first ferocious passions, the civilized loving, sweet, regular, orderly like hymn singing on Sunday mornings. He and Gabriella had not made love for several weeks now, as though saving everything for this trip, a dangerous overloading. There was too much riding on it now. Let it ride, Morgan thought, even for a fall.

Morgan did not sleep under his closed eyes; he measured the

speed and descent of this new despair. He could hope that it would leave in the morning, fade in the glare of the sun or die like a microbe exposed to this alien culture. He wanted Gabriella back, he thought, but not Gabriella as she had become lately with all her eagerness to be away from him and the life he offered her. He had imagined his fight for her finished now, the years of making a setting that suited her; he'd given her space to dance in and a shape to lean against. He had imagined them on a safe plane, the dangers past. They were used to each other, had worked for so long to make each other familiar, cherished territory. Homelands.

Then why had she flown from this home to surround herself with the creatures of her present life? Morgan's ego raged inside him; *he* should have been enough. Gabriella said he lacked gaiety; she meant that other thing, the floating on surfaces, the glide of unseriousness which in her friends was now beginning to sicken him. Even Claudio, after that scene in the restaurant, had begun to sicken him. Morgan didn't float. Life was more vertical than that. Nor did he think that Gabriella would herself be able to float for long. She would get tired of surfaces, sink with the weight of her own complex needs to the bottom, where he and they necessarily resided. Under was her element, and she would tire of the ducks on the water.

But she was so defended against him, and he didn't think he had enough will and desire for both of them to win her back. He was tired of the life with Gabriella that was always now a pulling of equal wills, like opposed to like. For a long time now they had ceased to travel side by side and had made, instead of progress, the undignified halt and shuffle of confrontation.

Gabriella came out of the bath wrapped in a towel and eyed him warily. Morgan's heart ached for that wariness, but he said nothing.

"Are you still tired?" she said. He heard the other question, "How difficult are you going to be tonight?"

Morgan sat up and took her hand, drawing her toward him. He read her nervousness, and she read his reading and looked away. He let go of her hand and sat back. Wearily, she leaned toward him and stroked—as you stroke a difficult child—the arm that lay like a battle-severed limb on the bed before them.

"Quite," he said.

"Shall we stay in?" Gabriella bluffed. Morgan caught her eye, and she said, rising, "No, let's go out."

"Yes, all right. You get dressed. I'll follow." Morgan made each sound heavy so that his voice would blame her. But it was also a challenge and a game: she would have her evening, he would have his sabotage. Or else he would join her in apparent good spirit and hope that her sense of fair play would carry later when he wanted to make love. And inside them both these calculations registered and the weight of them, even here, high up above a new city, at the start of this new start. Yet they played this game for all the world as though it gave either of them pleasure.

They got out on the streets and began to walk in their unfamiliar, last-summer's clothes toward the square where the mariachi bands gathered, the Plaza Garibaldi. The afternoon's dust had disappeared and the night was clear, the air cooler but still warm. Their movements changed; they relaxed; their bodies felt the walk and the air; they spoke and were companions again. They could do this, both in relief to be away from the hotel room questions and in simple, friendly pleasure that Gabriella was once again with Morgan, whose intelligence she knew and loved. They were away from the sexual pressure; they could be friends; they could and would enjoy their evening.

They walked along the Paseo de la Reforma, looking in the windows and into the side streets, idly chatting. There were three kinds of movements out on the streets. The tourists wandered for pleasure, took their time, retraced their steps, stopped and consulted maps. The Mexican men, distinct from the colorfully clothed and bangled tourists walked sullenly in dark suits; and the Mexican women, hurried one by one to get home off the streets, which belonged to the tourists and the men. On nearly every corner an Indian woman sat holding a baby in wildly colored rags and trinkets, lifting it high toward the passers-by, displaying its scabs and bruises and begging, *"Por favor, por amor de Dios,"* with a face melting sideways in near-parody of grief. And yet the tourists passed them, and the Mexicans. And each cry, each theatrical raising of battered child by teen-age mother found its response in the near-theatrical indifference of the implored, making it all comic, except for the bruises of the babies, which seemed quite real enough.

Gabriella and Morgan stopped to ask the way once or twice and then arrived at a large square seething with tourists and garishly costumed Mexicans. Over this mass floated the noise of a hundred small brass bands, each playing loudly and passionately in utter indifference to the competing noises of the square. Groups of players and their audiences stood with their backs to each other. Musicians who had not yet drawn their hearers walked in and out of the streams of tourists offering to play, or beginning to play, in passionate haste, two or three bars of hideously cheerful song while the chosen couple lowered their eyes to indicate no contract was made and no payment would be given, or wildly looked about for a means of escape. All over the square the brass noises started up ten, twenty times a minute, and the portly Mexicans in white clothes and mustaches, striped blankets, huge straw hats, waylaid the tourists and dropped ardently into song, attacked them with the mindless cheerfulness of the mariachi music and begged to be heard, to be paid. Just stop, *"Por favor, señores,"* and listen to this song, full of the spontaneous love of life, *"Por amor de Dios."*

Like the others, Gabriella and Morgan had to harden their

faces against the strolling musicians to get through the throng to the other side of the square. At the edge of the plaza two young mariachi players lay on the ground cold drunk, dangerously near the curb where the cars passed fast enough for injury.

"Why doesn't someone move them?" Gabriella said. She looked about her into the surrounding faces, and these stared back, fellow tourists in irony, Mexicans in contempt.

"They'll be all right," an elderly American said to her, "can't hurt a drunk."

They stepped past the bodies and crossed the street to where the restaurants were, choosing a large rose-colored cantina whose plaster walls were hung with pots and painted birds and signs offering music and food at cheap prices.

Inside, it was dark and suddenly silent after the noise of the square. Against a long bar dozens of tired mariachi players drank beer, their instruments hanging over their serapes, their embroidered sombreros on their backs. Potbellied and vacant-eyed, they drank in earnest and addressed no one. In the large back room were tables of tourists eating from large plates of brightly colored tacos, enchiladas, the cheerful Mexican food that was served to them by funereally mournful waiters.

"Maybe upstairs," Morgan said.

They passed through to the stairway, neither stopped by the waiters nor beckoned ahead, and came upon a small upstairs room where groups of mariachi players sat silent over their drinks. As Gabriella and Morgan passed, one or two of the players rose, grinning, to offer music, but then sat down again, almost gratefully, as Morgan politely refused.

A waiter approached them, fierce, handsome. *"Señores?"*

"Can we eat up here?" Morgan asked. He tried to say that it was too noisy downstairs.

"Cómo?" the waiter demanded.

"Es posible comer aquí?" Morgan tried again.

"Qué quieren ustedes comer?" the waiter challenged them.

"My Spanish isn't up to this, Gabriella. Can you say, 'May we see the menu' or 'What do you suggest'; but say it politely, for Christ's sake."

The waiter was not going to help them. If they were not going to sit downstairs with the other tourists, they would not be treated like them. Apparently they were not even to be given menus.

Gabriella smiled at the waiter, to no avail, and asked for *"la specialidad de la casa."*

The waiter hardly responded, but winced slightly.

"Obviously that doesn't mean much," Morgan said, and then, defeated, said, *"Tacos, por favor, enchiladas, mixtas."* *"Por favor,"* he said again as the waiter nodded, in contempt for the gringos who never ate anything but tacos.

"Y vino rosso," Morgan added as the waiter turned.

"I think that's Italian," Gabriella said.

"Well, if he doesn't understand *vino,* he's an imbecile," Morgan said. "Christ, tacos. We'll get a wordbook tomorrow."

"It's okay," Gabriella said. "Much better to be up here than downstairs. Listen to that strange music."

Protected by the restaurant, the sounds that came from the square made a solid bumbling noise, punctuated by bursts of brass at the outer edges and counterbalanced by the low solemn Spanish of the men upstairs. Morgan looked around him at the Mexicans and wondered whether, if Claudio had been with them, they would have been served at all, thought that if Claudio and Gabriella had even begun that scene of flirting here, there would have been serious trouble; they might well have been killed.

"They seem like Italians, but they're not the least like them," Gabriella said, as though reading Morgan's thoughts.

"How like Italians?" Morgan asked her.

"On the square," Gabriella said, still listening to the music, "the bright clothes, the flowers, the singing, the big plaza. Except inside all the *joie de vivre* there's something angry, sinister even."

"That's what people say about Mexico," Morgan said, "a death culture, the Indians and their blood sacrifices mixed with all the Moorish-Christianity of the Spanish. Under all the sun and fiesta, the seventeenth century lurks. But maybe it's only us, jet lag and language barriers."

"Shall we have a good time?" Gabriella asked Morgan suddenly. She took his hand. "Shall we bury the Jacobeans under the flowers?" She smiled.

"Let's have a good time," Morgan said. He held her hand on the white tablecloth and for a moment felt her with him.

"Enchiladas," the waiter said. He held out two plates of garishly colored food and set them down heavily. Next to these he put the glasses and a carafe of dark wine, forks, knives, methodically, fiercely.

They ate the thick, pasty food which seemed only to feed their fatigue. Nor did the wine revive them. Afterward they sat heavily and drank tequilas. The liquor jangled them, lifted their spirits for a moment, then set them down lower than they'd been before.

"I can see where the death wish comes from," Gabriella said, "if this is the national diet."

"We'll find the good places tomorrow," Morgan said. "This'll do for tonight."

"I wasn't complaining," Gabriella said.

"You were a bit," Morgan said, "my brave traveler."

Gabriella heard Morgan's irritation under the old joke and felt the contest again. Avoiding it, they finished their meal in silence.

"Shall we go?" Gabriella said.

Morgan asked for the check, too tired now to try his Spanish. Having dined like a tourist, he felt entitled to speak like one.

They paid—rather a lot, it seemed to Morgan—and left, crossing the square again, which was still jammed, still joylessly singing. They walked home in silence, neither touching nor looking about them, each one anxious inside his thoughts of the other. In the hotel elevator Morgan leaned against the back wall under the bright lights and pulled Gabriella toward him.

"Don't," she said. "I can't breathe for all that food."

"You didn't have to eat it," Morgan said.

Gabriella pulled away a little, "I think the word 'tacky' must come from *tacos.*"

Morgan watched Gabriella's maneuver, putting the joke between them to soften the fact that she wanted to be left alone. But Morgan did not want to be left alone. Alone was where she had no right to leave him. He'd been alone with her all day; alone, now, he wanted her company. Again, he tried to hold her.

"I feel sick, Morgan," she said to him.

"You'll be all right."

Gabriella hated this. She wanted to be asleep; relied on the wine to carry her out of consciousness. If there was to be a struggle, the struggle would wake her, not let her sleep. And she loathed it that Morgan insisted on his rights, having been nice, obliging her to be nice. It was a commercial game: she refused to play courtesan.

She led the way out of the elevator and walked ahead of him toward their room. In a drunken saunter, jangling the key, Morgan exaggerated his slow command of the struggle. At the door he took a long time with the lock, genuinely because the drink had made him clumsy, and in cruel sport because she was waiting and all her pride had been in that fast walk up the corridor without him.

He opened the door for her and she angrily passed in front of him, through to the bathroom, then out of the bathroom, passed him again and sat on the twin bed that was hers. She took off her clothes in the dark corner near the window and got quickly into bed while Morgan watched her, slow from his drink but beginning to be angry.

"Don't go to sleep," he said. Morgan meant it as a plea; Gabriella heard it as an order.

"I must," she said.

"Why must you?"

"Don't be a sadist," Gabriella said. "I'm fucking tired."

"You are always fucking tired."

"Fuck off, Morgan, don't ruin everything."

"You've ruined everything."

"Just let it pass."

"We let everything pass; you let our life pass down the fucking drain: your tiredness, your flu, your nights out. I'm here now; I'm asking."

Gabriella heard the tender message inside Morgan's attack, and turned her back on it.

"You're not asking very nicely," she lied.

"For Christ's sake, Gabriella." Morgan got up angrily, defeated, and got undressed.

Gabriella had cheated, she knew, but Morgan would not let her breathe. When Morgan came out of the bathroom, Gabriella, sleepless, feigned sleep and felt her tension slip the moment Morgan turned off his light and with a rhetorical heave inside the other bed made a sign of his capitulation to her will.

They held like that for whole minutes, Gabriella listening to Morgan's movement inside his bed, and his hurt, angry breathing, and he listening for signs of her relenting. She knew that if she turned to find a comfortable position, relaxed toward sleep, Morgan would hear that as a sign of guilt or apology, a relaxing toward him. Frozen in one position, Gabriella's anger swelled against this constraint; and he, sighing and turning, seethed in anger that she had removed speech from them and set up this humiliatingly wordless and crystal-clear communication of their anguish.

While they lay there, suspended in hatred and need, fighting for sleep, there came from the room next door wild, cheerful noises, the shrieking of children at play. A very late hour for children, it seemed to Gabriella, perhaps a delayed arrival of tourists. Between this and Morgan, she was doomed to a sleepless night. There would be an exhausted, dragged-through day and another fight for sleep tomorrow. The holiday was heading smoothly for disaster. The children next door shrieked again, then began their regular cries and ceased being children. Oooh, ooh, aaah, aah, ooh, eeeh, excessively, comically.

"Oh God," Morgan said. You could tell from his voice he was more excited than alarmed.

"It's quite something," Gabriella said. There was genuine admiration.

"Oh, oh, aaagh, aagh!"

"He's strangling her," Gabriella said, "or she's faking like hell."

Eeeeh, eeh, eeh, it was all her noise; the man had made his groans and stopped. Now they were both climbing down, soothing each other's feathers on the downward flight, arghing and cooing and growling low in the throat. The man made another loud groan and the woman replied.

"Is she a hooker?" Gabriella asked. "I didn't know they made so much noise. God, these walls are thin; tacky hotel, isn't it?"

"Maybe she's what they call a screamer," Morgan said. It was odd the way Gabriella and he had become the tourist companions again; though something made him sick that they were mocking the sex next door. However fake it had been, he was excited by it. Yet they were speaking again, he and Gabriella, using language.

"Gabriella?"

"What?"

"Are you asleep?"

"Not after that."

"Can I come into your bed?"

Gabriella held still.

"Let me."

"Oh, all right."

"Don't say it like that." Morgan was hurt and he had little pride left. He got into bed with his wife and touched her.

"I'm terribly tired, Morgan."

Morgan began to retrace his irritation; he could feel the steps toward his anger and his climb upward. He held it down, dying. "It doesn't matter," he said, dead-voiced.

Gabriella heard Morgan's despair and felt how her own constraint held her inside the false coldness; she felt all the day's angers swirling about her, blocking everything; and she knew in her heart it was hopeless. Morgan's skin next to hers forced her to feel it. If he had let her sleep, she could have gone on not knowing, thinking instead that they were on holiday, living happily on the vagueness that after Mexico it would be all right. She loathed the self-deceit which Morgan's body, taut, needful, next to hers made her see. She would have bad sex with him now, the outer forms and movements only, and again she hated herself and Morgan that he made her take him in this way.

The couple next door started again, at length, ecstatically, with the woman making her comic, grateful noises and the man silently humping the music into her.

Gabriella felt the floor of her despair and just gave up, capitulated to all the pain of her loving Morgan and not wanting him, to all the pain of their missed connection, of his needing her and her wanting to fly from him, of all the months when she'd thought she'd been happy and been happy only in her escape from him, and to all the pain of her knowing finally that she was damaging herself by all that running, able in the end to escape nothing at all; to all that hopelessness she now capitulated. And toward this Morgan now reached, forced himself through her despair, touched Gabriella's awful sadness, and there finally connected.

THE FOLLOWING DAY THEY HAD lunch on the terrace of a large hotel in the suburb where Diego Rivera's house was. In the sun Morgan read to Gabriella from his book on Aztec life.

They had spent the morning wandering with bands of small black-haired, blue-smocked schoolchildren among exhibits of tribes that had lived in the Valley of Mexico. They had admired the images of the Aztec gods of death and war, which came to the Mexicans in the forms of dogs and vultures, hummingbirds, snakes and falcons. These were depicted on pots, flutes, bracelets, in mosaic and jade, confections of feather and gold. The objects were intricate, exquisite, and dedicated to the most horrible practices.

"That huge Aztec calendar this morning," Morgan said, "was for the worship of the gods, it says here, 'each month, each solstice, each change of sun demanding its ritual sacrifice. The Aztec religion was one involving continual homage to the gods by the immolation of thousands of human captives yearly.' Thousands," Morgan repeated. "Think what that means."

"They set their watches by it, then," Gabriella said, "measured time by the sacrifice of other people."

"Yes," Morgan said, "but," he quoted, " 'The victims themselves considered it a glorious death to be seized by the priests and stretched on their backs over a stone on the temple summit, an incision made in the chest with a flint knife, the heart ripped out and placed in the *cuauhxicalli'* ''—here Morgan made theatrical choking noises, taking a long time with the imagined pronunciation—'' 'or "eagle vase" to be burned for the consumption of the gods.' ''

"What are *we* going to eat?" Gabriella said, looking at the menu, trying to interrupt him.

"Listen," Morgan went on. '' 'Quickly the head was cut from the corpse, and the body flayed. Priests and those doing penance garbed themselves in the victim's skin, which was worn for twenty days, at the end of which the god impersonator "stank like a dead dog." ' ''

Gabriella sighed and crossed her legs. "Revolting," she said.

'' 'Every priest had been to a seminary at which he was instructed in the complicated ritual which he was expected to carry out daily. Their long unkempt hair' ''—Morgan's voice slowed down again for Gabriella to follow—'' 'clotted with blood, their ears and members shredded' ''—"shredded," Morgan repeated—'' 'from self-mutilations effected with agave thorns and sting-ray spines, smelling of death and putrefaction, they must have been awesome spokesmen for the Aztec gods.' ''

"It's revolting," Gabriella said again. "Do you have to read this now?"

"Listen," Morgan said. '' 'The most famous among the Aztec sacrifices was that of a young captive annually chosen to impersonate the god *Tezcatlipoca*. For one year he lived a life of honor, worshipped literally as the embodiment of the deity; towards the end he was given four beautiful maidens as his mistresses. Finally he left them sadly, mounted the steps of the temple, smashing one by one the clay flutes' ''—Morgan's voice dipped poetically—'' 'on which he had played in his brief moment of glory, then' ''—Morgan waited—'' 'he was flung on his back so that the flint dagger might be plunged into his breast.' ''

"It really excites you, all this atrocity, doesn't it?" Gabriella said.

" 'The most horrible of Aztec practices,' " Morgan continued in a triumphant, low voice, " 'was the mass sacrifice of small children on mountain tops to bring rain at the end of a dry season, in propitiation of *Tlaloc*. It was said,' " Morgan ended, snapping the book shut, " 'that the more they cried, the more the rain god was pleased.' "

"It's horrible," Gabriella said.

"That is what is under all the gold and jade and plumage, homage to the carnivorous gods, not to life but to the glorious death that will placate the monsters that rule the universe."

"I don't see why all the bloodiness excites you so much," Gabriella said. "It was a horrible culture."

"You excite me," Morgan said, smiling.

"I'm not sure I see the connection."

"Anyway, some of this is quite beautiful," Morgan said. "There are Aztec battle songs. Listen to just this one and then no more." Morgan found his place and chanted in a full strong voice, oblivious to the people at tables around him:

The battlefield is the place:

> *Where one toasts the divine liquor of war,*
> *Where are stained red the divine eagles,*
> *Where the tigers howl,*
> *Where all kinds of precious stones rain*
> *from ornaments*
> *Where wave headdresses rich with fine*
> *plumes*
> *Where princes are smashed to bits.*

Morgan fell silent, moved by his reading.

"Beautiful," Gabriella admitted, "but vicious."

Back and forth over the lawns, waiters in pale-rose jackets and black shoes carried trays of glasses for a reception that was to take place in the hotel grounds. Three heavy women in tight black dresses brought cake boxes to a distant table. The puffy, lacquered hair and the severe black/white/red make-up seemed perilous in the sun. The nylon-covered legs would be sticky and confined in the heat, and their spiked shoes moved them awkwardly across the soft ground.

Half in shade, half in sun, Gabriella closed her eyes and drank peacefully while the waiters made the pleasing noises of cutlery and china in the open air. Above her, under a stucco arch, hung baskets of geraniums, camellias, bougainvillaea. A long, green lizard held alert and suspended on the arch, contemplating the dangerous climb down. Gabriella watched the little pulse in his throat beating fiercely and the black, darting eyes, as he held his head out and listened to the sounds around him.

"It's lovely here," she said to Morgan, "lovely to be in the sun."

Morgan was now also relaxing in the sun, letting the heat warm through his clothes. He was good in the open air. His pale skin tanned easily without first going red—unlike his New England family, the bright-pink or peeling towheaded cousins Gabriella had seen in summer photos from the Cape. Morgan's coloring changed as smoothly as the lizard's; he was beginning to look at home.

As the gardens began to fill with expensively dressed Mexican women in pale silks and noisy bracelets, Gabriella caught, among the many scents of the garden restaurant, their scent, of colognes and lipsticks. They moved excitedly, chattering, bearing gifts for the bride, greeting one another with bird cries, swoops of pleasure. Behind them darkly dressed husbands followed, new shoes pinching, uneasy in the narrow-waisted suits; they hung behind in groups and seemed to look at nothing.

"This could be happening on Long Island," Gabriella said, "except for the men. What a clump of malcontents."

"It's a macho culture," Morgan said. "The sexes don't mix very much unless they have to."

"They don't seem happy in their clothes, either," Gabriella said. "Why don't they wear white?"

"Or would you prefer ponchos? This is the tango-singer look, just as authentic as serapes, Latin, brooding," Morgan said admiringly.

"And why should the men be so brooding when the wives are so cheerful?" Gabriella asked.

"Latin culture," Morgan said. "The men still have it, though the women are a little Americanized, I admit." He indicated a florid blonde in chiffon at the moment embracing a cousinry of brunettes.

"But the men are still linked to the authentic Aztec past?" Gabriella mocked.

"Something like that," Morgan said.

"Kate might like it here," Gabriella said. "She always said being single in New York was like being the last animal invited on the ark. She said you only had to be suddenly single to watch the world divide into twos. Not many twos here."

"It's not macho," Morgan said. Gabriella looked at him across the table. He was pleased by the word, you could see that, and he despised the women in chiffon.

"You'd prefer the women squatting in the dirt and breast-feeding, wouldn't you?" Gabriella said. "And the men off in groups hacking each other to bits."

"I'm only saying this isn't the only way, or else they haven't entirely successfully got from one culture into another."

Gabriella looked again at Morgan, changing color under the sun, becoming Mexican before her eyes. "You don't believe any of it," she said. "You'd be terrified with a heap of dominated women on your hands, imagine all that responsibility, like a lost boy scout leader with a pack of crying children."

"Real Mexican women look after themselves far better than

that, Gabriella; anyway, I'm not talking about survival, but acceptance of a male culture. And perhaps it is true that someone always has to lead; it might as well be the man."

"The tango dancer," Gabriella said. "Someone *doesn't* always have to lead."

"You think frequent access to that," Morgan said, indicating the noisy flowery-dressed women, "would cheer the Mexican male? You think these dark looks come from exclusion from tea parties?"

"Maybe at some stage when the tea parties were his mother's and the future Aztec was a little boy banished from the room."

"That's sentimental crap," Morgan said. "It's in the blood. And the women, not these poor fucked-up half-Westernized wives, but the real ones, get a great deal from it, perpetuate it not out of ignorance but because it works."

"Works? You mean hundred percent alienation as opposed to simple cultural fragmentation?"

"They know what's good for them," Morgan said. He smiled.

Gabriella did not want to ask if he was joking; she had to suppose he was.

"It's all that blood from this morning; it's got you going. I suppose you want now to see a bullfight."

"No, lovely," Morgan said, smiling again, "now I want to go to bed. With you."

"Here?"

"We could get a room."

"You're awfully extravagant all of a sudden."

"You'd be worth it." Morgan smiled.

"No," Gabriella said. "Rivera's house first, and for the blood-lusting Morgan, the death scene of Trotsky."

"Suit yourself," Morgan said agreeably. "Trotsky's house, Rivera's house it shall be."

He was awfully happy, Morgan, all of a sudden.

On the lawn in front of them the bride and bridegroom arranged themselves to be photographed. After the series of them and family, the ceremonial children, was the series of them alone. The bridegroom smiled an embarrassed smile of a caught and dutiful male; the bride smiled neither the smile of triumph nor the traditional smile of modesty, but another smile, distinctly nervous. Perhaps it was nervousness of the day, not of the future, but Gabriella commented on it now to Morgan and said she guessed it came from the sudden proximity, beyond all previous preparation.

Late in the afternoon Morgan and Gabriella drove in the rented car out of Coyoacán on the main road back to Mexico City. Again the roads filled with dust and noise as the work population emptied the town and headed home. In the heavy rush-hour pollution the skies had darkened oddly and the air become bitter.

They had been talking about Rivera and Frida Kahlo and the *santos* collection in the little museum.

"Did you have a good day?" Morgan asked Gabriella.

"Wonderful," Gabriella said. "Is it too late to see the frescoes?"

"We have tomorrow."

"Or we could go now," Gabriella insisted. "It's not dark till eight, once the pollution lifts."

"All right." Morgan put his foot on the accelerator and passed two farmers' trucks tipping dangerously left and right under their loads of melons, tomatoes, more bright heavy food.

In the center of the city the traffic moved steadily and thickly in the heat. Morgan halted at the red lights of the first intersection, waited for the green and drove off. Suddenly he pulled the car over to the right-hand side of the street. The face of a motorcycle-goggled Mexican stared at them through the open window; under the mustaches he spoke a fast, angry Spanish.

"What's the matter?" Gabriella asked. "What does he want?"

"Money," Morgan said.

"Money? Is he a bandit?"

"A cop," Morgan said.

"What's he want the money for?"

"For not taking us to jail."

"But what have we done?" Gabriella asked.

"Nothing."

The Mexican stood now patiently next to the car and watched Morgan explaining to his wife what had happened.

"He says we went through the red light."

"We didn't."

"No, we didn't. But there's a fine for it."

"What?" Gabriella demanded.

"Five hundred dollars."

"Five hundred dollars! Morgan, that's ridiculous."

"I said all that. He says we can come with him to the police station. What he means is that for five hundred dollars he won't put us through the ordeal of Mexican justice."

"But he can't just do that," Gabriella insisted, "invent a crime and then fix a huge price on it! Is he crazy?" Gabriella peered across Morgan's lap at the cop, nonchalant in the sun, and tried to glare at him through his goggles. *"Demasiado!"* she shouted at him.

The policeman looked in on them, unperturbed.

"We won't pay," Gabriella said to Morgan. "Tell him it's highway robbery."

"He's the highway patrol."

"Demasiado!" Gabriella shouted again. "Morgan, tell him even in New York you don't pay so much. Of course not. *E más que en América,"* Gabriella shouted at him. *"E muchisimo más, muchisimo demasiado."*

The Mexican shrugged his leather shoulders.

"Offer him fifty dollars," Gabriella suggested. "Here." She

reached into her bag and brought out her traveler's checks, waved a fifty at him.

"*No* tcheckes," the policeman said, "*solamente dinero, pesetas.*"

"He wants it in cash!" Gabriella said.

Morgan fumbled in his pockets. The day had left him with little change; he found about twenty dollars in Mexican money and spread it on his lap.

The Mexican smiled.

A great noise of horns and angry drivers started up behind them. They had caused a traffic jam. Morgan got out of the car and began to negotiate with the cop, holding his money out in front of him. Then suddenly the policeman turned from Morgan, or pretended not to see him, mounted his bike and drove off.

"Where's he going?" Gabriella asked. She was also out of the car, watching as the Mexican revved and drove through the streams of other cars. Several angry motorists swore at them as they too moved past. Otherwise they were left alone, Morgan's pesetas dangling from his hand.

"What was that all about?" Gabriella said. "He's not off for reinforcements, is he?"

"Ha, very interesting," Morgan said. "See, the deal must be to show them up in public. God, we're lucky, or else he's awfully stupid, that cop, right here on the main drag, probably new to it."

"You mean they're not allowed to do it?"

"Of course not," Morgan said, staring at Gabriella.

"Then why do they?"

"Because they can. We've just had a very lucky escape from the notorious Mexican police."

"But what kind of country has a system like that?" Gabriella asked.

"This country; let's get a drink."

They got back in the car, still shaky, and cruised toward the city center, where the Riveras were.

"You can't prey on your own citizens," Gabriella said. "No wonder Rivera wanted a revolution."

They parked the car near the Zócalo and found an ordinary workers' bar. There they stood at the brass-fitted marble counter and drank tequila.

Gabriella looked around her at the bar and noticed once again that there were no women. Not much *joie de vivre,* either; perhaps that was the drink: the tequilas made you drunk but not high. After three, Gabriella was almost mournful.

They left the bar and walked through the dark narrow streets toward the huge Baroque public ministry where the frescoes were. The Indians and their babies were not yet out on the street corners, but everywhere women hurried home, and men walked at a different pace toward a different kind of evening.

Gabriella and Morgan entered the courtyard of the ministry and found the monumental paintings ignored by the passers-by, faded by the sun, that dimly promised a better life. Gabriella did not mind the crude and cruel parodies of the capitalists and the bourgeoisie inside the great socialist vision. She admired Rivera's other feelings, and the great flat passionate art with which he expressed them. She liked the brotherhood, the great mix that Rivera wanted for the Mexicans, unburdened by castes or sacrificial religion. In her drunken sadness Gabriella felt a retrospective pull toward Claudio and her band, their crowd scenes; in their white clothes and mustaches, dark faces, the Rivera workers might have been gay New Yorkers.

She thought now of Morgan's excitement over the Aztecs and his nonsense about macho culture at lunch, the unloving sex of last night, and felt again a kind of revulsion toward him. Separating from him, she walked alone through the frescoed arches.

Perhaps in Rivera's heroic socialist vision there was none of what Gabriella in her drunkenness read into it: a hope for a new system of relationship between humans. Perhaps she confused these frescoes with the ones that Giotto had made in Padua, of which her band had once reminded her, with their kissing apostles and promise of new life. But in her sentimental confusion she felt an overwhelming sadness for the loss of her band in New York. Avoiding Morgan, Gabriella walked faster and faster around the pictures, letting the tequila take her into Rivera's belief in the possibility of change, his hatred of the old dead system of power, capitalist over peasant, American over Mexican, the weight of the past over the fragile life of the moment.

But Morgan followed her heavily, watching, growing excited by her drunken movements and his own desires of the afternoon, his memory of the previous night, and he leaned on her almost tangibly with the weight of his will and intention. He caught up with her and took her arm.

"Why do you keep moving? It's too hot, and the pictures are too good."

Gabriella stood still next to Morgan and looked at the banally innocent faces of Rivera's peasant women and children, remembering with loathing how they had come to make love last night, the brutal noises of the couple next door and how she had heard them first as the shrieks of children, how she and Morgan had reached each other through all that thickness of hatred and misery. She thought with loathing of Morgan's pride in the Mexican men, his mockery of the wives, and she thought with loathing of herself that here she was again pulled in two by things she did not understand, loving Morgan and feeling that love at war somewhere with something that was better in her, some higher instinct or need for a different love.

Morgan swayed next to her and tilted his head against hers.

"Shall we go back to the hotel?"

Gabriella moved away from him. "How is this the Mexican death instinct, Morgan? Where does this fit in?"

Morgan sighed; in the language under the language they used

he heard her refusal. Mood, perhaps his own drink-fuddled mis-timing. He tried to answer her question.

"More sacrifice," Morgan said, "this time the whole nation for Rivera's great revolution. But it's the same war god as the Aztecs fed their captives to. You admit they're heartless pictures."

"No," Gabriella said. "I don't admit that."

"Icy, flat, larger than life, all surface. That is Rivera's modern-ism, but it's his philosophy too: banal, shallow. It's a monumental art, it ignores the individual, flattens appearance; there is no perspective to indicate where the figures have come from in spatial terms, and therefore no sense of history for all the histori-cal figures in them. The art doesn't exist in time or space, it's as unreal as Rivera's great revolution."

"The revolution did happen," Gabriella insisted.

"But not in Mexico. Rivera's revolution is Mexican, not about the future, but about death. You know, if Cortés hadn't arrived when he did, there might have been no Aztec civilization left, given the blood cost of their religion, thousands, Gabriella, every year, over and over. And if Rivera's revolution had transpired—no future, just a lot of corpses for burial."

"But they're beautiful," Gabriella insisted.

"Yes, and brutal."

"They remind me of Claudio and the gay bars," Gabriella said simply. She wanted Morgan to see it, or tell her why it wasn't there.

But Morgan said, "Probably for the same reason."

"What do you mean?" Gabriella turned to him. "I don't mean just the mustaches and white shirts."

"I know," Morgan said, "but it's the same over-and-over-again quality of gay life that gets nowhere, has been nowhere, constant mobility, constant now, what you call the dance. It's just a fren-zied running in place. The flat appearance of life, but without roots and without future, and amounting to death."

"But gay life isn't about death," Gabriella insisted, "it's about joy."

"Is it really?" Morgan said. "It felt more like desperation to me."

It was getting dark now in the courtyard; they could barely see the pictures.

"Shall we go?" Morgan said again.

"Not yet." Gabriella leaned against one of the arches.

"Why do you always bring them up?" Morgan asked her. "Why do you need to?"

"I don't always."

"Always, when we're having a good time. It's as though you do it on purpose."

"Can't I think about them? What do you mean?" Gabriella heard her dishonesty. Morgan was truthful. In the middle of his happiness she had felt obliged to confront him with their past life. She knew he was trying to win her back, and she did not know why she was resisting.

"I'm with you now, here," Morgan said. "Forget that stupid life in New York, be with me."

Gabriella stood away from the arch and broke their contact.

"It's only the mustaches," she joked. "Don't be so threatened. I am with you. Where shall we go?"

CAREFULLY, THEY DID NOT GO
back to the hotel; they went
instead to a restaurant in the Zona Rosa, old Mexico, eighteenth-
century charm. In such prettiness Gabriella felt herself free again,
indulged in Claudioisms, noting the antiques, the pale pink lighting. She ignored her own day's dust and Morgan, who was watching her with an irony bordering on rage. She sipped the ice water,
counted Mexican bankers and French wives, and made believe
she could stay on that level.

She knew that they had come close to a point of confrontation,
and that it was her own cowardice that had driven them from it.
There was a moment when she might have said that the Riveras
had reference to them as much as to gay life, their power struggle
and the weight of Morgan's hand and values on her. She had been
near enough to say that something in him subjected her and that
she too wanted to rise up against him, but she had retreated into
the image of herself as weak and had scuttled away again from
direct speech with her jokes and evasions.

But as much as Gabriella feigned her ease and pleasure in the
restaurant, Morgan displayed his discomfort and impatience. In
the end, and familiarly, he forced her into his, not her, present.

"What now," she said finally. "Can't we have a pleasant evening?"

"On your terms, always," Morgan said. He shifted. A waft of

Morgan's day sweat hit her across the bowl of gardenias and held. She sighed; he was going to win again, and again. He would always, however much he conceded to her, manage to win.

"What is it, Morgan?" she said in challenge. "For God's sake."

"We should have gone back to the hotel. At least to change. I feel filthy."

"It's all right, we'll be there soon," Gabriella said; she picked up the menu. Fatigue again.

"Always on your terms," Morgan repeated.

"There are always two of us."

"But why can't you ever just say yes? Why is it so important to you?"

"Oh Morgan, please, let it pass. Enjoy this. Don't always hold on."

"You make me want to smash things," Morgan said suddenly.

Gabriella looked at the expensive glasses and china before them. "Smash?" she asked.

"Smash the thing in you that always says no."

"You're so violent."

"Gabriella, you know what I'm talking about, you are pretending. I can't do it anymore."

"Do what?"

"Play these games. I think I've really had it now."

The waiter came for their order.

"I'm not eating," Morgan said.

"Morgan, please don't make a scene, for my sake."

The waiter retreated.

"A scene! I'm dying."

"Morgan, you're not dying, for Christ's sake."

"Something in me is dying," Morgan said seriously. "You are killing it."

"What is all this talk of smashing and killing? It must be the Riveras."

The attempted joke died before them, a genuine corpse.

"I'm going," Morgan said. "You can find your own way back, I'm sure; your own way is what you know best, after all."

Morgan rose and emptied his pocket onto the table.

"Morgan," Gabriella said, "please don't go. Talk to me, let us talk."

"We don't talk," Morgan said, "we tell lies."

Morgan hovered over the table while the waiter watched anxiously from the door of the kitchen.

It seemed to both of them now hopeless. In the hopelessness, Morgan foundered and then sat down. A word crossed Gabriella's mind then and made her ashamed. Capitulation. She had won. Capitulation. She had lost.

"Have something to eat, at least," she said to Morgan. She waved to the waiter.

"All right," Morgan said. "You order it."

I N THE DARK OF THE HOTEL room Gabriella heard two sounds simultaneously, one over the other: a long, complex noise of smashing glass, and a series of repetitions, of Morgan calling her name from his single bed to hers.

She came slowly awake and heard an odd quality in Morgan's voice, a kind of childish guiltiness about waking her; and then the other sound grew worse and mixed itself with a peculiar groaning, as of a ship swaying in a rough sea with its ropes and wood creaking. Then Gabriella was wide awake.

"Gabriella?"

"Yes."

"Listen."

She listened again; things were sliding about in the room now, falling and making noise. The room, in fact, was moving.

"What is happening?"

The room swayed gently back and forth and shuddered, and then not so gently began to swing so that the city outside tilted inside the panoramic window frame. Gabriella remembered that they were on the twenty-ninth floor.

"I think, sweetie, it's an earthquake," Morgan said, again in the child's voice.

A terrific crashing sounded outside on the streets below. A huge bomb burst of green illuminated the right-hand corner of the panoramic view, followed by another great flash and explosion; all over the city, glass fell and shattered and made a horrifying sound.

Gabriella got out of her bed and knelt on the floor next to Morgan.

"Don't be afraid," she said, holding him. "It's all right."

There was no reason to think so. The rumbling and swaying grew worse; bits of ceiling came down around them falling on floor and bedding; a reproduction Picasso bullfight slipped off its hook and slammed onto the dresser. Mexican construction, Gabriella thought, own nakedness, undressed corpse, last words; was it better to be down out on the street hit by buildings or a thing falling from this height onto others, a flying object or a buried one? Better to be dressed perhaps, in either case.

The groaning and shuddering stopped; there was a noise of shouting and laughter from the corridor. Laughter again; perhaps it was not so serious. Gabriella got dressed quickly and turned to see Morgan, sleepily fussing with shoes and laces.

"For Christ's sake, Morgan, we have to move out of here."

They got out of the room and ran with other hotel guests into the corridor; at the stairs was a bottleneck of people in varying degrees of dress and panic. Gabriella turned and led Morgan to the elevator. There she remembered it was the one thing you didn't do in earthquakes, fires, bomb scares. The doors closed on them; the thing moved downward. On the sixteenth floor the elevator stopped, opened and admitted a civil-defense worker with helmet and flashlight.

"It's crazy to be in the elevator, isn't it?" Gabriella asked him.

"Crazy," he said, "but it's a long way down."

Plaster covered his helmet and shoulders; he stared mournfully at them.

"Is anyone hurt?" Gabriella asked him.

"Not here, not too bad."

"Outside?"

"Yes."

The elevator shuddered and swung and slowly descended to the lobby. A large fallen mirror lay under a dust sheet in the central hall. Gabriella and Morgan joined the other hotel guests as they wandered about, already bored. The locals wore only nightgowns and pajamas under coats; two Frenchwomen wore sheets; the American businessmen were fully dressed, ties knotted, shoes on, briefcases in hand.

"We left the passports and money," Gabriella said, looking at them.

"No one's going to go back up to raid rooms," Morgan said. He too was already used to the quake.

"Why not?" Gabriella said. "If the Mexican safety officials can take elevators, Mexican thieves can take wallets."

The building shuddered again, but it seemed better being in the crowd, and the marble walls of the lobby promised solidity. A cornice over the coffee shop trembled, came loose and fell, slowly, in muffled bits onto the carpet; somewhere to the left, glass was breaking again. It would be awful to die in a Hilton, Gabriella thought; she wondered vaguely what Claudio would say, whether he would be able to resist the joke.

One of the Frenchwomen in sheets had hysterics on a sofa in the lounge as the Mexican staff wheeled out a large metal coffee trolley; a few of the staff got into a party mood as they handed out paper cups.

"Why don't they open the bar?" Gabriella asked. "Drinks are what we need."

"Coffee is cheaper," Morgan said. "Anyway, it's after six."

"Six?" Gabriella.

Out in the street beyond the cracked glass doors, there was a gray light. Now Gabriella could hear the noises of ambulances and fire engines, remote, frequent; no one knew the extent of the damage. By six-thirty the general opinion was that the quake was over; sleepily, irritably, the guests walked toward the stairs or waited for the elevators. The hotel staff smiled, reassured them and bid good morning. Normality was once again upon them; no one seemed even grateful as danger slid retrospectively into nuisance.

Once inside their room, this fact seemed odd to Gabriella. She watched Morgan yawning, making his way sleepily toward the disturbed bedding. Around them were signs of what had just nearly happened: the knocked-over lamps, the plaster, the clothing scattered in what had been an emergency exit. Only half an hour ago Gabriella had known clearly that they might die. Inside that knowledge she had held Morgan and comforted him. Did that mean that she *really* loved him? Was it proof or a sign? It had been a strong response; it wasn't courage, it was a powerful cutting through of her feelings for him. And now, once again, and so quickly, they receded.

She sat on the bed and began to undress, thinking only vaguely of what might be happening on the streets outside. As she sat there working her way back to her sleepiness the room began to shudder once more. "Oh God," she said, "Morgan, it's going to happen again."

There was a slow, low rumbling lasting several seconds, growing more and more violent. Then it suddenly stopped. In the meantime Gabriella had put on her shoes and stood up, ready again to bolt from the room. Morgan, however, had barely stirred.

"It's all right," Morgan said, "we can sleep. That was it."

"How do you know? It might begin again."

"We'll just have to risk it. Get some sleep."

"How can I sleep with the building shaking! Jesus, what a place."

"It's only aftershocks, Gabriella."

"How can you tell?"

"Be brave," Morgan said wearily. "You were so brave when it happened."

"Yes, but now that I know what it was, my legs are shaking. Oh Christ, again now."

"That's nothing."

"Can't you feel it?"

"You're imagining it."

"No."

"Aftershocks."

"How many will there be?" Gabriella sat upright on the bed, shaking and addressing Morgan's back.

"There could be hundreds," he said wearily.

"Christ, Morgan, I'll be a nervous wreck."

"Go to sleep now." Morgan said, turning over to look at her. He saw that she was serious.

"I can't." Gabriella was pale and convincingly tearful.

"Come to bed with me then, there's nothing happening. Come on, I'll hold you."

Gabriella was herself shaking, but the room, as Morgan said, seemed to be still. "No," she said weakly.

"Come on." Gabriella got up obediently and slid into bed with Morgan, letting herself be held and comforted.

"It takes a whole earthquake to get you into bed, doesn't it?" Morgan said.

"Hemingway says the ground has to move." Gabriella made her melancholy joke.

"After, usually," Morgan said; "it's all right now, it's over, let me hold you."

They woke late in the afternoon; the large mirror in the lobby remained in state under its dust sheet, otherwise all signs of the early-morning quake had been removed. The Mexican staff was no longer under obligation of cheerful effort and went about its business as before, with a bare tolerance for the activities of the guests. Many of these had departed, were departing as Gabriella and Morgan came downstairs. The new arrivals had not yet heard of the events of the morning, or were indifferent, and their ignorance mingled with the general amnesia. Out on the streets, however, the quake was still news. Television in the bars, news posters on the sidewalks gave the latest figures of the disaster. On the Richter scale the quake had registered a huge 8 points, its epicenter 200 miles from Mexico City. Where it had struck, schools and hospitals had collapsed and hundreds of people had died. The word *muertos* was on newsstands everywhere, and certain key pictures, again and again as Gabriella and Morgan walked the streets: wailing women, bleeding rescuers, aerial shots of the damage. They walked along the glass-covered sidewalks, noted the cracked buildings, listened to the sirens. It was true, as Morgan said: it might have been worse.

Gabriella accepted Morgan's view of it and retreated into her own fears. There were thirty aftershocks in the days that followed the quake, and continually revised body counts. All these Gabriella registered. When the aftershocks came, she became nervous and quiet. Sometimes her legs would begin to shake, or her hands, as the tremors started, and she would stand. Lying down made her more sensitive to the disturbances, like a builder's level, and she would need to move, confuse her sense of balance or keep alive until the vibrations passed. Morgan felt only a few of these, the larger ones, which had their own drama, drum roll, pause, and which to Gabriella threatened to be final events. As they subsided she felt drained and humiliated. There were smaller vibrations, as of a passing subway train, but even these made her dependent. She would stand up, move around, and then go docilely to Morgan to be held.

On the streets she let him carry their courage for them both, along with the passports, let him steer her past the official notices, the photos of the dead and the boasts of lucky escapes, distract her with visits to the pyramids and the park. Neither strong drink nor sex made any difference to her; she slept badly and was jumpy during the day. Occasionally she would rebel against the humiliation. "How can they live here?" she would demand of Morgan, "with that police force, and that religion and the quakes?" Morgan's own calm would answer her nervousness, and Gabriella would let him comfort her.

He was amused by her docility with him; her sudden acquiescence. To him and to the people they spoke with, the deaths and near-deaths were historical facts that retreated, with bureaucratic assistance, into the past. But Gabriella was stuck at the point of impact and could not adjust. She forgot that, at the very moment, she had actually been brave, and let her current cowardice remove her into a conviction of fragility. She was stuck, through a misreading of her weakness, in an eternal and precarious present.

She was not alone in this, however. In the days that followed the quake, in the papers she bought—forcing her Spanish through the accounts of the deaths, matching her reality (and not Morgan's) to the one she read there—small notices appeared regularly, placed by Mexican psychiatrists offering comfort for victims of hysteria, for those who couldn't sleep, for those who dwelt on death; experience and cures were promised, fees to be arranged.

When it was clear that Gabriella could stand it no more, they decided to leave, flying a little earlier than planned to Acapulco, hoping the sun would calm her nerves. Richard and Liza met them at the airport in a hired VW and complained that they had missed the quake by forty-eight hours. "Just our luck," Liza said; "from here it would have been fun."

"But it wasn't from the twenty-ninth floor," Gabriella said.

"She was very brave," Morgan told them. "She is having retrospective fears."

Richard drove them up along the coast of Acapulco, past the big hotels, describing the house they had rented and Claudio's first two nights, spent according to Richard dealing with assault by Mexican food. "He wouldn't have noticed a quake if he'd been there," Richard said, "he's been in the john since he arrived. He went for one of the waiters at what is clearly Acapulco's Greasy Spoon, had the local specialty while he waited—you can imagine

Claudio, eating casually in that civilized manner, waiting for the boy, loins and stomach burning . . . Needless to say, we were not with him. He didn't even get to make his pass but had to rush out and taxi home. Actually, it's not that funny, he's been horribly sick."

"He's lucky he didn't get to the point of proposition," Morgan said. "He might have been killed."

Gabriella imagined Claudio not noticing his food, or the sexual pride of the Mexican, and his impractical nature struck her and for the first time seemed exasperating. He *would* get food poisoning on his first night; he was too vulnerable.

She looked out of the window and forced her irritation to pass into the un-Mexicanness of the scene outside, the characterless tack and flash that could have been any international beach resort.

"Don't look," Liza said, "all this is dreadful. But our place is beautiful and far away from the center. Well, how are you two, then? You look wonderful. Earthquake apart, how has it been?"

"Marvelous," Morgan said.

F OR THE FIRST FEW DAYS IN
Acapulco, Gabriella remained
withdrawn and death-haunted. In part it was the constant drum-
roll of *muertos* that assaulted them on television and in the local
papers. It was partly the strange brutality of the place, the Mer-
cado, for instance, that Claudio and Liza found so colorful and
lively, and where Gabriella saw only the slaughter, the pathetic
stiff chickens and the idiot-mouthed fishes, the huge carcasses of
meat, with the forms of the living animals still horribly clear to
her. It was the churches, and the religious effigies sold everywhere,
the dead Christs with their wounds and victim's stare; the pictures of the *penitentes*, of the knee-scraping fanatics of Guada-
lupe, the self-flagellating Indians; the religious-art reproductions
that were always of the deposition, the corpse itself, unresur-
rected.

Not even the mindless hotel culture interfered with Gabriella's
obsession. She saw inside the tinkling, sunning crowds, its isolat-
ing touch, the future coronary, the living cancer, everywhere the
hand-picked ugly endings.

Once she told Morgan about these visions and he read to her
an Aztec poem, in his full, triumphant voice:

> *Even jade is shattered,*
> *Even gold is crushed*

193

Even quetzal plumes are torn . . .
One does not live forever on this earth:
We endure only for an instant.

Morgan liked that, it made him happy; for him it was only bravado. But for Gabriella it had become the only thing that was real. Like a figure from one of Rivera's frescoes, the hooded figure entered their crowd scenes, lounged by the pool, drank with them at the hotels; it also came to lie with Morgan and Gabriella between the sheets.

Her dependence on Morgan now became sexual. In bed Gabriella demonstrated her existence to herself and attempted to catch up with the time that was slipping. It seemed to Gabriella that the earthquake had shaken her loose from her previous opposition to Morgan. It wasn't in fear of their own deaths any longer, but in a kind of general despair that she saw the folly of their ancient struggle: the proposal and counterproposal, desire and its refusal, the system of checks that had seemed for so long to each of them to have been necessary to dignified survival. Only in a measureless time scheme could their one-step back-step make any sense. As death became real to Gabriella, time became real, and the stasis-loving maneuvers of their marriage came to seem insane to her.

She began to resent other people's waste of time, Claudio's particularly. His languor offended her now, and his characteristic andante. She measured her own time by a constant, ferocious love-making, born of despair and remorse, matched by Morgan's own appetites and need to unbury his long-suppressed self. Claudio's calm seemed to her due to an ignorance of which she was now intolerant; she despised his incomprehension of what she thought she knew—that there was not much time left and what there was, was there to be used in acts of love.

When they had first been lovers at college Morgan had used

to read to her Marvell's poem. In his sonorous, hammy voice he'd recite, holding his book with an arm under her head:

> Now let us sport us while we may;
> And now, like am'rous birds of prey,
> Rather at once our time devour,
> Than languish in his slow-chapt pow'r.
> Let us roll all our Strength, and all
> Our sweetness, up into one Ball:
> And tear our Pleasures with rough strife,
> Thorough the Iron gates of Life.

" 'Had we but world enough and time,' " Gabriella would say to herself as they stood by the car waiting for Claudio. Or lying on the beach in the sun, she would say, " 'The Grave's a fine and private place/ But none I think do there embrace.' "

Gabriella surrendered to these feelings, let Morgan possess her as she submitted him to her own desires. Together they abandoned all separateness, guardedness, the sense of boundary that they had been used to for so long. Ruthlessly they sacrificed their old timid, orphaned, resentful selves to the maw of the monster, the carnivorous love that seemed to give them new life.

"Why is this happening?" Gabriella asked Morgan. "It can't just be Mexico, the heat and the strangeness; that would make it as obscene as our first night in Mexico City."

"It's the tequila," Morgan would say, pulling Gabriella on top of him.

"Don't joke, Morgan; if it's the tequila and the sun, it's going to disappear as soon as we get back to New York."

She would look clearly into his eyes; she could do it all the time now without flinching; there was no deceit any longer between them, and therefore nothing to shame them.

"It won't disappear if we hold on to it," Morgan said; it amused him still the way Gabriella put herself so docilely in his hands.

"What if 'it' can't be prolonged?" Gabriella asked. She was childlike with Morgan now and trusted his answers. "What if work and people and city life interfere?"

"We can't let them, that's all, it's all too late now." Gabriella waited. "I used to come home," Morgan said, "and hear Claudio talking about our 'miraculous marriage' and want to throw up. To him all the props were real, to me it was an archaeological museum, our 'lovely' expensive home, with everything in it divorced from its first use and purpose years ago. The Museum of the Marriage, with two stuffed exhibits, two speak-your-weight machines. I'd like to get rid of everything, live with you in one empty room."

"Cut off from the world," Gabriella said, "real Dover Beach stuff. But you love the world, Morgan, and your job is part of that. It'll erode everything."

"No," Morgan said, "my job should support all this; there's no contradiction. It's your job that contains the contradiction, because until you take yourself seriously in your work, you can't take yourself seriously with me. And this is us being serious, at long last. You nearly blew it."

"I did?"

"Yes, and I never stopped it."

"You want me to give up the clubs; but I have."

"Not just the clubs."

"Claudio, you mean, but you love him too."

"I think I loved him out of missing you," Morgan said. "But now he only gets on my nerves. I spend a lot of time trying not to show it—I don't want to hurt him—but frankly, I don't much care if I never see him again. He reminds me of how sick we've been. How much a failure we've been."

"I can't just cut Claudio," Gabriella said. "Yet it's so strange the way he begins to irritate me, too. I can't understand why you've replaced him so brutally, why it's not possible to love you both in different ways."

"It just isn't," Morgan said. "The noble experiment is over. Claudio will survive. As Kate says, 'People adjust.' "

" 'Too damn easily,' Kate always said."

"Well, as you so often tell me, friendship is Claudio's great gift. Don't worry about him," Morgan said to Gabriella. "He'll find another couple with a shaky marriage; he'll find the hole and then he'll build his nest inside."

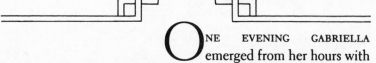

ONE EVENING GABRIELLA emerged from her hours with Morgan changed and dressed for dinner. For the past few days she and Morgan, Liza and Richard, had taken the period after lunch as regularly theirs, abandoning Claudio, who could not drive the hired car, in the house above the Pacific. Alone for long hours he would swim or read, patient and undemanding; only occasionally would he ask to be taken down to the bars and brought back before dinner. Claudio seemed to be unable to score in Acapulco, and though he made no complaint, his single status weighed a little on them all. Tonight they were going to a gay disco, for Claudio's sake.

Gabriella left her room, closing the door on Morgan still in bed under the fans, and came upon Claudio standing by the balcony that overlooked the cliff face above the sea. He stood as though waiting for her first sight of him, leaning against the rail in his white jacket, a long iced drink in his right hand, a cigarette in his left. His hair was immaculately brushed and pomaded, his cheeks were awash in verbena. His features, set in anticipation of a wonderful evening with his friends, bore also a slight anxiety about his appearance. For in addition to the Ricardo Montalban tuxedo jacket, and a pale silk ascot, Claudio wore sharply pressed knee-length khaki shorts, and below these, short white socks and sandals. He looked, to Gabriella, suddenly ridiculous. And pathetic, the hopeful self-presentation, the waiting to be taken out, the awful willingness to please: Claudio's fearful friendliness.

Claudio stood for a while frozen, high above the Pacific, amid the bougainvillaea, under the full moon, sipping delicately on his rum and tonic, puffing from time to time in his precise way, for all the world as though Gabriella were there to film him, so delicately did he move, so fearfully, as though, were he to disturb the angle of these poses, the camera would show, Gabriella would see, how fragile his image was and then how collapsible Claudio was, like some poor aging beauty who feared movement and natural light.

Watching him, Gabriella remembered how recently she had looked at Claudio with the admiration he now seemed so unsure of. He had seemed an enviably discrete being to her once, a finished artifact ready to be presented to the world. In himself, he had always been perfect and complete, both seer and seen. Whereas she and Morgan had seemed to spill incontinently from one to the other, to dip and leak into each other's lives, neither contained, both dependent. Each the other's surroundings, as it seemed to her, their world had been unreal, contingent, made not of objects and people but of feelings, derived like sustenance, or poison, each from the other.

For Gabriella only recently Claudio had carried his space in the world differently, neither pushing through it like a young stud, nor leaning back into it like a vamp, nor hobbling and slumping inside it like half of a married couple; Claudio had seemed to bop and play in the world like Uncle Remus in the film singing zippity-do-dah.

And now Gabriella saw that it wasn't so, that he was a creature dependent on Gabriella's approval, and this hopeless need to please revolted her and she wanted terribly to laugh.

"Come and sit with me," Gabriella said abruptly, forcing him out of his pose and back into movement and insecurities about himself and his dress. She did not comment on his clothes; she was not cruel yet, but she had become callous.

The household woke and slowly appeared as Gabriella listened, irritable now, to Claudio speaking nervously, wittily, about his afternoon and his reading. She felt her face tense whenever he laughed his great artificial laugh, which was now, she deciphered, growing lighter and gayer the more he felt his fears. When Liza came and then left them, taking a drink to Richard, Claudio abandoned his hope of winning Gabriella through charm and wit and entertainment, and made a direct appeal to their friendship, the former girl-to-girl intimacies.

"You seem," he said, "to be getting on better with Morgan."

Shame at his euphemism, shame at her feelings for Claudio held Gabriella. She would not discuss Morgan with him; it was repulsive to her. "Yes, much better," she said coldly.

"You only needed a holiday. That's what Liza and I said."

Liza and I! Gabriella said to herself. Liza and Gabriella, yes, Liza and Richard, but no kinship in Liza and Claudio—and yet this brutal conviction horrified her because it was so sudden and so close in time to her tender feelings for Claudio.

"Did you really?" Gabriella began but backed down, seeing Claudio's incomprehension. "Well, I suppose you were right."

"I'm very happy about it," Claudio went on, pushing his love at her, longing to trigger the recent responses, Gabriella's confidence. "I was getting a little worried back in New York. You two are so important to me—you know?" he added slowly, venturing gently to take Gabriella's hand.

Her hand lay in his as disconnected as she could make it. Her desire was to pull it back, to take it out of the range of Claudio's sticky love. "Were you worried?" she asked sourly.

The sourness and the question were in conflict. Claudio decided to hear the question. "Oh yes, sweetums," he went on. "You have an incredible marriage. I know how much you have to put into it, and it's so worthwhile."

"Thanks," Gabriella said. "You're very nice, Claudio." The dismissal in the tone ran up against the words; Claudio chose again, or could not choose, not to hear the tone.

"Sweetums," Claudio said. He brushed the side of his hand against Gabriella's and let it hover affectionately. A frightening wave of physical revulsion hit her then, so strong she nearly stood. She felt a flash of hatred for him, a longing to hit. The feelings scared her; she thought that if he touched her again, she would scream.

Claudio saw nothing but Gabriella's nerves. "Sweetums," he said again, "no drink in your little hand. Can I get you one?"

"Yes, thank you." He would be away from her.

"Pina colada?" Claudio mispronounced and drifted lethargically over the few syllables.

"Christ no!" Gabriella said rudely; then herself again, her old self, "Vodka and tonic, please, Claudio."

Claudio went to the little refrigerator in the salon bar and made Gabriella's drink, talking while Gabriella tried not to listen. Everything he said now rang trivial, camp, idiotic. She calculated that they had five days of their holiday left. She must get through it without hurting Claudio, and then, somehow, they would arrange not to see him again. Most of his things had been moved out of their apartment. With Kate gone, they could use the excuse of wanting privacy. She could say that they were going to try to have children. Claudio was so benign and sentimental it would seem excuse enough: even he had the heterosexual priorities. Perhaps she and Morgan really would have children out of this new union.

But where was the mysterious loathing for Claudio coming from? Had she merely pulled all the strength and virtue out of everyone else and fastened it on her husband? Had her own fears following the quake made him seem so strong, herself so dependent; and did she now loathe the dependency she read in Claudio, projecting her weakness onto him? Or was it a simple equation:

of death and quakes and Mexico having changed sex for her, and sex having changed her attitude to Claudio? Bed was the crude explanation of what had happened to their friendship.

Liza re-emerged now from her room, perfumed and braceleted and friendly. Claudio leaped toward her, burying his face in her neck and moaning a little as he swayed his dance of greeting.

"You smell in*cred*ible," he said and laughed his joyous laugh.

"And you smell in*cred*ible," Liza mimicked him and gently tried to disengage him. But there was no urgency in it, it seemed to Gabriella; Liza had never got so dangerously close.

"Where's Richard?" Gabriella asked, a little loudly, intent on drawing Liza from Claudio's disgusting nuzzling. She remembered how his lips on her neck had always been wet and soft, like a baby's genitals, how she would pull away, even in the past. Liza stood with Claudio's head on her still and looked, clear-eyed, at Gabriella. "He's coming. Are we late? Where's Morgan?"

They sat for a while and waited for the men while Claudio made piña coladas. They discussed the color of the moon, whether it was pink or beige.

"Apricot cream," Claudio said. "Wonderful with burgundy."

"Sounds like a repulsive drink," Gabriella said.

"Did you ever see Mickey's Hudson Street loft?" Claudio asked Liza.

"No, tell me."

Gabriella drank her vodka and watched them warily.

"It was a seven-layer lacquer job that took us four weeks, right?"

"Right," Liza said.

"We got a gold peach color that picked up any evening light; touches of brass throughout, a deep-maroon carpet, not wool unfortunately. The whole idea was for it to last, which I told him, but he had to save and get acrylic. Anyway, he sold the interior to a New Jersey queen before the nap wore. But it was an absolute spectacle in the summer with the light coming off the Hudson."

"And the lint coming off the carpet, and the boys bouncing off the walls," Gabriella said.

"What a nasty mood you're in tonight, sweetums," Claudio said, looking at her. "Isn't she?" he asked Liza.

"Is she?" Liza asked her.

Richard arrived among them, wearing an unfamiliar tropical suit.

"That's pretty snappy," Claudio said to him.

"Is it all right?" Richard went to the bar and poured himself a whiskey. "Liza's idea . . . she said it would do for the office in the summer."

"A bit flashy for your office, isn't it?" Claudio asked him.

"Richard'll pull it off," Liza said.

"You know what Otto's like," Richard said to Claudio.

"It sounds a little sartorially restricted over there," Claudio said, "as Morgan tells it."

"Well, any veering from seersucker, Otto questions your morals."

"Oh, Richard can stand up to Otto." Gabriella tried to pull Richard away from his friendliness with Claudio.

"Where's Morgan?" Richard asked, lost in this feminine sea.

"I'll get him," Gabriella said.

Inside the room with Morgan, Gabriella was calm again. She sat next to him on the bed, where he was reading.

"Do we have to go?" he asked. "I mean, a gay disco . . ."

"We have to go. Perhaps we can leave early. Maybe Richard and Liza can bring Claudio back."

"But he's on the scrounge."

"That's true; well, he can take a taxi back."

"Taxis stop at one; Claudio doesn't warm up till then."

"He can find his own way back for a change," Gabriella said.

"Well, let's go. Oh fuck, what a holiday. I'd rather be with you."

"I know. But it's sort of Claudio's big night, and he's all dressed up. A little weirdly. Can you wear a white jacket? We don't want to shame him at the disco. And aftershave, it seems expected."

"Come here, Gabriella." Morgan tried to pull her down to him.

"They're waiting for us, Morgan; this is awful."

"What's awful?"

"Wanting to be with you; having to camp around with Claudio."

"You wanted him," Morgan said, delighted.

"That was before I wanted you."

"Well, now, lucky girl, you can have us both."

"As though that were possible."

They rode down from the hill resort into the town of Acapulco, Gabriella and Morgan in the back, Claudio in the front next to Liza and Richard, who was driving. As they passed through the streets Claudio made a continuous report, laughing at the poor dolled-up women and the men with paunches, admiring the well-dressed and the occasional young boy. For half an hour he kept up his acid comments, in a speedy, comedian's monologue. Liza egged him on; to Gabriella it was numbingly depressing. "Why do you care so much what people look like all the time?" she said finally.

"What should I care about?" Claudio snapped back. He had felt her hostility behind him; he knew. "You tell me, you tell us all."

"About who they are," Gabriella said.

"But I don't know who they are, sweetums; you want me to get out and fucking interview them?"

"It would be a start," Gabriella said. "Instead of always clothes. I'm sick of clothes and looks and fashion."

"That shouldn't change your life much." The nastiness was on the surface now, she had tapped it.

"Children," Liza said, "of course clothes are interesting; self-presentation is always interesting."

"Thank you," Claudio said. He smoked his cigarette defensively and laughed again. But Gabriella had silenced him, and dampened them all.

"I'm sorry, Claudio," Gabriella said finally. "Forgive me, too much sun."

"Sweetums," he said, but there was an edge to it.

Richard parked the car opposite the discotheque. The sight of the clients waiting to get into the club cheered Claudio. He began to bop a little on the sidewalk in time to the music, and then, happy again, hugged Gabriella. "Have a good time," he said to her, "you can do it." He kissed her on the neck and she held still for him. "Just relax," he said.

They sat at a table on the circle around the dance floor, where gay and straight American couples moved without much energy to the disco music. Watching them, above little pots of camellias and red lanterns, was the seated crowd, largely gay, older, likewise foreign. No one much scrutinized the T-shirted dancers, except for Claudio, coolly still down to his crossed naked legs and sandaled feet, his cigaretted hand immobile over a pack of Gauloises, his head tense as an eagle's as he sorted desirable from dross, available from attached. Next to him, Richard loosened his jacket and fidgeted; the Callaghers watched dully and ordered long decorative drinks from the waiter when he came.

When the music stopped, the stage went dark and the dancers moved off the floor. "We get a show," Liza said. Richard straightened a little in his chair and looked into the blackness. Under the table Morgan took Gabriella's hand. Claudio clinked the ice in his glass and poised himself for what was coming.

A long, wailing siren blasted from the back of the stage, stopped, made a space for a microphoned Spanish voice to welcome them to the Cactus Club. There was a flash of lights, instructions to greet Señorita Rosa. A wavering red spotlight, a few bars from "The Stripper," and Señorita Rosa in sequins and biceps, arms shaven, torso plucked, made her way to the center of the stage. Slowly, ineptly, she removed a red feathered boa, two strings of pearls, a pair of long black gloves, the sequined skirt, sleeves and middle of her dress, until she stood like a wide-waisted matron in red bikini and bra, fishnetted and stilettoed on perfect legs under bizarrely narrow hips. There were appreciative catcalls and requests for songs.

In the darkness Gabriella listened to Claudio's laughter as it questioned his companions, and Liza's laugh that reassured him. "Very nice, very nice," Richard said.

"Look at the beehive," Claudio said, and his laugh ascended.

Señorita Rosa, left on stage with her man's waist and chiseled profile, did suggestive things with the microphone and sang bland show-tune medleys, and the audience applauded. She bowed and blew kisses, and was followed by Dorita, in long lashes and black cape, pushing three large stuffed black poodles on wheels. Waiting for the backup music, she smiled, played with the dogs and then sang a song called "Bitch in Heat." Rhinestones, teeth, applause, laughter.

"This is pretty lame," Richard said. They ordered more drinks.

There followed an act with whips and Dracula costumes, impersonations of Dolly Parton, Sophia Loren, the Queen of England and Blondie.

Gabriella was at first simply curious at the tameness of the drag compared with New York, and then she was bored. She focused on the sound of the laughter around her, wondered if it was real, and then heard in it the part that was directed against herself. She began to feel menaced, then humiliated and outraged. The impersonations seemed now to have more hatred and fear than admiration in them. It seemed that the audience, and Claudio, was laughing at her, or at least at a grotesque caricature of something that she was part of. She would have liked to leave for a while, but the acts followed one another in mindless speed: a blonde, a redhead, a vamp, a schoolgirl, Ursula Andress, Marilyn Monroe, one woman after another cannibalized and abandoned to the audience in a primitive ritual of desecration. The trite and tinny music blasted at them, and the padding and false hair, simpering and strutting, the cheap rhetoric named her again and again a poor stupid bitch, a joke, a grotesque. She tried to look elsewhere in the room until it was over; she tried not to listen to the music. But around her, she saw the faces turned happily, greedily toward the performers, lustful, malicious; and everywhere she heard the laughter and approval.

Gabriella was humiliated and beside herself. Morgan, simply bored, bent to hear what the trouble was.

"I am hating this," she said.

"Pretty silly, isn't it?" He took her hand, but she removed it.

"Worse than that. Oh, look at Claudio. I want to go."

"Stay," Morgan said to her, "it'll be over soon."

"No, I can't. I can't stand it," Gabriella said.

Only Morgan could hear. "It doesn't mean anything," he said.

"It does. It means I'm hated."

Just then a burst of Claudio's laughter covered her words, and she said loudly, yet under the music, "Shut up, damn you, Claudio."

Claudio, hearing only his name, turned his joyous face in Gabriella's direction and there stopped, struck by her fierce expression. And then all happiness left him, and a great doleful inquiry lifted his brows and drooped along his mouth as the word "What?" formed a giant childlike wail.

Gabriella turned away quickly. Claudio was quiet and did not laugh again, except in a kind of defiance, until the show was over. In the sudden silence Richard said "Marvelous. Let's get some drinks. I loved Judy Garland—was it Judy Garland? Didn't you?"

"Great," Liza said.

"Wonderful," Claudio said. He laughed again and turned his back on the Callaghers.

"It's nothing," Morgan said to Gabriella, "just Acapulco show biz. Calm down." They drank the drinks. The disco music took over again and Claudio took Liza off to dance.

"I think we'd better go before I say something awful to Claudio," Gabriella said to Morgan.

"We can't go, we've only just arrived. Control yourself," Morgan said. "Drink up."

Gabriella drank up and then ordered more drinks and got drunk until she slid out of anger into a kind of reckless disdain for the place and for Claudio, whom she then in careless deceit invited to dance.

Gabriella's drunkenness gave them an excuse to leave the club early. But in the back of the cab, as it made its long trip up the tiny hillside roads, she found her anger again. She tried to explain that to Morgan as between directions and warnings to the driver he held her and tried to calm her down. At the villa Gabriella found a bottle of rum and took it to the pool, where with Morgan she watched the distant boats of Acapulco harbor and tried to rid herself of all the hatred she had felt that evening.

"But you used to love it," Morgan insisted.

Now Gabriella renounced it for him, and through her drunken tears, and in her long *mea culpa*, Morgan saw the old willingness and meekness that made him, too, mournful for the time that had passed between them, wasted, it now seemed, in all those years of egalitarian struggle that had only made the space between them, the hole into which Claudio had crawled and flourished. He could not share her grief in the present because he was happy now to have her back, broken over nothing, the trifling humiliation of the drag show. He held her, as again and again she filled their glasses from the bottle of dark rum, until the violence abated and Morgan could take her, drunk and exhausted, away from the pool and back to bed.

In the morning Gabriella woke early, before the boy who cleaned the little pool had arrived and while the air was still cool and fragrant. Wrapped in a towel, she passed over the terrace with all its littered ashtrays and abandoned drinks, and despised their life once more. She swam naked and chilly in the morning air and then lay in the patches of sun that were warmest at the side of the pool. It would be hours before anyone came; she lay naked in the sun, admiring herself and her brownness and her own female beauty. The rum and the swimming had bathed away the horrors of the night before; she had only to manipulate herself around Claudio—Claus, as she was beginning to call him to herself—to survive the rest of the stay. She didn't mind that Richard and Liza had had to take the burden of him last night. She would let them take over.

She listened to the noise of the birds in the trees along the hillside, and the distant sounds of early traffic in the village below. She was happy, Morgan had made her so; she was happy thanks to Morgan, with nothing more than this present of sun and noises and her own health.

She found her cigarettes, abandoned last night by the pool, and lit one, wishing she did not smoke. Four years ago she had stopped smoking for a whole year and had been proud of that. It had been power over herself, one of the few things she had been able to control. It seemed to her now that her distance from Morgan in the past years had likewise been an attempt to control what was outside of herself, that she had feared Morgan's closeness to her. Too dangerous. She had perceived herself weak and had not been able to risk capitulation; and she had kept him, as he always said and as she always denied, at arm's length, filling the space between them with all the signs of apparent ease of concourse, their abysmally free and eloquent words. Morgan had not been deceived; only outsiders had been. Now with Morgan she had capitulated, and survived. More than survived. She had given up cigarettes to tighten her control on life, and around the same time, it now seemed, she had given up Morgan; carved a space around a tightly regulated island and there had suffered appalling loneliness which she only now recognized, and for which she felt a retrospective pity.

Liza had been braver. Liza risked more with Richard. Liza even smoked. Nor, as she watched her here, did it seem that Liza played the manipulating games with Richard that Gabriella had learned with Morgan. Perhaps Kate had played them; perhaps young people, appalled by the costs of intimacy, all played those games until one partner awoke to find himself simply alone. Perhaps Liza and Richard could now be free of all that, having seen, and unlike herself and Morgan, not having to relearn that there was nothing to fear. Kate, it seemed to Gabriella, had mourned only the outward forms of marital harmony; the substance had vanished long ago.

It seemed paradoxical to Gabriella that it had been the earthquake, and her understanding that she was weak yet could survive, that had let her surrender again to Morgan. It was all right to let Morgan be as strong as he was; she could descend through her own terrors until she hit bottom, where there was ground and footing, and through which she would not fall. Accepting Morgan this wholly, she saw that she need not herself seem fractured; she was whole and sound and happy. She felt she was living correctly, as she always ought to have if she had only had the courage. There was that "ought" again, and now it meant something. Courage to be weak. And something else, she thought, she was now, in her own way, out of her own closet. She had come out.

Gabriella lay in the sun for a long while until she heard the young Mexican at the villa gate on the long steps above her. She took up her towel and stepped past last night's bottle of rum and the glasses, past an early lizard, likewise admiring himself outside the shadow of the bougainvillaea, and went inside to find Morgan.

On the top level of the three-tiered villa she came across Claudio making coffee. "How long have you been here?"

Claudio stared at her, startled by her rudeness, but uncertain that she meant to sound as she had. "Not long."

"I thought I was alone." Gabriella hovered in her towel, trying to conquer her surprise and irritation.

"We saw you down there. Don't worry, sweetums, it was only a flash; we made a chaste withdrawal."

"We?"

"Peter and I."

"Peter?"

"Yes, Peter."

"Where is he?" Gabriella looked around her on the upper terrace of the villa, proprietorial and curious.

"He's just phoning his parents."

"Phoning his parents?"

"Christ, Gabriella, do you have to repeat everything I say? He's phoning his parents to tell them he's all right."

"Who is he?"

"We met at the club."

"Last night?"

"Of course."

"Je—sus!"

"What the fuck's it got to do with you?" Claudio reached suddenly for a cigarette, lit it, regained some calm and stared coolly, insolently, at Gabriella.

"Why are you such a little whore?" Gabriella had not meant to say it; it came from nowhere, blasting across her morning like a jet. But she had said it, and she looked now at Claudio, stunned, silently smoking on the canvas chair in front of her.

"Peter," he called, "come and meet my friend Gabriella."

Peter came up to them, a young man in faded jeans.

"I hope we didn't disturb you," he said. "I guess we thought no one would be up. I had to call my parents." He looked at

Claudio. "Not in," he said to him. "I'll try again later. They might be playing tennis."

He turned and smiled at Gabriella, shy and accommodating, a polite boy, taught to shake hands with his parents' friends. Claudio turned a challenging face to Gabriella. "Coffee?" he asked.

"I'm going back to bed," Gabriella said. "Thanks."

She turned and smiled at the boy. "Nice to meet you," she said and walked toward the door where Morgan was, lay down on the bed and closed her eyes.

In the afternoon they all went down to the beach at Acapulco and lay in the sun until Peter left them. The sun was hot, and the beach flat and littered, noisy with tourists, heavy with the smells of lotion and sweet drinks. Liza had talked a great deal to Peter throughout the day, and in gratitude for this, Claudio lay close to her, chatting in a low, intimate way. On the other side of them, Richard and Morgan slept heavily in the heat. Gabriella read her paperback and tried not to hear Claudio's absurd laughter as it drifted over the sleeping men. Around them, family life, singles life, honeymoon life grouped and parted until the beach seemed to seethe with combinations, and the noise and movement became unbearable.

"It's so depressing here," Gabriella said to Liza and Claudio, "shall we go?"

"What's depressing?" Liza said.

"All these people."

"You've been in a foul mood all day," Claudio said, safe behind Liza. "Just relax."

"Come on, Richard, get up," Liza said, "we're getting bored and roasted."

"Go into the water," Richard said sleepily.

"There isn't any room; anyway, the water's warm."

The men stirred and shifted and stood up to shake the sand

from their suits. Elsewhere on the beach, patches of sunbathers were standing, shaking out blankets, organizing children, lighting up cigarettes. Richard and Claudio went off to get beer, Morgan followed sleepily behind.

"Thank god Claudio's found Peter," Liza said to Gabriella. "At least the cruising is over; I had no idea what a slow worker he was."

"We don't have to have Peter from now on, do we?" Gabriella was appalled. "It was bad enough spending the whole day with him—you mean for the rest of our stay?"

"Well, it's Claudio's holiday too."

"Yes, but he's not going to be at breakfast from now on? Did Claudio say that?"

"No, but I assume . . ."

"We'll have to tell him. It's no good. I don't want him."

Liza looked over to Gabriella. "What's the matter with you?"

"What's the matter? He's about seventeen. I mean, it's not very interesting, is it? He's a bore."

"Well, he's Claudio's bore. You don't have to talk to him; you haven't so far. Don't be so intolerant, Gabriella, what's gotten into you?"

"I'm just bored with Claudio. I don't know why. He gets on my nerves. Doesn't he irritate you?"

"Irritate?" Liza repeated. "He's adorable."

"Adorable," Gabriella said. "They're a bore his drag clubs, shepherding him toward his pickups."

"Well, he's got Peter now; you don't have to take him to clubs."

"Has Peter got a car at least?"

"I don't think so."

"Oh Christ."

"He's only a high school kid."

"That means we have to take them both all over the place now. Liza, this is awful."

"Well then, you tell him. I'm not going to. What do you care, anyway, you've got Morgan."

"I don't like him."

"Who?"

"Peter."

"Well, that's tough, you're stuck."

"No." Gabriella got up and walked to the booths where the men stood drinking beer and smoking. Even now, Gabriella noticed, Claudio's eyes never stopped, but cruised the bodies as they passed along the beach.

"Claudio," Gabriella said to him, "can I ask a little question?"

"What?" A small exasperated look changed his face as he turned toward her.

"In private," Gabriella said. She smiled.

"What's happening?" Richard called to them as they moved away.

"Private matter," Gabriella said to him. Claudio held his glass of beer and looked directly at Gabriella, challenging her to speak.

"I'm sorry about this morning."

Claudio relaxed, paused, then stroked her lightly on the arm. "Forget it. No one should be held responsible for what they say before eleven." He was happy, he had a bridge back; he waited.

"But this guy Peter . . ."

Claudio's face changed again. "What about him?"

"He isn't going to be with us from now on, is he?"

Claudio turned from her and walked toward Morgan and Richard. Gabriella stood in the sun with her question hanging in the air. Over Claudio's shoulder Morgan watched her and saluted with his glass of beer. He had missed out on this all day; Gabriella had said nothing to him.

Gabriella walked back to Liza, lying, eyes closed, in the sun.

"Did you tell him?"

"Not exactly."

"Good. It's none of our business what Claudio does. Get some sun. We'll be back in New York in five days. You can smash your friendships then."

They lay for a while without speaking. She would explain to Liza later about Claudio, about Morgan and herself. Liza would understand the priorities; she must have them herself with Richard; that was simply the way things worked.

"They're crazy, did you see him?" It was Richard, breathless, without his T-shirt, his brown belly bare over the stripes of his suit.

"What?" Liza sat up first, her master's voice.

"Got a cigarette, Richard?" Gabriella asked him.

"Sorry. I left them with Claudio. Did you see Morgan?"

"Where?"

"In the sky. Those fools have challenged each other to hanging off some plane that goes around the bay." Richard looked up into the sky.

"Claudio must be up there now. Morgan's just down. It's two hundred feet up; he says he's never been so scared in his life, thought he was going to spray vomit all over the beach."

"Good God," Gabriella said. "Up there? Why?"

"Who knows?" Richard said. "It was Claudio's idea; some Mexican with a one-propeller plane actually charges for it."

Liza and Gabriella were now both standing with Richard, scanning the skies. "But why would they do it?" Gabriella asked again.

"Claudio insisted."

"But Peter's gone; it can't have been to show off to Peter."

"Why are you so nasty?" Liza said, turning to Gabriella. "Maybe it's simple high spirits."

"High spirits!" Richard said.

"There he is," Liza cried. She pointed and they saw, drifting very slowly toward them, the tiny suspended form of Claudio, his pink bikini drooping in the sunset as he floated over Acapulco Bay, his chest covered in Richard's blue shirt, his eyes protected by his silver shades. Strapped and hanging from the underbelly of the small glinting plane, he was calm and radiant as he sailed high above the hotels and the bathers, like a Christmas angel on its wire.

"Look at him," Liza shouted. "Bravo, Claudio, bravo!" Again she shouted and waved.

Claudio saw them and lifted one languorous hand, faintly, weakly, like a dying pope. From where Gabriella was standing and peering as Claudio drifted overhead, she could make out between the fingers of his long, elegant hand as it made its benediction the little white flash of a cigarette.

AT THE EDGE OF THE LAGOON, among the fishing boats, Mexican women washed their clothes in muddy water. The Americans that came to water-ski bought Coca-Colas from a nearby shanty and drank them at tables set out night-club style on the long palm-shaded dock from which the skiing could be watched. Here, looking out on the abandoned ski jump which rose out of the oily green, splintered in the afternoon sun, Gabriella sat with Liza. They were waiting for Richard to take his turn around the water. Morgan and Claudio were down by the boats with him, and for the first time in several days they were alone.

The issue of Claudio hung in the air between them, and Gabriella's disappointment that the days, given over to other things, had not made them friends. She suspected that Liza no longer found her even likable; the irritableness with Claudio was constant now, seemed unprovoked and willful. In Gabriella the physical well-being, from hours of sun and sea, the hours with Morgan, jangled with guilt about Claudio, and a sense of loss of the opportunity between herself and Liza. She had, too, the beginnings of an anxiety about Morgan, as the holiday drew to a close and the old life and its habits loomed before them. There was beginning to be some stress in maintaining the ardor, as the old selves slowly crept back inside the new beings. To Liza, and to herself, Gabriella needed to defend the high cost of her new love with Morgan.

"This thing with Claudio," Gabriella began. Liza turned her head slowly from the water and looked at her.

"Which you must have noticed," Gabriella added quickly. Liza nodded.

"Is as peculiar to me as it must be to you." The confession made her formal, remote. She tried again.

"It's been a sudden turning against him, which I don't understand and can't control. I just can't bear to be around him, can't bear his voice or his laugh or those damn ice cubes he clinks all day long in his drinks. I can't stand how nice he is or his loyalty to me." *Mea culpa* was becoming relief. Gabriella back-tracked:

"And yet nothing has changed. He is as he always was, and I did love him. The worst thing is I don't really feel guilty, though I should; I feel embarrassed by it, its effect on all of us, what it's doing to our holiday. God knows I try to keep it from Claudio, but I'm very bad at that; he senses it, but, I suppose because it's so unreasonable, can't quite believe it."

Liza said nothing.

"Has Richard noticed anything?" Gabriella asked her.

"No. Not much. Not as much as I have."

"And what do you think is happening? It's so strange."

"That you've just fallen in love with Morgan," Liza said. Gabriella waited for rebuke, but that was all Liza said. She played idly with her cigarette. Under them, the dock rocked slightly on the water, reminding Gabriella of the sensation of the earthquake, the peculiar origins of her recent feeling for Morgan.

"But why does it automatically involve Claudio? And so brutally?" Gabriella asked her.

"Not only Claudio," Liza said gently, "but Richard and me, and all your other friends." Liza stopped and saw that Gabriella was waiting. "Listen, Gabriella, when Richard fell in love with me, in the beginning, he turned against Kate like that, physically, though he's better than you at hiding things. I suppose he must have been, because we were together six months and he was still living with her."

"Six months?" That long. Even Gabriella was shocked.

"Yes. Now there's treachery for you. It happens. Richard fell in love with me and turned not only against Kate but against most of his other friends. You wouldn't have noticed, perhaps, but he was just no longer interested. He was consumed by me—and he consumed me," Liza said, "before I saw what was happening and pulled out."

"Pulled out, how can you 'pull out'?" Gabriella asked; How can you want to pull out? was what she thought.

"You take your life back," Liza said, "you put yourself back in the world."

"But, Liza, if you knew," Gabriella insisted, "if you knew the way Morgan and I were before, the 'world' just wasn't enough."

"Wasn't it?—didn't that larger world of Claudio and his friends make you happy? I thought it did."

"For a while, but then I tried to force a romantic love inside it, and it all fell apart. I think . . . I don't know. But this with Morgan now is real." Again Gabriella put herself into Liza's hands, and waited for confirmation.

But Liza said unhappily, impatiently, "Oh, this is nothing. The honeymoon stuff just doesn't last. Don't worry about it. You can't maintain this with Morgan, you won't. You're a human and you live with other humans. It's not just you and Morgan, and if you let the sacrifice become so large, just for sex—"

"It isn't just sex," Gabriella insisted.

"Well, whatever it is, the cost is too great. You'll see that, you'll pull back. You don't throw the world away. You don't make monstrous sacrifices for your passions. You'll become sick of yourself if you do."

"But, Liza, the isolation before."

"Is terrible," Liza said, "but marriage doesn't prevent it. And friendships can't be pushed very far. And living alone is hell. I know; but you have to live in the world with a patchwork of companionships and sort of jumble along—not this all-or-nothing business. And one thing, Gabriella, you have to put yourself in the center of all of that."

"But I do; I am horribly selfish."

"That's not what I mean. I mean, you must not let other people save you all the time, Claudio or Morgan; you have to take yourself seriously."

"Seriously?" Liza was sounding like Morgan.

"You can't throw yourself around the way you do, throw yourself at Morgan, at the gay world—with all your gay abandon, you're only abandoning yourself. Why don't you have a job you like? Why is Morgan so damn important? If you let him be everything, the thing that you 'do,' you'll be left with nothing. Look, Richard did it. Richard sacrificed Kate for the great love, threw himself into this with me. And now what is it? Of course we love each other, but I have my work and friends and Richard knows he's just a part of all that. And Richard is beginning to find his way back into the world, in a way that's what this holiday is about."

"Oh," Gabriella said guiltily.

"I wasn't everything," Liza went on, in her own confession now. "It didn't justify sacrificing Kate."

"Do you mean that?" Gabriella asked.

"No, it didn't," Liza said. "But then, it's not a question of justification; it's something else that just happens, desire, greed, will . . . I don't know."

"But, Liza, surely it was worth something," Gabriella tried to comfort her.

"Oh, of course, Richard got out of something that wasn't working. I didn't say it wasn't worth it, I say it's not justifiable. It just is; but there's no higher rightness about the thing. And I feel awful about Kate the whole time. It poisons things. And I can't think it was all in a great cause, her pain—I just can't." Liza turned from herself back to Gabriella. "You think sacrificing Claudio for Morgan is all right because of what you get instead, but what you get goes too. Because there isn't anything permanent. It's just feelings, and feelings change."

"Oh, Liza," Gabriella said sadly, "you sound so bitter."

"I'm not," she said defensively. "I'm just sorry. I'm sorry for all of us. We're all so terribly greedy, crashing around taking things, smashing them up when they're not enough."

"Is that how you see Morgan and me?" Gabriella asked.

"No," Liza said suddenly. "And, Christ, Gabriella, I'm not lecturing you. I'm talking about me. But be careful how reckless you are, Gabriella. Be kind. Claudio is special. He doesn't take the way we do."

"There's Morgan," Gabriella said. She saw him over Liza's left shoulder. He was as yet a tiny figure, moving steadily across the far side of the lagoon. She felt him rather exposed now as Liza turned to watch. Morgan, so infinitesimally small that Gabriella could blot him out with an eye movement. The tiny figure on the horizon hardly seemed worth so much upheaval. She had surrendered herself to an image so faint she might be imagining the whole thing.

And at the same time, she now invested the disappearing fleck with the weight of their shared history, the long uneven past and the claustrophobic sensuality of their days here, and felt herself solid again on the unsteady dock. It was the mere notion of Morgan that gave her stability. Sensing the paradox, she felt ashamed and confused.

"What does it mean, Liza, 'take yourself seriously'? I'm not a painter."

"What has that got to do with it?" Liza said, turning back to Gabriella.

"Well, it can all be one for you, your private self and your work self. I have to divide those people."

"I only mean you should do something that matters to you. You

221

don't like your job; why not get out, or make something of it?"

"That's what Morgan says."

"Well, why not?"

"And do what? I used to paint and act and all that at college, but you have to be good to go on. *You* paint because you're good at it."

"I'm not a good painter," Liza said, "I know that."

"Aren't you?"

Liza laughed. "Come on, Gabriella, don't be dishonest. But I can't do anything else. And you should find the thing you can't do anything else but—other than Morgan. Obviously the agency is wrong. It's not as though the money matters. Claudio has to work, for the cash and the freedom. No, for the freedom. Freedom is what he does; that's his profession, and of course"—Liza smiled—"a certain amount of sexual traffic at the restaurant, and being in elegant surroundings and seeing people who might be coming to his house for dinner only just happen not to, just happen to sit down at the restaurant table instead."

"Is that how you see it?" Gabriella said, laughing.

"Sure, it's a kind of para-hospitality. It's lovely. It suits him."

"Talk to Claudio about whether he'd like most of those people to come to dinner."

"Well, he's happy and you're not."

"He's not very happy now," Gabriella said.

They were interrupted by the sudden arrival at the next-door table of a large American in cowboy clothes—a hand-tooled leather belt buckled by a huge steer's head that cut into a vast girth, a string tie, denims—noisily organizing his family around their Cokes. A tiny boy of two blinked palely into the sunlight, then wriggled off his chair.

"Jessie, I'm warning you. Get your ass over here," his father said loudly. The mother, ignoring them both, bent over her Coke. The family looked weary, battered, yoked. Liza and Gabriella watched for a while, forced by the proximity to listen as the father spoke.

"He's got to learn sometime, Tessie." It was about the eight-year-old boy he was speaking. That child, thin and rigid, tried to disappear like his mother into the Coke as his father harangued. He had misbehaved in the morning, gone off at the beach; they had found him an hour later. He'd been punished. Tessie had protested weakly, but given in. The ritual of the drinks was intended to end the episode. All had been forgiven: they had their Cokes.

Jessie slid off his chair again and stood behind it, holding on to his mother's skirt. He too wore a cowboy belt and a string tie, the strands held in place by an ugly clasp in the shape of a horse. As his father talked to Tessie he wandered off a little, fingering the stalks of the palm trees. Then he found one of the plastic meshed lanterns that had been placed at the edge of the dock, squatted over it, lifted it and watched in surprise as it slipped out of his hands and bounced on the wooden dock.

"You break anything here," his father said, "and I'll bust your ass."

"It's not broken," Tessie said.

"He didn't break it," the eight-year-old said.

"Get over here, you," the father said again. "I'll whip your ass."

"Jesus!" Gabriella said loudly. The man turned in her direction.

"Jesus!" Gabriella swore again. "He's only a baby."

"Family life," Liza said. They both felt a little sick. Now all six of them at the end of the dock looked ill.

"I think that's Richard," Gabriella said in relief as another small figure appeared on the other side of the lagoon.

Liza turned to see. "Not Richard," she said with excitement, "Claudio."

"Claudio?" Gabriella said. "He can't water-ski, can he?"

"Why not?" Liza challenged her. "You think it's such a butch sport?"

"I didn't mean that," Gabriella said. "I just thought he said he couldn't."

"Well, he's doing it," Liza said happily. Claudio's form, as he now hove into view, was unsteady. He hunched like a boxer over the skis. He wore his shades, however, which meant that he hadn't yet fallen and was determined not to. His knees looked a little shaky, but the boat was moving fast and he was following doggedly and impressively behind.

"He's doing well," Gabriella said.

"He's pretty game, old Claudio." Claudio's form, still crouched, came into closer view. He seemed to be approaching the dock.

"He should straighten up," Liza said, "he's going to have a terrible backache."

"But he stays on."

The boat turned in a large arc and Claudio took the small jumps over the wake, catching his balance each time at the last moment. After a few of these, he raised his arm and waved the driver on.

"I think he wants to show us, he's coming this way."

The boat turned again and pulled at accelerated speed toward the dock; behind it Claudio moved, his knees firmly bent, his shades set straight ahead.

"Jesus," Gabriella said, "I think he's going for the jump."

"He can't," Liza said, "the driver must know. It's dried out, they'd have to wet it. *Claudio, stop!*" she shouted, now standing.

The cowboy family turned to see what was going on.

"*Stop!*" Gabriella, too, was on her feet. They ran to the edge of the dock and shouted again as Claudio headed for the jump, head down, knees bent, at terrific speed. In a second his skis hit the jump and his body came apart over it, knees and glasses and head, moving in the air as though the limbs were already broken; the body spilled skiless over the jump and crashed into the water.

Gabriella and Liza stood stunned at the edge of the dock and said nothing. Then Claudio surfaced, slowly paddling behind one ski, his glasses in his left hand. There didn't seem to be blood. The driver arced back across the water, cut his engine, and Claudio climbed into the boat, moving normally. He seemed to be all right. Gabriella and Liza shouted again, out of hearing, and then sat down.

"He's *crazy*," Gabriella said. "He could have killed himself."

Liza was still pale. "He's a maniac at the moment," she said quietly. "He almost drowned this afternoon. We didn't tell you."

"What?" Gabriella was feeling sick, and just faintly, oddly, guilty.

"Well, after lunch when you were off with Morgan, we went down to the little beach here, which is quite rough. There are caves on one side, and Claudio somehow got stuck."

"Stuck?"

"Well, he walked into the cave as a wave went out, and then when it flooded back he couldn't get out. But he didn't call us; he just stood slipping on the rocks as the waves went in and out. He was exhausted by the time Richard saw him. And then Richard couldn't get to him. He had to get two Mexican boys who happened to be there, thank God; it took the three of them quite a time to free him."

"God," Gabriella said, "was he all right?"

"His feet were cut badly and his hands, didn't you notice?"

"No," Gabriella said quietly.

"And he was exhausted. He lay down for a while and then we came back to the house. Richard was furious with him, and quite scared too, I think, because they both could have drowned. But when Claudio felt better and Richard attacked him, he said we were making a fuss about nothing; he was very odd, he just pretended it hadn't happened and made us promise not to say anything to you. I thought that was embarrassment at having been so stupid, but I think he really just doesn't think about things like that."

"Since when? He's never been reckless before. He's always careful."

"Think of his life in New York," Liza said.

"But what's he doing it for, and the hang gliding?"

"I don't know. He won't talk about it."

Just then Morgan arrived at the table, followed by Richard and Claudio.

"I didn't get my turn, I'm afraid," Richard said.

"Are you all right, Claudio?" Liza said.

"Just about."

"Are you really?" Gabriella asked him; her voice was unnatural, Claudio heard it. "Fine," he said, "I'd like a drink, though."

"Sit for a while, Claudio," Richard said. "I'll see if I can get you something." He went off to the shanty to negotiate tequilas. Morgan sat with the three of them, in silence.

Gabriella looked at Claudio, unable to see his expression behind the silver glasses; but she noticed the cuts on his legs and feet, the deep scratches on his hands.

"You've had quite a day," Liza said to him.

Gabriella didn't speak, feeling that she had no right to say anything to either of them. Nor did she speak to Morgan.

I N THE LAST DAYS OF THEIR STAY,
the air went out of the holiday,
expectancy collapsed like a balloon, as people rose late, ate at odd
hours and drifted off to the beach only late in the afternoon, as
though obliged in the final hours to justify the day itself. None
of this interfered with Gabriella and Morgan's routine amatory
schedule, but Gabriella, coming out of the warm bedroom, was
surprised, and then a little guilty, to find the others drifting
around the house, purposeless, Claudio dedicated to his reading,
Richard and Liza dedicated to a wary companionship of Claudio.
Late in the evenings they bought their food in the village shops,
took it back and cooked it at the house. Nights out weren't even
suggested, the arguments being too near, the under-arguments
too bitter. It was as though the friendships were finished, or the
great friendship, the noble experiment, and no one had the heart
to talk about it.

Even on their last evening they did not go out, to stay up all
night in Acapulco dancing till dawn, dragging the body, fun-
weary into the airport lounge, the hangovers as heavy as the
luggage—obeying the holiday duty to expend all that is left, like
the last pesetas, before the flight out.

Because they were so clearly not doing this, the thoughts rose
and the half-recriminations as the five of them sat, not in awkward
silence, but in performance of civility, over the remains of the last

dinner, festively prepared, of guacamole, ceviche, guavas and tequila, which burned all the way down and left the head disconnected, disconsolate, somewhere else.

Behind them, over the balcony of the little house, somewhere the Pacific rose and fell in its night breathing, sending up amid the scent of mimosa and almond the warm salty exhalations that should have bathed them all, blessed them, on their way home to New York.

In the silence where they sat at the table, the pottery dishes still out before them, the food wet and bright on the plates, the air could be heard, and the rustlings from the terraces below where other tourists, or Mexican families, sat out, had their meals and felt the night. And over this human movement there was stirring in the trees as the night birds called to one another, brightly and without fear. A chorus now, almost deafening in its happiness, came from a nearby growth; they listened to the birds and tried to hear their different languages.

"There's a lovely poem . . . do you know it, Gabriella?" Liza said, " . . . a couple in love stand in a garden at night and listen to all the noises around them. Oh—who *is* it?"

"Who?" Gabriella said.

"No, I can't remember, or the lines. But the man says 'Listen, my darling, to the nightingale' and they kiss under the stars; the birds are making this wonderful noise and the lovers make love to the chorus of birdsong. But, as the poet explains, the beautiful sounds are not love calls but hunting calls, and somewhere while the couple is sighing and swooning an owl is ripping a rabbit to shreds, and a hawk is devouring a sparrow. The night is full not of love talk but of the noise of killings and appetites and death cries."

"Sounds like a beautiful poem," Claudio said ironically. "You have a morbid taste, Liza."

"I always think of it when I hear the birds."

"Sounds like an answer to 'Dover Beach,' " Morgan said. Gabriella looked at him. He was sleepy from the tequila, and replete, with food and with her.

"Is it Baudelaire?" Liza asked.

No one answered her; they were all now listening to the birds.

Claudio moved and then pulled himself together like a woman withdrawing into shawls. He stood up.

"You're not leaving, are you?" Richard asked him.

"I think I will. I'll read a little. What time's the plane?"

"Twelve."

"All right. I'll see you tomorrow." Claudio spoke formally, unnaturally.

Gabriella watched him as he avoided her eye, but Liza, sitting nearest to him, reached up, put her arms around him and drew him down to kiss him good night. Then Gabriella leaned over the table and kissed him. The awkward position covered the coolness of their embrace. But Gabriella felt it, removed, dry.

"Good night Morgan, good night Richard," Claudio said.

Morgan and Claudio did not kiss good night as they used to in New York—a sweet, tolerant pleasantry to Morgan, a source of happiness and pride to Claudio. In front of Richard, Claudio would not have kissed Morgan, not wishing to distinguish between them, yet Gabriella, remembering how it had been before, faltered.

When Claudio was gone, the two couples sat and avoided talk. They passed the tequila, arming themselves with excuses for their distance, smoked their cigarettes and listened again to the birds.

Then, after a while, each couple got up and went to a bedroom, to make love or not make love, according to its desire.

About the Author

JANET HOBHOUSE was born in New York in 1948. She read English at Oxford and began writing about art in 1971. She is also the author of *Everybody Who Was Anybody: A Biography of Gertrude Stein* and of one previous novel, *Nellie Without Hugo*, and is currently writing a book on the artist and the nude in the twentieth century.